The Other Side
of War

Welcome to the
Other side
series.
Enjoy!

[signature]

Nov. 21, 2015

Canadä

The Publishers acknowledge the financial assistance of the
Government of Canada through the Book Publishing Industry
Development Program (BPIDP) for our publishing activities.

Library and Archives Canada Cataloguing in Publication

Calder, Marie Donais, 1948-
  The other side of war / Marie Donais Calder.

(The other side ; 1)
ISBN 978-0-88887-394-1 (paperback)
ISBN 978-0-88887-492-4 (ebook)

  1. World War, 1939-1945--Fiction. 2. Donais, Edmond--
Fiction. I. Title. II. Series: Calder, Marie Donais, 1948- .
The other side ; 1.

PS8605.A4564O85 2010   C813'.6   C2010-903155-5

Printed and bound in Canada on acid free paper.

The second novel in this series, *The Other Side of Fear*, continues the Canadian soldier's (Eddie) relationship with the German family which, like other people of Europe, faced fear of epic proportions. Sometimes this fear was produced by Hitler and his Hit men, and frequently by the treatment of the German people by members of the allied countries. For example, the family in these novels was forced by the Polish military to evacuate their home, dig a hole in the ground in their backyard and live in it for almost a year.

In *The Other Side of Pain*, the third novel in this series. Eddie continues to help the German family to deal with their wartime traumas. One of their sons returns from his army service in a war that he and his family did not support nor did men from this family volunteer to serve Hitler. However, if they refused, their loved ones would be killed. *The Other Side of Pain* portrays physical and emotional pain the German family and Eddie, faced in the aftermath of the Second World War.

The Other Side
of War

Marie Donais Calder

Borealis Press
Ottawa, Canada
2010

Acknowledgements

Thank you to all the war brides and others living in Europe during the Second World War for sharing their awe-inspiring stories of survival with me, to all the Canadian soldiers who helped me appreciate the sacrifices they made for our freedom, and to my family, for their support and understanding while I've been on this incredible journey.

I would also like to acknowledge Frank Tierney and his team at Borealis Press for recognizing the meaning and relevance of my Dad's contribution to changing "the family"'s future after the Second World war, and to Janet Shorten, my editor, for her patience, enthusiasm, and encouragement.

To Mom, Dad, and "The family" in Germany

as well as
to all others who were and are adversely affected
by wars of all kinds

Preface

May 1998

My daily phone call to my Mom resulted in a profound change to her life, my family's lives, and hopefully it will positively affect your life as well, when she uttered the words: "Marie, I would really like to meet the family."

I paused only briefly, knowing that she meant the family in Germany that Dad had saved over 50 years ago.

"Okay, Mom. I'll be right over. Can you just gather up your old photos, letters, telegrams and anything else you may have? We'll find the family."

"Oh, Marie, I think this is really just a lost cause."

"I'll be right over, Mom. We'll find them."

I hurried to the other side of Estevan, Saskatchewan, where my Mom lived in a tiny apartment. She always left the apartment door open when she was expecting a visit from me. I pushed the door open to see Mom sitting on her pastel floral chesterfield, the photo album on her lap. She looked up at me with a sadness in her eyes. "It's no use, Marie. We'll never be able to find them."

Spread out before her on the coffee table were a few letters from Dad, one from Karla from Germany, and some pictures Dad brought back from Germany in 1946. She continued to hold the old, dark brown photo album with a picture of a black sailboat on it on her lap.

I quickly read the brief letter from Karla, which provided

no information. She had signed it simply Karla. No surname. No address.

Mom was holding a 5 x 7 picture in her elegant hands with the perfectly natural fingernails.

"We'll find the family, Mom. I just know we will. What do you have in your hands there?"

Mom held the picture face up. "This is the brother who was a soldier in Hitler's army. He did not want to be a soldier for Hitler. But then he had no choice, did he?"

I gently took the familiar picture into my hands and looked into the saddened face of a Nazi soldier—a young boy, really.

"The family didn't support Hitler, you know."

I nodded, having heard this story so many times over the years but not understanding the gravity of that stance in wartime Germany. Slowly I turned my eyes away from the sad face before me. I turned the picture over and saw something written in German. I recognized my Dad's name and—the soldier had signed his name! Excitement coursing through my veins, I moved over to the chesterfield to sit next to my Mom. "Now we will find these people, Mom. We have a name to go on, see here? I can look them up on the Internet. I'll have to find someone to translate the message."

That very day I had the names of 10 people in Germany with the soldier's first and last name. I printed off the address labels for them and proceeded to write a letter to be translated into German. The letters were on their way to Germany by mid-June.

In July we began receiving letters in response. The letters stated that they were not the family we were looking for but they would really like to meet my Mom. Although we were touched by these sentiments from these sincere German people, disappointment began to set in. The third week of July we received a fax: "We are the family you are seeking. We would welcome a visit from you. We have much to talk about."

I called my Mom and told her I was coming over right away. Mom met me downstairs. I hugged her. "Just wait until you see what I have for you." We rode the elevator in silence.

Once inside her apartment I offered the fax to her. Her hands shook as she read the invitation. "Marie, I don't know how I can go to Germany." Mom sank down into her seat on the chesterfield.

"Arrangements are already being made, Mom. Blaine is going to take you to meet the family. I'm just relieved that my brother can do this for us. He has promised to videotape the visit for me since my health will not permit me to travel."

My Mom lifted her tearful eyes to meet mine. "Marie, I didn't think this would actually happen. This journey is for me, it's true, but it is also for your dad."

I smiled. "I know, Mom. But I think this trip is for the family too. I cannot wait for your return so you can tell me all about it."

Chapter 1

A whole weekend on kitchen duty was nothing to look forward to. I wouldn't have minded so much except that most of my buddies went to Portsmouth for the weekend for some sightseeing. My battalion of Canadian soldiers had arrived in England one month earlier, and this was our first opportunity to leave the barracks in London. I was with the RCEME division. This was the engineering division whose duty it was to repair the machinery used in the Allied cause. I was grateful that I had the skills necessary to join this division. I couldn't imagine being in combat duty and having to take another person's life, even if he was the enemy.

It was now April 1945 and the war was supposedly almost over. It was rumoured that the German war effort was hopelessly beaten, mainly because they lacked the necessary weaponry and transport to continue the war effort for much longer. We were anticipating being drafted to the Occupation Force as soon as the war officially ended. We knew we wouldn't remain in England. There was much speculation as to where we would actually be sent.

I was washing dishes in the cookhouse when my friend Earl burst into the room.

"Ed, I just overheard the Sarge say that we're going to be leaving England in a few weeks."

"Is that good news or bad news?" I asked cautiously. "Do you know where we're going?"

"I wish I knew. I definitely heard the Sarge say we're heading to Germany. That has me worried, Ed. He says the war won't last much longer than another week or two," Earl declared, a nervous twitch tugging at his left eye. "He said we'd be stationed in the northwest part of Germany, near Holland. He said it's a small port city, called Leer or something like that."

Physically, Earl and I were as different as night and day. Earl was over six feet tall while I stood only five feet, five inches. My coal-black hair contrasted with Earl's blond, almost white hair. My eyes were large and light blue; his were small and dark brown. I kept my face shaven, as best I could under the circumstances, while Earl sported a blond moustache. Yet we had bonded immediately when we met two years ago in training camp in eastern Canada. I asked, "Earl, are you absolutely sure the Sarge said Germany? Why would we need to go there when the war is almost over?"

"We're going as part of the Occupation Force," he said. "We'll probably be told sometime this week and leave a few weeks later."

I put my dishcloth down and turned to face my good friend. "I'm not anxious to go to Germany, are you, Earl?"

"No. We've only been on Allied soil so far. I think it'll feel strange to be in enemy territory, but then we don't get the choice, do we?"

"Not when you're in the army, my friend. I wonder how it will feel to be amongst the enemy. Will the people hate us, do you suppose?"

Earl shrugged. "I rather think they will be as uncomfortable with us as we'll be with them."

"We may not even meet any of the people. I guess it depends on what our duties are and where we'll live. I would imagine that the common people of Germany are not much different than any of us. People are people, don't you think, Earl?"

Earl smiled and patted me on the shoulder. He picked up the tea towel to dry the dishes for me. "Trust you to think the best of the Germans, Ed. I guess we'll find out for ourselves soon enough. I can't wait to see the look on Shorty's face when he hears the news. You know what he thinks of the Germans—he hates them with a passion. But then that's Shorty for you. He hates lots of things, doesn't he?"

I barely noticed Earl chuckling to himself. I was lost in thought about the next phase of my life. This re-location to Germany was going to have its challenges, I had no doubt about that. Most of the boys would adjust fairly easily. Shorty, though, was another story. I knew that Shorty did not accept change very well. This was one change he would resist with every bone in his body.

Earl's voice broke into my thoughts. "What say we go for a walk after these dishes are done? We may never get a chance to return to London once we're gone."

"That's a good idea. It's a nice evening for a change, so why not?"

Later that evening I wrote a letter to my wife back in Canada.

25-4-45

Dear Sweetheart and Family,

I thought I had better write to you while I still had a chance. How is everyone? Are you doing okay? Are you getting enough food and other necessities? And how are my three little sons? We haven't seen each other for more than a year now. Do you think you'll recognize me when we finally meet again? It makes me sad to think that my sons don't even know their own Daddy. They were so young when I left. We will be

together again, my love, and I'll cherish every
moment of our time together.

Earl told me today that we'd be leaving for
Germany in a few weeks. It seems that we'll be
part of the Occupation Force there. This is a scary
thought for most of us. I'm hoping that we'll be
able to come home as soon as our duties are over
in Germany. As for your radio, I'll move it for you
when I do get home.

I got a letter from Mother and she says that Gin
is in Holland. We'll have to go through Holland to
get to Germany. We haven't been officially told
anything yet, but once the announcement is made
I'm going to ask if I can connect with my brother.
It must be close to five years since I've seen him! I
don't even know if it's possible to arrange to meet
another Canadian soldier but it won't hurt to try,
will it? You know what they say, nothing ventured,
nothing gained. I'd give anything to see him again,
especially since Mother says he has enlisted for the
Far East. Apparently his whole division enlisted
together. From what we hear that will give them an
opportunity to get home sooner than the rest of us,
since we expect to serve here in the Occupation
Force after the war's over. That was a wise move
as far as I'm concerned. I tell you, if I weren't a
married man I would have enlisted myself, but it
may be a dangerous place to be and getting home
later is better than not getting home at all. Gin is
a single man so I can understand his wanting to
take the chance. You never know what's going to
happen, but the thought of getting home sooner is
an enticing thought. The good news is that this war

is almost over and we'll all be able to go home in time.

Mother also said that Little Joe doesn't have that windmill up and running yet. What's taking him so long? He was working on it when I was home the last time. I thought he would've finished it long ago. Has he forgotten all about it and gone on to another challenge? My brother is going to have to learn to finish the projects he starts. I guess I'll have to write to him and give him the what for, eh?

I ran out of soap again last night. It's almost impossible to get your clothes clean without soap. The worst part is the socks. We march up to 15 miles per day so clean socks make the marching a little more bearable. Oh, well, I did get a chit for a parcel so hopefully there will be some soap in it.

Shorty and Sarrasin went with some of the other fellas to Portsmouth for the weekend. They heard that this port city on the southern tip of England was pretty badly bombed. I was on KP duty all weekend so I couldn't go along. Earl is such a great guy that he decided to stay here and keep me company instead of going with them. I hope you get to meet Earl someday. Speaking of Earl, he just popped in to tell me that the guys who have enlisted for the Far East, like Gin, will be sent home to Canada for 30 days before going to the Far East. Then we understand they will have to undergo further training either in Canada or the States before being shipped out.

How is your Mother? I'm grateful that she has come to live with you and the boys. Will your lady teacher boarders be returning in the fall to stay with you for another school year? I'm so grateful that you live in a small community where you have the support of our family and friends. Some of the boys here have wives and children left behind in situations where they have very little support. At least we're lucky that way.

I'm a little apprehensive about going to Germany. We've never been directly exposed to the enemy here, not like Gin has. He's been in the midst of the combat for years. I really don't know how anyone handles that. He has seen some horrors as he drives the transport trucks through Italy, Belgium, and Holland, no doubt. I have to go to parade in a few minutes so I'll have to say bye-bye for now. Give my love to all that are dear to us. Give the kids each a big kiss from me, and to you Sweetheart, all my love,

Your Hubby

A few days later, on May 1st, it was reported that Hitler had committed suicide the day before. Everyone at the Canadian barracks wanted desperately to believe that Hitler was dead. The war without Hitler would end immediately. However, several conflicting reports were being heard every day. No body had been found when the Russians invaded the bunker where Hitler and his wife, Eva Braun, had been in hiding since January. No body meant there was room for speculation. Hitler's followers did not want to believe that their Führer had taken his own life. They chose to believe that he had escaped from Germany, and consequently many "sightings" were reported in remote parts of Italy, the Swiss Alps, and Ireland, to name a few. In fact, some believed that the war wasn't really over yet. Not until they found Hitler's body, at any rate.

It took a week for us to get official news that the war was definitely over. We immediately received our marching papers. The announcement of the war's end was made right after breakfast as we lined up for inspection. The men reacted with exuberance. Our joy was short-lived, though, as the other announcement was made immediately afterwards. We would be in Germany by the last week in June.

Later that evening, Shorty, Earl, George, and I went for a walk. We discussed the impending move to Germany. "I don't think I'll go to Nazi country," declared Shorty.

"What do you mean, you won't go? You have no choice," said George, as he looked down at Shorty. George, like Earl, was six feet tall, while Shorty was just over five feet.

"I do so have a choice," Shorty snarled, and stomped his foot on the ground. "I'll go AWOL is what I'll do." He planted his stubby hands firmly on his hips.

"Shorty, you can't be serious," I said as I turned to face my friend.

"I have never been more serious in my life." His defiance was evident as Shorty held his rigid body straight, his green eyes flashing.

Earl patted Shorty on the shoulder. "That's nonsense and you know it. None of us wants to go to Germany, but we don't want to go through a court-martial either. Think about your future, Shorty."

"It won't be all that bad," I reassured him. "After all, we'll all be together, right, boys?"

"That's right," agreed George. "And you never know, Shorty, you may meet a cute little fräulein while we're there. You wouldn't be the first soldier to meet your future wife over here." George jabbed Shorty in the ribs.

"I'm not interested in any Nazis no matter what they look like. How can you say such a thing, George? You know how I hate Nazis." Shorty was agitated enough to be near tears.

"George was just trying to lighten your mood, Shorty," I said, as I gave his shoulder a squeeze. "Enough talk about Germany. Now why don't we all take a walk over to the canteen and see what's new there. We may be well advised to get any extra supplies we can before we leave London. Who knows what kind of canteen we'll have in Germany."

Shorty huffed, "I doubt we'll have anything there. It sounds like we'll be the first to get there, so how could we have a canteen? The army doesn't exactly care about our needs. All they care about is us doing whatever they want, is what I say." Shorty's bottom lip jutted out as he reiterated, "That's all they care about. Nothing else." Shorty turned and headed for the canteen. He glanced at us over his shoulder. "Well, boys, what are you waiting for? Let's stock up before we go to No-wheres-land."

On the ninth of May, the general surrender was formally ratified in Berlin. The war was officially over. The Occupation Forces were deployed. My division was set to leave for Leer, Germany, soon. We would travel by ferry to Belgium. Transport trucks would then carry us north through Belgium and Holland.

Sarge caught up with Shorty and me just outside the room we shared with George and Earl. "Ed, your brother has been sent on a mission to Germany to take supplies for the Occupation Force divisions. They don't expect him back in Holland until a week or so after our division is expected to arrive there. I'm sorry, Ed." The Sarge left me alone with Shorty to digest this news. I was terribly disappointed.

Shorty wasn't surprised by the news at all. "I don't know why you got your hopes up in the first place, Ed. You should have known better. When was the last time anything good happened in this army?" Shorty kicked the ground with the toe of his boot.

"You can't blame a guy for trying. I would've seen my brother if he hadn't been sent on this mission. If he had known about this before he left, I'm sure his superior officer would have let him stay behind to meet me. I may get to see him yet, especially if he's hauling goods to Germany."

Shorty eyed me closely, then he shook his head. "You really amaze me sometimes, you know that? You never give up hope, do you?"

"Sometimes hope is all we have, Shorty," I replied wistfully.

My battalion left London on Thursday, June 21st. We ferried across to Belgium, where we spent the first night. Early the next morning we headed north in trucks. The weather was cold and damp—just the kind of weather I hated the most. We travelled throughout the day, stopping only for fuel.

We spent the first night at a British soldiers' base. Earl had a cousin in the British army. Coincidentally, Earl's cousin happened to be stationed at this base. He was from London, and Earl had visited his parents several times while we were stationed there. He had taken me with him on that last visit, so he made sure I was with him when he went looking for James. We found him in the mess hall where he was playing cards with some of the other Brits.

James jumped up from the table, his card game forgotten, at the sight of Earl. "How are you, old chap?" James enthusiastically shook Earl's hand.

"I'm fine, thanks. James, I would like you to meet my friend Ed. He was with me when I last visited your parents."

James extended his hand to me. "So you're the chap Mother was referring to. They had a jolly good time with the two of you. They wired me to say that you may be stopping here on your way up north. I'm very pleased to make your acquaintance, Ed."

"Your folks tell me that you're doing some writing for *The Times* of London. That must be exciting for you. I've often envisioned myself as a writer too," said Earl with a smile.

"What sort of things do you write?" asked James.

"I wrote some documentary articles for the newspaper back home before I joined the war effort. I've read some of your articles in *The Times*. They're quite interesting."

"Thank you, old boy. May I offer the two of you some coffee?"

The three of us sat down with our coffee cups. Earl said, "I've thought of writing a novel. Perhaps after I get back home, I'll do just that. Ed, here, can design the jacket for the book." Earl patted me on the back. "He's quite an artist, even if he doesn't realize it himself."

James looked over at me. "An artist, you say. That's a talent I only wish I possessed. What do you like to draw?"

I felt my cheeks flush. "I'm afraid your cousin here exaggerates a bit. I'm not really all that good at it."

"That's not true," stated Earl emphatically. "I've seen some of his sketches. He draws animals mostly. I especially like the horses he draws. They're quite detailed."

I turned to James and asked, "Have you ever been to Leer, Germany? That's where we're headed."

"No, I can't say that I have. Where is it exactly?"

"It's on the northern tip of Germany, right next to Holland. It's also on the North Sea."

"Oh, okay," said James as he looked upward as if at an imaginary map. "I have never even been to Holland yet. You never know, though, I may just come up to see you when you're in Germany. We've had reports that many of the people in Germany are nearly starving. They may be the enemy, but I still hate to think of women and children starving to death." He shook his head.

Earl nodded. "I suppose you could be right." Earl yawned and stretched his arms. He finished his coffee and stood. "I guess we'd better get back to the others. We'll have to get to bed right away. I understand we're leaving first thing in the morning."

James extended his hand to Earl. "It was great to see you again, old chap. It was jolly nice of the two of you to visit my folks. Before you go, I wonder if you can tell me how they are. I haven't seen them in months and they never tell me any of their problems when they write or wire me. Did they seem okay to you?"

Earl nodded his head. "They seemed very healthy to me. I only hope that I can be that energetic when I'm their age. They're in their sixties, aren't they?"

"Indeed they are. I was a change of life baby. Quite a surprise I was, they tell me." James extended his hand to me. "I really must let you go, old chap. It was great to meet you. Take care of my cousin for me when you're in Germany, won't you?"

I shook James's hand. "I'll do what I can, James. It was a pleasure to meet you. Perhaps we'll see you again someday. Hopefully in Germany."

"I would look forward to that." James walked us to the mess hall door. "Have a good trip north. Goodbye for now."

* * *

We were given a warm breakfast the next morning. We were treated to porridge, bacon and eggs, and fresh bread. The bread was much heavier than Canadian bread, but it was delicious just the same. We all ate heartily, knowing that we might not get a decent meal again for a while. We had sandwiches packed for us for the remainder of the day's meals. We would travel straight through once again. No breaks for meals, not when you're in the army and on the move.

The roads were in deplorable shape due to lack of repair and heavy equipment being hauled over them. The roads through the middle of Belgium were particularly rough. The trucks were only able to travel at a snail's pace. We didn't make our next scheduled destination where another Allied barracks was preparing to house us for the night. Instead, we slept upright in the trucks as the drivers took turns resting and driving. We finally reached the barracks two days later in the afternoon. We hadn't eaten for nearly forty-eight hours.

The barracks housed another British battalion. Several of the British officers made this barracks their home, so it was quite a deluxe facility. We Canadians were welcomed with the offer of showers. I had never had a shower before in my life. We were ushered to the sleeping quarters and given soap, a face cloth, and a towel. The shower was invigorating after the long road trip. The warm cascading water soothed my body. I lathered myself liberally with soap and rinsed it several times. Reluctantly, I finally ended my shower and dried myself off. I vowed that day I would make getting a shower in my future home a priority. My brother, Little Joe, was always looking for a new challenge. Perhaps we could rig something up together at some future time. Most people back home didn't even have running water in the 1940s but I was one who liked to dream of the possibilities that could lie ahead.

We had an hour to rest before the evening meal. We were delighted to learn that we would be treated to another hot meal as well. We had a delicious supper of roast beef, roasted potatoes, Yorkshire pudding, and canned peas. We were also treated to an English trifle for dessert. After the meal we were invited to listen to a British broadcast program on the radio, and there was even some music following the radio broadcast. Several of the soldiers fell asleep in their chairs. We were escorted to our sleeping quarters where most of the boys fell asleep within minutes. I was not one of them.

"Earl, are you asleep?" I whispered.

"Not yet, Ed."

"That was a great meal, wasn't it? I really enjoyed the beef, didn't you?"

"I enjoyed the whole meal," Earl yawned. "Now what is the real reason you're not asleep?"

"I don't know," I sighed.

"I think I've known you long enough to know that something is bothering you. Now what is it?"

"That roast beef reminded me of my wife. It was almost as good as hers, though don't you ever tell her I said that." I chuckled.

"Sometimes I'm really glad I'm single. I don't have to miss my girl because I haven't found her yet. On the other hand, when we get home you'll have someone waiting for you. I have no one special waiting for me. So, Ed, you just enjoy this pain. Pain is the flip side of the same coin as joy. You just remember that every time you feel the pain of missing your wife, you'll feel the joy of re-uniting with her just as much."

"Thanks, Earl. I needed that reminder. The right woman is waiting for you, old buddy. You'll find her when the time is right. Goodnight."

"Goodnight."

We thoroughly enjoyed a hot breakfast the next morning consisting of muffins, bacon, eggs, porridge, and coffee. We were supplied with sandwiches for the next leg of the journey. We would have been able to get to Leer by nightfall if the roads were passable. However, we discovered that the bombings of Belgium and Holland at the end of the war had taken a huge toll on the highways. These roads were even worse than the ones we had already traversed. At one point the trucks landed in holes so large that we had to get out and practically lift the trucks out. It took all the manpower from one truck to hoist and push it out. The drivers drove slower after that and often preferred the ditches to the roads. We spent another night sleeping upright in the truck. Finally we arrived in Leer, totally exhausted, on the evening of Sunday, July 1st. Even in our state of exhaustion and despair, it was not lost on us that we were entering enemy territory on Canada's birthday.

"Happy birthday, Canada." Shorty sneered as we entered our new barracks. This was one time I had no desire to deal with Shorty's negativity. I dropped into my bunk wondering what my life was going to be like in this enemy land.

Chapter 2

Kanadische Soldaten. Canadian soldiers. The words chased each other around and around in my head as I kept my eyes on the abandoned German railway cars. They were clearly visible from our house. My parents' two-storey brick home was on the southwestern outskirts of Leer. Thankfully, our home had survived the Allied bombings from this horrible war that was now finally over. Fields populated with sparse patches of thick brush surrounded it. Abandoned railway cars, directly to the south, momentarily blotted out my panoramic view of the canal. It travelled westward along the railroad track about two hundred metres before it curved northward, widening as it bent as if opening its arms to the mother sea several kilometres ahead. I was perched on my front step, a mere spectator in this still landscape. During the war there was much to observe as the railway tracks and the canal transported people, machinery, and goods from nearby Holland and the North Sea to points in Germany. There were times when I froze with fear when I saw Hitler's Gestapo ride the railway cars as they enforced Hitler's laws of madness. Activity had slowed down and finally stopped altogether as the war drew to a close.

My gaze returned to the intriguing railway cars. I had been sitting on the front step observing the lengthening shadows as I eagerly awaited the distant sound of trucks that would bring new occupants to the deserted railway cars. The sun was doing a slow-motion dive towards the canal across the field to my right.

My stomach growled again. Mama said I was going through a period of rapid growth. My shrinking trousers were evidence, she said. Recently Mama was putting more food on my plate. This, of course, meant that the others had less food to eat. Usually our portion at the evening meal covered approximately one-quarter of our dinner plates. Now my plate was about one-third full. When I protested, Mama assured me that the change was only temporary until my growth spurt was over. Then my portions would once again be equal to the others. As long as we were still able to use food cards, that is. Now that the war was over no one could predict what the future held for the people of Germany. Would life get better? Or was this just the beginning of something worse to come? That's what my sister Diane thought.

The beauty of my surroundings drew me back to the present. I longed to paint the scenes around me on canvas but there were no art supplies available to me. The urge to paint was so strong these days. Did that have anything to do with this period of rapid growth I was experiencing? I imagined the painting I would undertake of the desolate landscape, as it was now, occupying one half of the canvas, while the identical landscape with the new occupants would grace the other half. Empty/Full. That would be the title of the painting. I envisioned it framed and prominently displayed in an art gallery, the walls barely able to hold the numerous paintings by the most famous artist in Germany, Johann Schmidt. Me!

The last glint of the setting sun caught my eye. Just this afternoon, Andreas, my secret friend, and I were skipping stones right there on the canal. Andreas and I had a code so that we knew when to meet. He would leave the number of stones that indicated the hour he could meet at the northern end of our property. There was an area of heavy brush, and we had hidden a pile of stones in the centre of the brush. Today he had placed two stones out so we met at two o'clock.

I shuddered as I recalled the meeting. Andreas was nine years old, one year younger than me. He obviously hadn't had his growing spurt yet; he barely reached my shoulders. He had short blond hair, big brown eyes, and ears that stuck out a little. He had some bad news he needed to share with me. He couldn't tell anyone but his secret friend, he said. Andreas's father was a member of Hitler's feared Secret Police, the Gestapo. He told me that his father had been seriously injured in the famous Shell attack in Copenhagen, Denmark, on October 31, 1944. The British Royal Air Force bombed the Gestapo headquarters, destroying Gestapo records, killing 26 members of the Gestapo, and injuring several others. They bragged about this accomplishment because they did not harm a single Dane or any of the large number of resistance prisoners held in one wing of the bombed building. The British were very proud of themselves, but I wondered if they knew how badly some people were hurt by their "accomplishments." He informed me that the Russians had captured his father. Andreas said his mother was warned that they would probably never see him again. Andreas's father was young too, not like my bent, white-haired Papa. His father was only 35 years old, just five years older than my eldest sister, Diane.

I was so wrapped up in the memory of my friend's melancholy that I almost missed the anticipated sounds of the convoy of trucks. Shaking off the melancholy, I jumped up and darted into the house. I dashed past the dining room and through the French doors of the parlour. I bumped my leg on the side table on my left as I entered the crowded parlour. Marlene and Diane were sitting together on the smaller brown sofa to my left. Mama was standing directly ahead of me by the large beige sofa, upon which Karla and Papa sat. On my right sat the only armchair in the room, with a floor lamp standing sentinel between it and the beige sofa.

My three older sisters and my parents were patiently awaiting the arrival of the convoy. Rushing over to my two oldest sisters, Diane and Marlene, I reached out a hand to each of them and tried to pull them up from the sofa. "Come quickly," I begged as I pulled them with all my might. "Come, everyone. They're here at last." Diane resisted my pull and remained glued to the sofa cushion, wringing her hands in her lap. Marlene quickly rose from the sofa.

"Fine, little brother, I will follow you." She and Karla each extended a hand to one of our parents.

Diane's narrow brown eyes mirrored her panic. "No!" she shouted as she jumped up, and placed an iron grip on Marlene's and Karla's arms. Her face was ashen. Her head was lowered and her eyes darted quickly about. "No," she whispered, as she pleaded with her younger sisters, "do not go out there. They will hurt you. Please do not go out there." Diane's grip on my sisters' arms did not weaken.

Marlene's free hand tilted Diane's face to meet her gaze. "It is fine, Diane, really it is. The war is over now. These Canadian men are coming to keep the peace. They will not harm us." She squeezed Diane's chin gently and smiled into her frantic eyes. "Anyway, they will not even see us in the darkness of our porch. We will be safe, I promise you." Marlene hugged Diane's trembling body as Karla quietly put her arms around both of them.

I was only ten years old, but I had learned that Diane was filled with fears I did not understand. She was especially terrified of strange men. I think it had to do with the Polish soldiers who occupied our home a few years ago. Papa sighed as he ran his fingers through his thinning white hair. He slowly rose from the sofa and shuffled behind Mama and me as we hurried to the porch. The roaring engines of the army trucks caused me to become more and more excited as they pulled up to the railway cars just over the hill south of our house.

The railway tracks used to be off limits to us children during the war. The Nazi soldiers patrolled the area, around the clock, during most of the war. Once the ban was lifted I could not hold my curiosity in check. These cars had been moved here a few weeks ago. They were boarded up but I had managed to peek inside most of them between the cracks. The car on the east side was completely empty. The second car was like a kitchen with sinks, cupboards, and a small table with two chairs. The third one appeared to be a dining car filled with tables and chairs. The other cars were sleeping cars with four bunks in each, a small closet, and a bureau with four drawers. My vivid imagination ran wild as I pretended to travel the world inside one of these cars.

I had been born just before the Second World War began, so I had never had an opportunity to venture even to the other side of Leer. A few years ago, before my older brother Arthur was forced to join the war effort, we swam in the canal pretending that we were swimming in the nearby North Sea on our way to other lands. We knew that Holland was close to Leer and often secretly spoke of wishing we had been born over the Dutch border. But I discovered early in my life that escape from the horrors of the war was only possible within the confines of one's mind. We were German, and we could not change that fact.

My parents and I sat on our front porch as darkness fell and watched the trucks pulling up in front of the abandoned railway cars. We could only catch a glimpse of the men as they pulled away the boards barring the doors and carried their sleeping gear off the trucks and into the sleeping cars.

Mama looked over her shoulder and through the screen door at my sisters. "I wonder how long these Canadians will stay here?" she asked, as she rocked in her tattered wicker chair on this warm spring evening. She raised an eyebrow at Marlene.

Marlene nodded as her eyes remained on the soldiers' barracks. She glanced at Diane, then back at Mama as she replied, "According to my employer, Helmut, they will be here for a year or so. He hears all the latest news down at the railway station."

Marlene's quivering hushed voice alarmed me. I turned around to see Diane's knees buckle. Karla put her arm around Diane's other trembling shoulder. My three sisters stood quietly in the safety of the house, Diane with her eyes lowered, Marlene and Karla straining to see the action taking place over the hill. The soldiers were limping and hanging on to each other. They could barely walk the short distance from the truck to their new home.

Mama winced as we watched the Canadians. "What pain they must be in. They will need some good rest before they will be able to do any kind of work."

"Does Helmut know what duties these soldiers will have while they are here?" asked Papa.

Marlene squeezed Diane's shoulder. "He thinks they are here to repair many of the damages caused by the war. He heard that this particular troop is here to fix the broken-down machinery."

Papa reassured me with a pat on the back as I continued to glance over my shoulder at my sisters. He sighed. "There is a whole compound full of broken-down trucks, motorcycles, and other vehicles. Perhaps these soldiers will get them in running order again. If that is the case, they may be here for a whole decade." Diane moaned and swooned. I thought she was about to faint. Papa stood up from his faded brown bench seat and opened the screen door. He embraced my three sisters. "From what I hear of these Canadians, I think we will not have to worry about them hurting us. It will be fine, Diane. I just know it will." Papa looked over his shoulder at Mama and me. "In any case, we might as well go to bed now," he declared. "I think the Canadians will give us no more action tonight. They look like they have travelled a great distance and are ready for a good night's sleep."

Everyone followed Papa into the house except for me. My eyes were still riveted on the Canadians' new home. *I wonder what Canadians are really like? Are they any different than we are? Will they hurt my sisters?* I shuddered at the thought. I decided to find out what they were like for myself the next day. I felt a smile twitch at the corners of my mouth as I planned the strategies I would use to secretly observe the Canadians the next morning.

I had gotten proficient at secret meetings since I'd met Andreas. No one in my family knew of our friendship. I don't think they would understand how I could befriend the son of a member of the hated Gestapo. Papa often spoke of Hitler and his hit men: "Those people are despicable. They have done nothing but evil acts on behalf of their mad leader. Don't these men realize what horrible atrocities they are committing?" Papa had looked straight at me when he said this. Attempting to avoid Papa's scrutiny, I kept my eyes lowered. Did he know about Andreas? We'd been so careful with our meetings that Papa couldn't possibly know. Could he?

My reverie was broken by Karla's crisp voice through the screen door. "Johann? Where are you? It's past our bedtime." I reluctantly stood up and went back into the house.

I wasted no time getting washed up and dressed the next morning. I was anxious to satisfy my curiosity about the

Canadians. I gulped my breakfast down. I planned to spend the morning watching the soldiers, but first it was my job to dry the breakfast dishes.

"Karla, aren't you done eating yet?" I asked impatiently as I danced around the dining room table. We ate all our meals in the dining room. Seven dark oak chairs attended the matching table. The eighth chair accompanied the buffet and hutch on the west wall.

We used the good silver and china dishes every day. Mama insisted that our meals be as pleasant as possible. "We may not have much food to eat," she once explained to me, "but we can still have meals in style and with dignity."

Karla was six years older than me. She looked up at me as she carefully chewed her food. When at last she swallowed the morsel in her mouth she declared, "You must learn to eat your food more slowly, Johann. We have learned in our health class at school that you should chew each bite of food at least a dozen times. This helps your body to digest the food better."

I was in no mood for a lesson this morning. "Karla, please hurry up and eat. I can't dry the dishes if you haven't washed them yet," I said as I carried some of the dishes to the kitchen. I quickly returned to the dining room.

"What is your hurry, Johann? It's not like you to be so helpful." Her sky-blue eyes mirrored her curiosity. "Johann putting the dishes in the sink? Usually you wait until the dishes are almost dry before you lift your tea towel from the rack. So, Johann, what is your big hurry this morning?" Karla took another small bite of her bread. I was pleased to see that she was chewing her food a little faster now. Finally she swallowed her last bite and followed me to the kitchen.

"It's a secret, Karla, but I promise to tell you all about it later," I assured her as I lifted the hot kettle from the wood stove and poured the water into the sink.

"You are not going anywhere you should not go, are you?" asked Karla with a wrinkled brow. She approached the sink and looked into my eyes. "Johann, just where are you going this morning? You must tell me." Karla gently lowered her cup and plate into the sink.

"I'll be fine, Karla. Now let's please do the dishes," I pleaded as I grabbed the tea towel from the rack.

"Fine, Johann," declared Karla in her big sister voice, "but please be careful. I just do not want anything to happen to you. Then who would dry the dishes around here?" Karla gave me a little jab in the ticklish spot of my ribs. "Seriously though, Johann, you must promise me that you will not go far. That curious nature of yours could get you into trouble, you know."

"I promise," I said with a smile. After all, the Canadian camp was just over the hill. "I won't go far. Not far at all," I assured her as I looked forward to observing the Canadians on their first morning in Germany. Drying the dishes seemed to take forever this morning.

Chapter 3

My leg was going numb. I shifted positions as I squinted up at the bright sun that had snuck up from behind me unnoticed. I had yet to see a single Canadian. Most of the activity this morning seemed to be inside the railway cars. I counted 22 cars in all.

Finally the soldiers began to appear. They would walk towards my hiding spot and throw dirty water into the bush. Then they would go to a barrel sitting on one of the trucks and get a fresh bucket of water and disappear inside one of the cars.

I observed that the Canadian men, like German men, came in all shapes and sizes. Most of them were slim but not skinny. However, there was one man with bulging eyes and a tummy to match. I've never seen such a round belly. Where did he get enough food to fill it? The man not only looked different from the others but he also dressed differently. His pants, jacket, and cap were all white.

I heard the roar of a truck approaching from over the hill just to the east of my hiding spot. It stopped in front of the first railway car. The man with the bulging belly approached the truck as the driver jumped out of the vehicle. I listened intently and even managed to understand a few of these English words, thanks to my lessons at school.

"Time you here, Private," said the round man with his hands on his hips. "The men starving. We haven't eaten twenty-four hours." I decided to listen even harder to their conversations. Karla once told me that the best way to learn a new language is to spend time with people who speak that language.

"Sorry, Sarge. This old truck broke down," the truck driver said, pointing to the rusted-out, dented vehicle. "The spark wires slipping off. I re-attach them. I'm glad boys here fix problems, be treat one trip without problems."

The round man moved over to the rear of the truck. "I tell the Captain someone working on it you leave. We have no food, you to help unload the truck. I work on the meal. I can make coffee, find it, sooner we get food into bellies, the sooner you on your way."

"Wow," I thought, "I can understand a lot more English when I'm not scared of the teacher calling on me for an answer."

A short man with a blond brush cut jumped out of the first car. He looked towards me. I felt the hair on the back of my neck prickle as he stared my way. He didn't appear to be much taller than me but he had a menacing look about him. I was relieved when he looked away from my hiding spot.

"Boys, food truck here! Which boys hungry to help unload truck?" he hollered. Ten or so men stopped their cleaning duties immediately and rushed out to unload the truck. The boxes of food were hauled off the truck and stacked up neatly on the ground against the back of the rear car. My ears got a badly needed rest as the men worked without saying a word. The short man directed the others. He seemed to be responsible for stacking the cartons.

The man in white came out of the rear car and spoke to the short man. "Find the bread and canned meat Shorty? I want the coffee too. Bring me soon find them." The man's jovial voice contrasted with the short man's snapping tone.

I tensed as the short man peered in my direction and

replied, "Right Sarge. Found the bread, haul it the cook car for you." The two men disappeared inside the car. A few seconds later, the short man returned to the stacks of cartons and surveyed the contents. He leaned over to the right and peered at the cartons. He leaned over so far that I thought for sure he would fall flat on his face. Then he stood upright, stomped his foot, looked up with a scowl on his face, and shook his head. "How to read labels you boys putting them sideways and upside down? Get cartons right now. You boys do want to eat today, don't you?" That got immediate action. Three of them hurried over to the stack and moved some of the cartons around while the short man supervised. Finally the short man pointed to the tall husky man. "Okay, George, take carton of canned meat cook car. Sarge. Make sandwiches. Find the coffee, take the box in to Sarge. I go into the supply car and plan where put cartons." The tall dark-haired man shrugged his shoulders, picked up the box, and headed to the car where the man dressed in white had gone. The short man turned on his heel and disappeared into the second car from the rear.

I was so absorbed in the activity of the Canadian soldiers that I hadn't realized that my shadow had disappeared. It must be time to get on home for lunch. Hungry as I was, my curiosity about the Canadians held me fast as I slipped into reverie.

* * *

I was only four years old when the war started so I didn't really know any other way of life. I often heard my family speak of the good old days. I knew this meant before the war started. I also knew that my family didn't agree with the war. I wonder if my family's feelings about the German cause have anything to do with the fact that Papa has so much trouble finding work? No one spoke about their feelings except when Arthur turned fifteen and was called to serve his country. Even though that was three years ago I could remember that day clearly. I remembered when Mama gave Arthur the summons letter at the supper table. Arthur's hands trembled as he read the letter out loud:

Dear Arthur Schmidt,

Male German citizens who have reached the age of fifteen must serve their country. Therefore, you must report to the Director of Military Affairs in Berlin on April 25, 1942, at 0700 hours. You must bring your birth certificate, school records, and passport (if you have one) along with you. You will not be returning to your home in the immediate future. You will be enlisted immediately and begin training as soon as you are processed. Failure to report as instructed will result in immediate and punitive measures being taken against you and your family.

Arthur's voice broke as he read the last sentence. Mama and my sisters sobbed quietly throughout the meal. Papa scared me the most as he sat erect in his chair in stony silence for the remainder of the meal, his eyes glassy like marbles.

Later that evening when Karla and I were supposed to be getting ready for bed, we hid on the staircase. Mama was seated at the dining room table so that we had a clear view of her sad round face. Her large green eyes sparkled with tears. We had only a partial view of Arthur and Papa, but we could overhear the family discussing the letter.

"Mama, Papa, please don't make me go," sobbed Arthur as Mama reached over and wiped the tears from his eyes.

Papa put his hands on Arthur's shoulders and looked him straight in the eye. "You know we do not support this war, Arthur, but what else can we do? If you try to hide, they will punish your family. And you, Arthur, you will be killed when they find you. You do remember what happened to Stefan Hess, do you not? You have no choice, Arthur. You must do as they say."

Karla and I could hear Mama, Papa, and Arthur sobbing together. We hugged each other silently as we eavesdropped. Finally we heard Mama's soft quivering voice: "Arthur, we are sickened that this war did not end before you became old enough to join in the war effort. It is bad enough that Diane's husband and Marlene's fiancé are away at war. We know what a terrible thing this is for you, Arthur, but we are all powerless to stop it."

I didn't know who they were at the time but I understood that my family was in grave danger if Arthur didn't join the army. I had heard many stories of others who fled when *they* were called to duty only to be found brutally murdered soon afterwards. I had grown up with the fear that some day my family and I would be killed in this war.

The image of Arthur leaving on the train that day in 1942 flashed through my mind as I lay on the ground, oblivious to the action at the Canadians' new barracks. Before that day I thought Arthur was the strongest person in the world. Tears streamed down my cheeks every time I allowed myself to relive the day my family went with Arthur to the train station.

The night before he left, Arthur had spoken to me about his leaving to serve in the army. Arthur sat on my bed. I crawled onto his lap as I did every time Arthur read me a bedtime story. When the story was over, Arthur laid me down and covered me up for the night. His sorrowful eyes still haunted me. "Johann," said Arthur in his strong low voice, his Adam's apple bouncing, "I must leave the family for a while. You must not be afraid for me. I will be fine. I will be home before you know it." Arthur smiled at me and jabbed me in the ribs. I was not so reassured because Arthur's lips might have been smiling but his eyes were not. It was then that I realized that my big brother was not so formidable.

The memory of Arthur's fearful face in the window of the train car that next day brought a shiver to my body. We were allowed to say goodbye to Arthur. When it was my turn, I jumped into his arms. I locked my legs tightly around his waist and gripped my arms around his neck. Maybe if the army men saw that Arthur couldn't leave with his little brother attached to him they would let Arthur stay at home. I had promised Arthur I would be strong when it came time to saying goodbye but I couldn't help myself. I blurted out between the sobs, "Don't go Arthur, please don't go." A gruff soldier came over to Arthur and harshly told him he had to get on the train. Right now! Arthur hesitated for a moment. He looked over my shoulder at our parents and sisters, his eyes pleading for guidance.

Marlene broke away from Karla's embrace and gently unlocked my limbs from Arthur. "Come, Johann. Arthur has no choice. He must get on the train."

I clung to Marlene and stroked her curly blond hair. I helplessly watched as the man jabbed his rifle into Arthur's back and pushed him towards the train. Arthur stumbled and the man yelled at him, "Get on the train, you stupid kid, and stop your blubbering. Hey, Fritz," he hollered to his friend, "look at this one. He's crying like a schoolgirl." The two friends guffawed as they watched Arthur wiping the tears from his swollen red eyes.

"Marlene," I begged, "don't let that bad man take Arthur away. Please don't let him hurt my brother."

Marlene was shaking as she held me close. She whispered in my ear, "Arthur will be all right, Johann. Shh, shh. He will be all right." She rocked me from side to side.

As the train pulled away from the station I panicked, realizing that I might not ever see my big brother again. I broke away from Marlene and began running after the train, begging Arthur not to leave. I ran until the train was out of sight. I knew that Arthur's heart was breaking as he saw his little brother chasing after him but I couldn't help it. I just had to find a way to stop my brother from leaving. I ran along the tracks, stumbling on the uneven ties. Still I ran, until my breath came in gasps and my spindly little legs could carry me no more. I finally collapsed by the train tracks. My energy was spent but still my body produced racking sobs.

Papa had tried to run after me but his tired old legs couldn't compete with my speed. I didn't have any idea how long I lay alongside the railway tracks, hearing only the train's wheels clicking on the rails. The next thing I remembered was Papa lifting me up in his arms and holding me close as we sat there together on the cold hard ground. I recalled how Papa's tears joined mine. Together they flowed down my cheeks as Papa said, "Thank God I still have you and your sisters. Thank God I still have you." We sat there together listening to the last clicking sound of the retreating train. I remembered wondering if I would ever see my big brother again. I was only seven years old but I often thought of that day as the day my childhood ended.

Even though the war was now finally over and the Allies were here to keep the peace, I continued to be fearful of any new experiences. However, as I remained hidden and watched these strange Canadians jabber away in their foreign language, I felt a sense of comfort. I had heard the adults talk about the Canadians' kindness. I stretched my legs and rubbed my tired red eyes.

"Well now, who do we have here?" My heartbeat thundered in my ears at the sound of the unfamiliar voice. I was so caught off guard that all my English left me and my mind went blank. I sprang to my feet, my mind already carrying me to the safety of my home. The man placed his hand softly, yet firmly, on my shoulder. "Don't be afraid, Little One," said the man gently. I did not understand the words but the man's soothing voice calmed me. I got the message. My heartbeat stopped interfering with my thoughts. I looked up to see a face that I shall never forget. The soft blue eyes radiated a warmth like Mama's did whenever she needed to console me about something. There were crinkles around his eyes as he embraced me with his gaze. "No one is going to hurt you, my child; it's okay." The man had an olive complexion and coal-black hair. He was about five and a half feet tall, I guessed. He was wearing a white short-sleeved shirt and brown pants, like the others I'd seen this morning, but he looked different somehow. He smiled and gently patted me on the head. My tense muscles relaxed.

The man reached into his pants pocket and pulled out something wrapped in bright paper. Was this a candy bar? My secret friend, Andreas, talked about them but I had never actually seen one before. My eyes were riveted on the bright paper. Colour was not commonplace in Germany in the 1940s. I lifted my eyes to meet his when I realized the man was speaking to me again. The man seemed to be offering the candy bar to me. My thoughts scrambled around in my head. *Should I take this gift from a strange soldier?* I wondered. *Papa said the Canadians could be trusted. Would Mama be mad at me if I accepted this gift?*

"Go on, Little One. Take the candy and share it with your family." The English word family sounded much like the German word *Familie*. I could feel my face breaking into a broad smile as I envisioned the look on Karla's face at the lunch table when I presented this treasure to the family. I was surprised to see that my hand was outstretched. The man pressed the brightly coloured candy bar into my hand. I felt like I had just been given a fortune in pure gold.

"*Danke*," I said as I bowed from my waist in a salute. I lifted my eyes to see the man's friends watching in the distance; they were all smiling at me too. The short man and the man in white were nowhere to be seen. My feet retreated a few steps. I gave a tentative wave to the man and his friends. Then I turned on my heels and raced across the field and down the hill to my home.

Chapter 4

"Johann, what are you beaming about?" asked Karla as I entered the dining room. "Where have you been? We have been worried about you. Did you not hear me calling your name?" Karla's hands were firmly planted on her hips as she faced me.

Karla, like Mama, was about six inches shorter than our other sisters. I had been growing so much lately and now, at nearly five feet, I was almost as tall as her. I looked her in the eye. "I'll tell you all about it at the lunch table." I could barely contain my excitement. I had to look away quickly.

Karla gave me a questioning look and shook her blond head. She continued setting the table. "Hurry then and wash up for lunch. Papa will be home in a few minutes. You can help me set the table as soon as you are cleaned up."

Minutes later the family gathered at the dining room table with Mama and Papa seated at either end, Karla and Diane on one side and Marlene and me on the other. I sat up tall in my chair, next to Mama: "I met one of the Canadians today." My croaky voice betrayed me. I had pictured this moment as being the one time that I, the youngest of five children, would have something important to offer my family. All eyes at the table turned to me. I rushed on. "He gave this to me. I think he wanted me to share it with my family." With shaky hands, I proudly pulled the large candy bar out of my trousers pocket.

Karla's eyes were as big as saucers as she stared at the

brightly wrapped gift. "Is . . . is that a candy bar?" she asked in disbelief.

"Let me see it, Johann. I will tell you what it is," declared Diane. I got up from my chair and enjoyed the moment as everyone's eyes followed me to Diane's place at the table. With a flourish, I bowed at the waist for the second time that day, and proudly handed the treasure over to my sister. Diane turned the object over and over slowly in her long, slender hands as she carefully examined it. "It sure looks like a candy bar," she declared. "Does that not look like the word chocolate right here, Karla?" Still speechless, Karla nodded. Diane's hands trembled as she turned to Papa. "Is it safe for Johann to accept a gift from a strange man, Papa?"

Papa smiled and patted Diane's hand. "I think it will be fine, my dear. I hear good things about these Canadians."

Diane's voice quivered. "This man may be Canadian but he is still a stranger and a man, Papa."

Mama smiled reassuringly at Diane. "Not all strange men are bad, Diane. We must begin to trust again." Her eyes never left the chocolate bar as she spoke. "Let's examine this candy. Perhaps you should unwrap it," suggested Mama.

"I think Johann should have that honour," said Diane as she gingerly placed it in my outstretched hands. She turned her anguished gaze to Papa.

Papa reached out and patted her hand again. "Perhaps this is a sign that the Canadians are good people just as we heard they are."

I returned to my place at the table pretending to carry the candy on a silver platter, to the sounds of Diane's nervous giggles. When I arrived back at my place I carefully set the chocolate bar on the table. I ran my fingers along the joining edges of the paper. I remained standing as I lightly folded back the lengths of the paper. A long brown object was revealed. An unfamiliar scent of sweetness drifted into the air. A collective gasp was heard in the silence of the room. Everyone's eyes remained steadfast on the scented object. "Is this what a candy bar looks like, Mama?" I whispered, not wanting to break the magic of the moment.

"I believe it just could be a candy bar all right, son." Mama's eyes sparkled.

"Can we eat it for dessert, Mama?" I asked hopefully.

"What do you think, Papa? Would it be safe to eat a gift from a stranger?" Mama's eyes remained on the delicacy.

" I think it would be fine. We will all just have a tiny bite today. If we feel fine tomorrow, we can have the rest for dessert tomorrow night." Papa smiled as he saw the looks of anticipation on the faces at the dining room table.

I eagerly handed the chocolate bar over to Mama to be sectioned. "We must keep a portion for Arthur. We will surprise him when he comes home from the war," I suggested. Heads nodded in agreement around the table. With that settled, Mama prepared a tiny portion for each member of the family. Marlene carried the platter holding the sectioned pieces of chocolate. She followed Mama to each of our places at the table. With a flourish Mama placed a tiny section of the precious candy bar on our plates. It looked like a dot on my plate. When everyone had a portion we joined our hands in a prayer of thanks.

I placed the morsel on my tongue and closed my eyes. I let my senses explode with the sweetness of the candy. I rolled the morsel from the front of my mouth to the back, then from side to side. The chocolate slowly melted in my mouth, exposing a harder sticky candy. *So this is what a candy bar tastes like. No wonder people talk about them with such enthusiasm. I wish I could tell my friends from school but that probably would not be wise.* I smiled as I realized I did have someone to tell. My secret friend Andreas wouldn't tell a soul.

Papa must have been reading my thoughts. "I think it would be best if we did not tell anyone about this gift from a Canadian soldier," said Papa. "Even though the war is over, we still have to be very careful about what we tell others."

Heads nodded around the table at Papa's suggestion but no one spoke. We did not want to spoil the magical moment with conversation.

**

I arose on Saturday morning with an unusual sense of excitement. I did not want to waste any time. I needed to thank the Canadian soldier right away. I helped clean up the breakfast dishes without any of the usual prodding from Karla. I had noticed that everyone in my family seemed a little happier this morning. I even heard Mama, Marlene, and Diane singing as they prepared breakfast. I couldn't remember the last time I'd heard Mama sing, and I'd never heard Diane's sweet voice before today. They sang my favourite tune, about birds and their music in the springtime:

> Alle Vögel sind schon da,
> alle Vögel, alle.
> Welch ein Singen, Musiziern,
> Pfeifen, Zwitschern, Tiriliern!
> Frühling will nun einmarschiern,
> kommt mit Sang und Schalle.

Just as I was about to set off on my quest to find the soldier, Karla asked, "Could I go with Johann to meet this soldier, Mama, please? You know that I speak English. I could help Johann converse with the Canadians."

Diane gasped. Mama shook her head. "No, Karla, I do

not think that would be wise. You are becoming a young lady and we do not know these men."

I felt sorry for my sister so I gave her a tip-of-the-hat gesture and a shoulder shrug before I turned to leave.

I clambered up the hill at record speed. I spotted a group of men hauling more supplies from an army truck into the rear boxcar. My benefactor was not among them. As I cautiously approached I heard one of them call out, "Ed, your little buddy is back." Although I could not understand all the words, I wasn't surprised to see my new friend poke his head out of one of the boxcars. My friend waved to me and beckoned for me to come closer. As I approached, he asked, "Did your family enjoy the chocolate bar?"

"Chocolate bar," I repeated slowly as I nodded my head.

"Was the chocolate bar good?" asked the man with those unforgettable crinkly eyes.

"Schokoladentafel . . ." I shook my head. "Chocolate bar good," I stammered.

"You're learning English quickly, my little friend," announced the man proudly. "Would you like to stay and help us unpack the supplies?"

"Help," I agreed with a bobbing head and a beaming smile.

"My name is Ed. Ed, me," he declared as he pointed at himself.

"Name Eddie," I repeated.

"Yes, I guess you can call me Eddie," said the man. "What is your name?" asked Eddie as he pointed to me.

"Name Johann Schmidt," I replied as I mimicked Eddie and pointed to my chest.

"Welcome to our barracks, Johann." Eddie said each word slowly. He turned to the other soldiers. "Everyone, listen up. This is Johann. He's going to help us unpack our supplies." I found myself surrounded by a dozen boisterous soldiers. They each shook my hand and told me their names. The carousel in my head spun faster and faster with all the excitement. Their names sounded so funny to me. George, Mike, Earl. Such names were not often heard in Germany. "Come with me, Johann. I'm responsible for storing the food supplies. The cook car is at the rear over there. Do you want to give me a hand?"

"Hand?" Now I was confused. I had learned at school that the word for hand was the same in English as it was in German, but I just did not understand. Did Eddie want me to give him my hand? I'd heard of terrible atrocities occurring during the war, but people who did such things were not nice people with crinkly eyes like Eddie, were they? I didn't realize that I had my hands tightly clasped together behind my back until I heard Eddie talking to me. I unclasped my hands and shook them loose as Eddie began to speak to me.

"What's wrong, my little friend? Are you afraid of us? No one here will hurt you. That is a promise." Eddie took my trembling hands in his. "I have three little boys back home just like you. I would not let anyone hurt you." Eddie gave me a hug and said, "Would you like to be my young friend?"

"Friend," I sputtered, with my head nodding up and down like a daisy in the wind.

"Come along then. I had better get to work before I get fired." Eddie burst into laughter at that absurd thought. I found myself giggling like a schoolgirl as relief washed over me. I was amazed at how many words I was beginning to understand. Papa's advice when I began studying English at school rang in my ears: "Johann, you must pay special attention in English class. Do not daydream even though you will not understand everything your teacher says. English is an important language. Someday you will be glad that you have worked hard to learn this language." I was beginning to appreciate Papa's wisdom.

Eddie and I spent the rest of the morning arranging the food in the supply car. I had never seen so much food in my life. I found myself licking my lips many times as we opened boxes to reveal food that my family hadn't eaten in years. I didn't even know what some of this food was called. I did recognize the bags of potatoes sitting in the corner of the supply car. I pointed to them and Eddie said, "Potatoes."

"Potatoes," I repeated.

"Do you eat potatoes, Johann?"

I nodded my head. How could I tell him that potatoes were so scarce that my family only had a chance to eat them once or twice a year? We had nothing to trade with the farmers who grew vegetables so we were restricted to using the food cards at the market. Vegetables and fruits were hard to find at the markets.

The man dressed in white arrived just before the noon hour to inspect the job we had done. This round-bellied older man with bulging eyes looked me up and down. I was amazed at his jolly appearance. Frau Berg was the only person I knew who could be called plump, but even she wasn't this rotund. "This is the cook for our soldiers, Johann. He is also our Sarge. My helper's name is Johann, Sarge."

"I'm pleased to make your acquaintance, Johann," declared the Sarge as he shook my hand.

"Acquaintance, Sarge," I said with pride. *This English language isn't so hard to learn after all*, I thought as Sarge and Eddie shared a smile.

Eddie looked at Sarge and closed one eye, saying, "When we greet someone we say 'hello.' Can you say hello, Johann?"

Does Eddie have something in his eye? I wondered,

although he only closed it one time. I remembered getting an eyelash in my eye once and I couldn't keep it open for Mama to look into it. Mama had to pry it open with her fingers.

"Hello, Johann." My face turned beet red as I realized that I had just said hello to myself. I shook my head to clear it and tried again. "Hello, Sarge." Eddie patted me on the head and nodded.

"That's right, Johann. Good for you. This young man was a big help to me today, Sarge. Could we send something home with him for his family?"

The jolly man frowned. "Ed, you know we can't feed the people. We barely have enough for ourselves." This brought a sad look to Eddie's face. His eyes weren't dancing any more. "Now, Ed, don't look at me like that. You know it's true. We don't know when next truck arrives. We have to make grub last long time." I was having trouble focusing on the words now that Eddie looked so sad.

Eddie's brow wrinkled and his lips pressed firmly together. He placed his hands on his hips and said, "I can go without potato supper tonight." Eddie stepped outside of the cook car and hollered, "Is there anyone else who supper without potato tonight?"

"What's the problem, Ed?" asked the tall, dark-haired, muscular man called George. "Are you trying lose weight be slim when you back home to wife?" The other soldiers burst into laughter.

Eddie's face got that distressed look again. "No, George. Johann, here, big help to me today and I want to give family potatoes. You know how short food people are here in Germany. I can without a potato for one night. Does anyone else feel same way?"

A dozen pairs of eyes glanced at me. They were staring

at my exposed arms and legs. I looked down to see my knobby knees and my skinny bare feet. I hadn't really noticed how skinny my family was. It seemed like everybody I knew looked the same way. But these soldiers didn't have bones sticking out like we did. George pulled on his moustache as he stepped forward and said, "So, boys, what you say? Can we survive without potato tonight?" He raised his index finger and pointed it at the men. "If you can, cook car and potato on the table." Without turning to face Eddie at the supply car door he said, "Ed, I think little Johann need box put the potatoes in." He raised his voice as he crossed his arms on his chest and fixed a firm eye on the men. "Right, boys?"

George's words must have been important because they all rushed over to the cook car except for the shortest man in the group. He was the man in charge of unloading the food from the truck yesterday, I realized. Eddie stepped aside to let them enter. Then he fixed his eyes on the short man. "Why are you standing there, Shorty? Aren't you give up potato tonight?" Eddie shook his pointing finger at the short man. "You know if you don't your potato too, it won't too great with the others, now will it? And what Sarge say about it?" Eddie and the short man were facing each other with deep scowls upon their faces.

"I don't care others think." The short man's nostrils flared. "I'm not going to feed no Nazi family." Shorty might not be as big as the others but his voice was like thunder and he shook his finger back at Eddie with such anger that my fear returned twofold. My heart jackhammered in my chest. I began to shiver all over. Had I done something wrong when I was helping Eddie? He had gotten so sad and the short man sounded really angry about something. His voice rose to new heights as the other men gathered around the duelling pair. "I ain't helping no Nazis, is what I say. Not ever. No way!"

Now this man was shouting at Eddie!

Mama and Papa won't let me come back here ever again if I made Eddie sad and the other soldiers angry, I thought as I realized I was trembling again.

My alarmed thoughts were interrupted by Eddie's gentle voice. "Here, Little One. Take these potatoes home to your family. You earned every one of them." Eddie turned to look over his shoulder at the short man. "Shorty, you go and be selfish. This is just a little boy, no different my three little boys back home. You enjoy potato this evening, Shorty. You'll be one eating a potato tonight so you enjoy yourself." He began to hand me one of the boxes we had emptied earlier that day.

A tall blond-haired man with a moustache looked down at Shorty. "You know Ed is right, Shorty. This little boy is just like children back home and I bet the rest of his family is no different us either. Now you put your potato in box like the rest of boys have done." Shorty's face was red. His green eyes flashed as he glared at him. "Okay, Earl, you win this time." He slammed his potato into the box. When Eddie put the box in my arms it wasn't empty any more. It was full of potatoes!

Chapter 5

The box was so heavy I dropped it twice on the way home. The potatoes went rolling down the hill both times. I giggled and laughed as I chased these gems of food. I had just put the last of the potatoes back into the box when I saw Karla running up the hill, with her shoulder-length blond hair dancing after her. I was so out of breath I could barely speak as I ran to meet her.

"What is so terribly funny, little brother? I could hear you laughing from inside the house." Karla's clipped tone momentarily halted my breathless giggles. "Look at you rolling all over the ground. You are going to get so dirty. Don't you think Mother has enough work to do without washing more clothes for you?" Karla's hands were on her hips. Sometimes she thought she was my mother. In spite of the scowl on Karla's face, I could not hold back my giggles. All I could do was point to the box of potatoes behind my sister. She was so intent on lecturing me that she had stormed right past them without even noticing them. When she saw the contents of the full box her face went ashen.

"Where on earth did these come from? Johann, stop laughing at once and tell me where these potatoes came from." Karla's eyes darted from the box of potatoes to the hill, then to her left, then to her right as she checked to see if anyone was watching us. "We must return them at once," Karla stated in a tight voice. "Johann, I do not think you realize how serious an offence it is to steal food. Please Johann,"

Karla's whispering voice pleaded, "help me return them before it is too late."

"There will be no need to return them, Karla," I said as I got up from the ground and dusted myself off. "I didn't mean to frighten you. These are our potatoes. My new friend, Eddie, gave them to me for helping the Canadian soldiers unload their supplies today. Let's take them into the house and surprise Mama."

Karla's eyes bulged in disbelief. "But, why . . . ," began Karla. "I mean how . . . " It was a rare thing to see my sister speechless. I rather enjoyed this new experience.

"I will explain everything to you and Mama at the same time. Now please, help me carry this box home. It's much too heavy for me to carry alone." We picked the box up together and carried it to the house and straight into the kitchen.

Mama was on her knees scrubbing the floor in the dining room. She turned her head at the sound of our footsteps. She watched us as we passed by her and through the open door into the kitchen. Her tired eyes rested on the box we placed on the floor. "Oh, there you are, Johann. What do you have in the box there?"

"Mama, I think you should come and look for yourself. See?" said Karla as she tipped the box towards our mother. Mama's eyes mimicked Karla's when she first saw the contents of the box. She slowly rose to her feet with her eyes glued to the potatoes.

"Those are potatoes. But where did they come from? Who do they belong to?" Mama's voice was trembling and hushed. She looked into Karla's eyes and with pursed lips she declared, "We must return them at once, Karla."

"Mama, these potatoes are a gift from the Canadian soldiers," I replied with a tentative smile.

Mama took a step towards the box. Her eyes never left

the contents of the box as she declared, "You must take them back at once, Johann. They do not belong to us. You know what punishment we will suffer if we take things that do not belong to us. We cannot even get potatoes with food cards now. How would we explain where they came from?" There it was again, that look of terror that I had grown up with. For a moment I was convinced that perhaps I should return this wondrous gift. I had pictured a look of joy on my Mama's face when she saw the potatoes, but once again I was disappointed.

I decided I was not going to give up so easily. These potatoes were a gift from a bunch of Canadian soldiers. These men were going to bed a little hungrier tonight so that my family could enjoy their meagre portions of potatoes. I squared my shoulders like I had seen Eddie do just this afternoon. My voice was firm as I explained, "Mother, this box of potatoes is my day's pay for helping the Canadian soldiers unload their supplies. My friend, Eddie, said he would give up his potato for supper tonight to pay me. The other soldiers agreed to give up their potato as well. There is one potato from each soldier in this box. We can keep them because I worked to earn them. These Canadians really want our family to have this gift. They said so, Mama, they really did."

It's funny that I was telling my Mama about working for pay when all day I was having so much fun and feeling so important. I hadn't even thought of myself as having worked at all. I knew that these were an offering but I also knew that Mama would not be able to accept such an overwhelming gift from a stranger. A chocolate bar was one thing, but a box right full of potatoes was quite another thing. I could not ever remember my family receiving a gift from anyone outside of the family. My family, like some others, had never supported the German cause so we were somewhat ostracized by the officials and therefore by some members of the community.

Many of the German people were in favour of Hitler at the beginning because of his enticing promises. The economy was terribly weak and unemployment was extremely high for years before the war started. During the election of 1933 Hitler promised that he would restore prosperity to the people of Germany. However, once Hitler was in power the people began to see that he was not interested in their welfare. He became extremely powerful very quickly. He started a war that many of the people did not support. Public negative comments about Hitler or his men were immediately and severely punished. The German people were no longer granted the freedom to express their personal views without fear of being harmed.

Mama slowly approached the box as she tucked a stray hair into the bun she kept her long red hair in. "I have no doubt that you would have worked very hard for these potatoes, Johann." She looked into the box wistfully and sighed. "I suppose we can keep them since you worked so hard for them." She examined the potatoes in the box.

"Perhaps I could bake them." Mama held one to her nose and inhaled deeply. "That way we would eat the skin and all. There would be no waste and no proof that we even had them in the first place." She counted the potatoes that lay in the box. "It looks like we would have enough potatoes here for four or five meals. We must all remember your friend . . ." She paused. "Did you say his name is Eddie?" I nodded my head. "We must remember Eddie and the others in our prayers," she declared as she put the potato back in the box.

Karla let out a whoop. She grabbed my hands and we jumped up and down together. "Just wait until Papa gets home for supper. He is going to be so surprised. When was the last time we had potatoes to eat, Mama?"

Mama took the box from Karla and me and hoisted it up onto the kitchen counter. "We were able to save some potatoes for our Christmas supper last year. I will clean just enough for supper tonight and hide the others in the larder." Mama carefully lifted the six smallest potatoes out of the box and laid them on the kitchen counter by the sink. "We will not eat them every day. We will save them for special days." She began to carefully scrub the skin of a potato. "Perhaps . . . " Mama placed the clean potato on the baking sheet. "Perhaps we should ask Papa if we can invite your friend Eddie to supper on Sunday."

My eyes lit up at the prospect of inviting Eddie to meet my family. "Karla, do you know the English words for come to supper?" I asked hopefully. Karla had been studying English for six years longer than I had. "I could visit the soldiers' freight cars after church tomorrow and ask Eddie to come for supper." I hummed a merry tune as I danced around the room with excitement.

"We will have to make sure it is fine with Papa first," reminded Mama. She smiled. "He is going to be so surprised when he sits down to the supper table this evening and sees potatoes on the platter." Finally I was rewarded with a look of real joy on Mama's face as she prepared the potatoes. The scrub bucket lay forgotten on the dining room floor.

Karla gave me lessons right away just in case Papa was in agreement with our plan. We practised the words of invitation until our other sisters arrived home from work. They were just as excited as we were about the surprise we had in store for Papa at the evening meal.

As soon as Papa arrived home we all took our place at the table except for Mama. The sauerkraut and biscuits were on the table. Papa was waiting for Mama to come to the table so that he could say grace. Finally he grew concerned. "Diane, what is taking your Mother so long in the kitchen? The food is on the table already. Why is she not here? Is something wrong?"

"I do not think anything is wrong, Papa. I will just go into the kitchen to fetch her."

Diane left the room and Papa turned his attention to me. "Johann, what did you busy yourself with today?" he asked.

I did not get an opportunity to reply, for just then Mama and Diane entered the dining room with radiant faces and a small platter of potatoes. Papa's eyes widened in surprise. "Mama, what is this you carry to the table? We already have our supper before us, do we not?" I sneaked a peek at the other faces at the table. Karla had tears streaming down her face. Diane was wringing her hands like she always did when she was anxious. Marlene's grey eyes sparkled as she anticipated Papa's surprise. Mama placed the baked potatoes on the table in front of Papa. We all held our breaths. "Mama, what is this?"

"You do not recognize a potato when you see it, Papa?" she teased, with a strained chuckle. The sound was strange to me. Laughs and chuckles were seldom heard in our community.

"Yes, of course I know these are potatoes, Mama. But where did they come from? I have not seen a potato for a very long time. Last Christmas, was it not?" Papa stared at the potatoes. He frowned and asked, "Did someone offer these potatoes in return for a favour, Mama? You know we agreed not to help the cause in any way. I will not permit these potatoes to be eaten if that is the case."

"Mama, please tell Papa about Eddie," blurted Karla. My heart sank. I felt nauseated. *Was my friendship with Eddie over? Would Papa forbid me to visit Eddie again?* The faces of the others around the table reflected my anxiety.

"Eddie! Who is Eddie?" demanded Papa loudly, his brow furled, his cheeks flaming.

"Eddie is the Canadian soldier who gave Johann the candy bar. Johann has made a friend of Eddie," explained Mama staunchly, with her head held high.

"A Canadian soldier, you say? Sure we hear that the Canadians are kind people. But I do not understand. Just what does this Eddie have to do with these potatoes?" He searched Mama's face as he awaited her response.

My heart settled down as Mama firmly replied, "Johann, tell your father what happened today."

Papa listened intently as I related the day's events to him. He smiled and nodded his head when I told him the part about all of the soldiers going without their potato tonight so that we could enjoy a treat. I left out the part about the short man's anger. I had often heard Papa say that some things are better left unsaid. I was beginning to understand what that meant.

Papa rubbed his chin as he listened. When my story was done he suggested, "You must invite this Eddie to our home Sunday evening, Johann. Then I will know if it is all right for you to be his friend. I need to see for myself if these Canadians are such good people or not. Does he speak German, this Eddie?"

"No, Papa. He speaks English but I am learning English from him. Karla helps me too." Karla smiled at Papa and proudly nodded her head.

"I can translate the English Eddie speaks," announced Karla with glowing eyes. "You know that I get good grades in English class at school, Papa. I have been teaching Johann the proper English words to use for the invitation al—"

Karla's hands flew over her mouth as she realized that she had just admitted to Papa that we all expected him to agree with our plan to invite Eddie to our home.

"Oh, you have, have you?" asked Papa with a smile.

Mama served a potato to each of us. "We thought perhaps we could invite him for supper, Papa. That is, if you are in agreement."

"Very well then," replied Papa. "You can invite this Eddie to supper Sunday night, Johann. Perhaps we can find a way to thank this generous man for his kindness. I hear that the Canadian soldiers do not have so much food that they can afford to feed others. I think that Eddie and his friends will go to sleep hungry tonight. Let's pray for their comfort and safety." We all bowed our heads in prayer, the aroma of baked potatoes floating in our nostrils, and said heartfelt thanks for the gift of a new friend.

Chapter 6

My family seemed to have a renewed spring in their steps as we walked to church Sunday morning. It was as if we shared a joyful secret. We waved to others as we approached the church grounds just as we had every other Sunday that I could remember, but this Sunday was different for us. Could the others see how different we felt? Our family had agreed not to speak to others of our Canadian friend.

Andreas and I exchanged a darting glance as my family walked past him to take our place in a pew near the front of the church. We knelt down to pray. I felt a sense of hope as I prayed. I could hear whispers behind me but I was trained to never turn around in church and look at the people behind me. My family considered that to be very rude. Ignoring the persistent whispers with great difficulty, I focused on my prayers. This morning they were extended to include Andreas's family as well as the families of the Canadian soldiers. I had never felt such hope since before Arthur had been forced to join the army. We had seen Arthur only once since that day. He was allowed to come home for a brief visit before he was shipped out. We had heard from him only a couple of times since. I prayed today, as I did every day, that Arthur would be returned to us soon.

Mid-way through the mass my heart leapt into my throat. Eddie was in our church! He was wearing a white shirt, a tie, and grey pants. He walked back to his seat after Communion with his hands clasped in front of him. Our eyes met and he waved with just his forefinger. His eyes smiled along with his mouth. My shaking hand returned a tiny wave. *Should I tell Mama and Papa that Eddie is here? Or should I wait until after church when the people are returning home? What if someone saw him wave to me?* These questions swirled around in my mind. It's no wonder I didn't hear another word the priest said for the remainder of the service. I was extremely upset about my situation. *If I do not acknowledge Eddie will he feel insulted? If I do speak to him will my family be in danger? We will be walking home in the same direction so maybe I should wait until we are close to our home before I speak to him. But then maybe he will think my family doesn't want me to have anything to do with him. I think that will make him sad. Oh, what should I do?*

Karla jabbed me in the ribs. "Johann, what are you doing? Church is over. You can stop praying now and come home with us." I realized I was still kneeling in the church pew. The church was empty except for Karla and me.

"Where are Mama and Papa? Is everyone gone from the churchyard?" My eyes flitted around the church.

"Mama and Papa sent me back to get you, silly. They have just started walking home. Come on. I am hungry."

"Eddie was in church this morning. He waved to me."

"He was here? This morning?" asked the dumbfounded Karla.

"Yes, Karla. He waved at me when he was returning to his seat after Communion. Karla, should I tell Mama and Papa he was here? Should I introduce him to them on our way home? Or should I just say nothing about it? Please, Karla, tell me, what should I do?"

"We need to get going. We will catch up to the family first. Then if you see Eddie walking we can decide. Come on! Let's go before it is too late to catch up with him."

Karla and I hurried out of the church. We soon caught up to the family as they made their way home at a leisurely pace. Up ahead I could make out a figure of a man. I grabbed Karla's hand and said, "Let's run ahead, Karla. See if you can catch me."

She looked back at the others and said, "Johann and I will have a race home. We will meet you there; will that be fine with you?"

Papa nodded his head absently as he was in the middle of a discussion with Mama and my older sisters.

By the time we caught up to Eddie he was just walking by our house. I stole a glance behind me down the block but my family was nowhere in sight. Neither was anyone else visible on the street, I was relieved to see. Our house was off by itself, two blocks from any others, so we didn't have any neighbours to worry about.

"Hello, Eddie," I said, my voice reflecting my excitement at seeing him again.

Eddie turned on his heel. His face broke out into a familiar smile. "Now, who do we have here? Could it be my new friend, Johann?" I felt Karla's jab in my ribs again.

Practising my English with Karla the night before certainly proved to be helpful.

"Yes, Eddie, I am Johann." A harder jab steadied my voice as I introduced Karla to my new friend.

"Hello, Eddie," said Karla as she gave Eddie a little curtsy and bowed her crimson face. "Would you like to come to our home for supper this evening?"

I gave Karla a sideways glance. *There goes Karla, showing off her English skills.* Even as this thought crossed my mind I felt gratitude. The conversation was about to go beyond my limited grasp of the language. I realized it was time to let Karla take over the conversation.

Eddie's eyes widened in surprise at the unexpected invitation. "I don't know if your parents would be in agreement with the invitation, Karla, but I am very glad to meet you. Now I have two new friends in this country. You speak very good English, by the way."

Eddie began to walk towards the boxcars. I grabbed his forearm and guided him to our front steps.

"Here comes our family now. Let me introduce you to them, Eddie," said Karla. Before he could reply we both rushed up to meet the family.

Mama thanked Eddie for the potatoes.

Karla relayed the message to Eddie. He said, "Tell your mother that we were glad to pay Johann for his hard work."

Papa smiled at me and patted me on the head.

"You should have seen my friend Shorty. He's the youngest member of our battalion at twenty-one years of age." Eddie burst into laughter. "He made rumbling sounds with his mouth all evening and tried to convince us that his stomach was empty just because he didn't have his potato for one night." Eddie grabbed his stomach and made a funny rumbling sound as he tossed his head from side to side, his face all screwed up and his cheeks puffed out. My entire family was laughing. Diane had tears running down her cheeks. I couldn't remember seeing these kinds of tears before. These were happy tears.

"Karla, please ask Eddie . . ." Papa was laughing so hard he could barely speak. "Ask Eddie if he would join us for supper this evening."

"Are you sure that would be all right, Mr. Schmidt?" asked a once again serious Eddie. "It wouldn't be too dangerous for you to have a Canadian soldier as a guest in your home?"

Papa was sombre now too. "No, Eddie. I think it will be

just fine. It would be our pleasure to have you as our guest this evening." Papa looked up and down the street. "I would ask, though, that you be careful that no one knows where you are going. We do not want anyone to know of our friendship just yet." Karla gave Eddie a weak smile as she translated this message.

Eddie glanced at me. "Yes, I understand. The war is barely over and I don't think any of us know what to expect just yet." Eddie smiled reassuringly at my family. "It was very nice to meet all of you. What time should I arrive this evening?" Now it was Eddie who was glancing up and down the street.

"If you come from the west no one will see you so you can come during daylight. Please come around six o'clock if you can," instructed Papa.

"Six o'clock it is then. I'll look forward to our evening together." With a tip of a hat gesture and a nervous grin, Eddie turned south to walk to his barracks. My whole family stayed on the front steps watching our new friend until he was out of sight.

"How lonely it must be for these men. I wonder how long it has been since they have seen their families," said Mama thoughtfully.

"It's just like with Arthur, Otto, and Friedel, Mama. They must be missing us badly too." I said. Diane and Marlene had tears in their eyes.

"Maybe we can give this Canadian soldier a family here in Germany so he does not have to be so lonely. At least we expect to see our boys soon now that the war is over," declared Mama.

"I hear that these Canadians may be here for a very long time," offered Marlene, "as much as eighteen months, according to my employer, Herr Vogel."

Our family was quiet once again, each with their own thoughts of how devastating this war had been for us all. I said a silent thank you to Eddie for making my family laugh. I was proud that I had been the one to bring Eddie into my family's life.

Chapter 7

Karla and I spent most of the afternoon in the parlour nestled on the sofa looking at our English textbooks. We soon discovered that I had learned a great deal even in the last few days. We decided that my textbook was too elementary, and concentrated on Karla's level of English. We were concentrating so hard that we didn't notice Marlene and Diane enter the room. I jumped at the sound of Diane's voice: "Karla and Johann, we need your help."

"Our help?" I asked.

"Yes, could you teach us a few English words so that we can speak to Eddie too?" Marlene asked shyly. Diane stood beside her, eyes lowered, wringing her hands.

"You want me to teach you?" My voice betrayed my surprise. It had never occurred to me that I could teach my big sisters anything. Big sisters were supposed to know everything, weren't they?

"What would you like to know?" asked Karla in her matter-of-fact manner.

"Just teach us how to greet Eddie and how to introduce ourselves properly in English for now," requested Marlene.

"I think that will be easy enough. You can both repeat after me: How do you do?"

Diane and Marlene repeated the words but they sounded so funny that I couldn't help but giggle. "Let's try that again," said Karla. "How do you do?" My older sisters repeated the words in a halting fashion.

"Johann, this is not easy for us. Stop giggling," admonished Diane. "It is not so funny. Marlene and I did not have a chance to study English at school like you did. Let's hear you say the words. Maybe it will be easier if we hear them from more than one person."

"How do you do?" I said in a slow staccato voice. Now Karla was giggling at my antics. Marlene couldn't hold a straight face either. Before long all four of us were giggling. We began dancing around the room repeating "How do you do?" and slapping our thighs to the rhythm of the words.

Mama and Papa heard the commotion. They peeked into the room to see the four of us dancing and repeatedly singing the words "How do you do?" They smiled at each other, shrugged their shoulders, and joined in the fun. "How do you do?" chorused my family as we danced together in a circle. Laughter filled the room. This house must be wondering what had happened this day as the long-forgotten music of frivolity bounced gaily from its walls. Finally, we all collapsed on the sofas and allowed ourselves to revel in the joy of the moment.

I heard a faint knock at the door. Mama had instructed us that, when Eddie arrived, she wanted to be the one to answer the door. She was pleased that we had been practising the words she would need to use. I jumped off the sofa and dashed to the front door with Karla at my heels.

"Mama, come quickly," I called over my shoulder. I was breathless with excitement. "It must be Eddie at the door. Didn't you hear the knock?"

"Is it that time already?" asked Diane with a shaky voice as she headed to the kitchen to place the baked potatoes back into the oven to keep warm.

"I think everything is ready, Mama. Perhaps you should open the door," suggested Marlene, as she untied her apron and headed to the kitchen to put it on the hook by the stove. She and Diane quickly returned to the dining room.

Mama's eyes were wild. "Johann, you will come with me. And you too, Karla," instructed Mama. "I will say the greeting, and then you will need to continue the conversation. Marlene and Diane, you may take your place in the parlour with Papa."

"Mama, please hurry," implored Karla. "Eddie will think we are not at home."

"Yes, Mama," I added as I hopped from one foot to the other. I couldn't stand still no matter how hard I tried. "Please hurry, Mama; Eddie may think we have changed our minds. Come, Mama," I said as I pulled Mama towards the door; "hurry."

"Yes. But is everybody ready?" My sisters were still in the dining room fussing at the table. Diane went to join Papa in the parlour. Marlene steered Mama to the door but by this time the knocking had stopped.

"Oh, no!" I exclaimed. "Do you suppose he has already left? We should have hurried faster, Mama." Tears slipped down my cheeks.

Marlene instructed, "Open the door, Mama. He may still be there."

Mama rubbed her hands on her apron. "Oh no, I am still wearing my apron. I cannot answer the door with my apron on." Mama's eyes were filled with panic. "Maybe Papa should answer the door after all." Mama turned towards the parlour.

Karla placed her hands firmly on Mama's shoulders to stop her retreat. She began to untie Mama's apron. "It is fine, Mama. You can do it. I will just take your apron to the kitchen while you say your greeting. I will be back to help you before Eddie has an opportunity to respond." Karla spun on her heels and darted for the kitchen, apron strings billowing out behind her.

"It's fine, Mama. Please open the door now," I said quietly. I really didn't expect to see Eddie standing on the other side any more anyway. It must have been at least five minutes since I'd heard that last knock.

Mama straightened her hair and flattened the skirt of her best dress. She put her trembling hand on the doorknob and slowly turned it. She tentatively opened the door only a crack. I was peering anxiously from behind her and, just as I feared, there was no Eddie standing on the doorstep. Mama flung the screen door wide open. We both stepped out the door but there was no one in sight.

Karla came rushing up behind us. "Mama, are we too late? Where is Eddie?" Her voice broke as she realized Eddie was not there.

"Did I hear somebody say my name?" My heart leapt in my chest. Eddie was coming around the side of the house. No one spoke. We had agreed to let Mama say her greeting before we said anything to Eddie.

Karla gently took Mama's hand and whispered, "Go ahead, Mama, say the greeting."

Mama cleared her throat and raised her lowered chin. "How . . . how do you do, Eddie?" With that formidable task over, Mama's shoulders relaxed. She extended her hand to Eddie with a smile. Karla and I stepped forward to take the pressure off Mama and begin our roles as interpreters.

"I'm fine, Frau Schmidt, and you?" Mama was bathed in those incredibly warm blue eyes as Eddie gently shook her hand.

"My family does not speak English, Eddie." Karla stepped in front of Mama. "Mama practised the words to greet you. Now Johann and I will have to speak for the family. We will interpret what is said as well as we can." Karla cocked her head and looked up at Eddie. "Will that be all right with you, Eddie?" she asked shyly.

"I believe that will work just fine. Please tell your Mama that she did a fine job of greeting me." Karla quickly relayed the message. Mama's face was glowing as she beckoned Eddie to enter our home.

"Where you go?" I asked Eddie. I looked over at Karla to see her nodding her head in approval of my English skills. "Mama open the door. You not at the door, Eddie."

Eddie burst into laughter. "No. You're quite right. When you didn't answer the door after several minutes, I thought that perhaps you used a back door. I was just walking towards the back of the house when I heard the front door open. Did you think I had left, my little friend?" Those blue eyes weren't laughing any more. "Friends keep their promises to each other. I wouldn't have left so easily." Eddie patted me on the head. I found myself beaming back at him.

"Did you see the back yard, Eddie?" asked Mama with alarm. My legs felt weak as I realized that Eddie might have discovered the dreaded shelter connected to the back of our house. What if he wants to know about the many months we had to live in that hole? Eddie gave Mama a quizzical look. He glanced at me, then at Karla for interpretation. Mama quickly recovered and asked, "Or did you hear us first?" she asked with a smile.

"I was just heading around to the back yard when I heard you at the front door. I wasn't sure if I should be seen hanging around on your front step." Eddie searched my face, then he turned back to Mama and asked in a hushed tone, "Did I do something wrong, Frau Schmidt? I'm not accustomed to Germany yet, having only just arrived. I'm really sorry if I've done something I shouldn't have."

"No, Eddie, you have done nothing wrong," assured Mama. "We are still not sure ourselves what is acceptable and what is not. The war is just ending and we do not know what to expect of life in post-war Germany." Mama shook her head. "You have done nothing wrong. We have done nothing wrong. The war is over. We just want our old lives back. I did not mean to alarm you, Eddie." Mama beckoned Eddie to come inside as she looked up and down the street once again. Eddie joined her in the street surveillance but he also glanced towards his barracks just over the hill.

We wasted no time leading Eddie into the parlour, where the others sat rigidly in their seats. I took Eddie by the hand and led him to Papa. Papa rose from his seat and offered a hand to Eddie in greeting. He even said the words we had all practised earlier that day: "How do you do, Eddie?" The words were uttered slowly and precisely.

"I am pleased to be invited to your home, Mr. Schmidt." Eddie and Papa shook hands enthusiastically.

Diane and Marlene were still sitting together on the sofa. They stood up in unison and came to Papa's side. "How do you do, Eddie?" they said.

Eddie smiled. "Please tell your sisters I'm fine, Karla."

Marlene extended her hand to Eddie and said simply, "Marlene."

"I'm very pleased to meet you, Marlene," replied Eddie as he shook her hand.

Diane kept her eyes lowered as she said her greeting. She did not shake Eddie's hand. My two older sisters did not resemble each other even though they were the same height and only two years apart in age. They both had pale complexions but Marlene had fine curly blond hair; Diane's was wavy and jet-black. Marlene had a cute upturned nose, full lips, and happy grey eyes. Diane had serious brown eyes and thin tight lips. Marlene was easy-going and fun-loving. Diane, on the other hand, was serious and full of angst. They smiled at Eddie and sat back down on the sofa.

Papa asked Eddie to sit down on the family's most comfortable chair. Usually Papa sat in the worn beige armchair but on occasion he would relinquish it to a special guest.

Karla sat on one of the dining room chairs brought in for this occasion and placed opposite Eddie so that she was well positioned for her duties as an interpreter. I snuggled on the smaller sofa with Mama and rested my curly red head on her chest. Papa sat between my older sisters on the larger sofa, one of his arms around each of them.

"You just arrived in Leer two nights ago?" inquired Mama.

"Yes, we were in England before that," replied Eddie.

"What will you be doing here?" asked Papa.

"We're here to fix the machinery that has been abandoned."

"Do you know how long you will be here?" asked Karla.

"We're told that we'll be here for a year or so," Eddie got a faraway look in his eyes.

"That is a very long time to be away from your family," Marlene said quietly. Eddie nodded sadly.

"Well, then." Mama nodded her head. "I think we should move to the dining room. Our supper is keeping warm in the oven." Mama and I rose from the sofa. Papa led Eddie to the dining room while Mama and my older sisters disappeared into the kitchen. Papa pointed to the chair he wanted Eddie to use. This spot at the table was left empty when Arthur had to join the army. Now it was in use once again. I found myself smiling. Eddie joined my family as we said words of thanks for the food we were about to eat. Before we touched the food, Papa addressed Eddie: "We want to thank you again for the potatoes, Eddie. We understand that all of the soldiers gave up their potato for that one meal. That was very kind of them," said Papa.

"It wasn't such a big deal after all. Cook simply made a stew without any potatoes. It was a little watery but not all that bad," replied Eddie.

"Tell us again about your friend Shorty acting funny last night," begged Karla.

"Shorty is the one who doesn't like me," I blurted out.

Eddie must have noticed the hurt in my voice. He looked at me and asked Karla to interpret what I had just said. Karla looked over at Papa. Papa nodded his head. Karla relayed my statement.

"You need to know that Shorty likes to complain about a lot of things. He spends a lot of his time scowling and grumbling about the little things in life." Eddie then turned to me and said, "I'm sorry if he upset you, Johann. I think you'll get used to him after a while. Sometimes he's a very funny person. Like last night for instance." Eddie chuckled, and he repeated the antics from that afternoon. This time, however, he went into great detail. He pretended he was eating watery stew. He searched around on his plate with his fork for the potatoes. Then he set his fork down and with a scowling face he picked the plate up and looked under it. He placed the plate back down on the table with a grunt. Shaking his finger at the air, he grumbled under his breath. Then he looked under the table. He lifted the tablecloth at the edge of the table. Still shaking his head, he looked under the candlesticks. By this time we were laughing uncontrollably. I took a great deal of pleasure in observing my family's reactions. Marlene had her arms crossed over her middle and was holding her sides. Mama was wiping tears from her eyes. Papa pushed his chair away from the table and slapped his thighs as he guffawed at Eddie's clowning actions. Eddie imitated Shorty's contorted face. He rolled his eyes and billowed out his cheeks. My cheeks were sore from laughing. Now Diane was holding her sides with laughter too. Eddie made some strange low rumbling noises. Karla went to the sideboard to get a hanky to blow her nose. She was laughing so hard she got the hiccups. I was thoroughly enjoying the moment. After all, if it had not been for my meeting Eddie, this family would be having another solemn meal, just like every other night since I could remember.

Finally Eddie sank back down in Arthur's chair and revelled in the hilarity around him. Karla handed him a hanky to wipe his laughing eyes. Papa finally gained control of his voice and declared, "Eddie, you have made my family laugh tonight." The laughter continued to roll out of his body. "I thank you for that, Eddie." He smiled as he looked around his jovial table. "Perhaps we had better eat before everything is too cold to enjoy."

The remainder of the meal was much more subdued. The family wanted to know more about Eddie. "What part of Canada are you from?" asked Marlene. She had a penchant for world geography but she didn't know Canada all that well.

"I'm from the province of Saskatchewan. Canada has nine provinces and two territories," Eddie informed us.

"Where is this Saskatchewan?" pressed Marlene as she tried to get her tongue around the strange word.

Eddie asked for everyone's napkins. He folded each one and lined them up in the shape of the country, explaining that each napkin represented two provinces. He folded one in quarters to represent the ninth province. Then he placed two unfolded napkins across the top to represent the territories. When this was done he placed the salt shaker on the one representing Saskatchewan. Then he pointed with his finger to the southeast part of "Saskatchewan" and said, "I live right about here."

"Do you live in a big city?" asked Diane.

Eddie's eyes crinkled as he chuckled, "I live in a tiny village. It's so small that we even count the dogs and cats when we take our census." Again the room filled with laughter.

My cheeks and sides already hurt from the evening's jocularity. *How much more of this fun can we take in one night?* I wondered. *Maybe it's possible to have a future filled with hope and joy after all.* I delighted in the sight of my parents' and sisters' sparkling teary eyes. I couldn't wait for the day when Arthur would return from the dreadful war and meet our new friend. Arthur needed to learn what the word fun meant. I suspected that the war would have taken Arthur's sense of fun away from him. I just hoped Eddie could help Arthur learn to enjoy a laugh once in a while. Until Eddie came into our lives we had all forgotten how to laugh.

Chapter 8

Later that evening Mama finally asked the question that she had wondered about ever since she first met Eddie. "Do you have a family back in Saskatchewan?"

His answer was given in a quiet tone. Karla had to strain her ears to understand his reply. "Yes, Frau Schmidt. Besides my parents and siblings, I have a wife and three little boys." Eddie's melancholy was infectious.

"When was the last time you saw them?" asked Diane in a halting voice.

"I haven't seen them for seventeen and a half months. I haven't even seen the baby yet, and my two-year-old I've only seen once since he was born." Eddie's voice broke.

"You must miss them very much," said Marlene. "How old are your three boys?"

"Frank will be five this summer, Armand is just over two, and Edmond is fifteen months old."

"Do you have any pictures of them?" asked Marlene gently.

"I don't have a camera so, no, I don't have any pictures. I sure wish I did though. I would like to know what they look like now. You know how fast children grow." Eddie turned to me and smiled. "Like you, Johann. What did you look like when you were a little baby? Did you have pointy ears and a flat nose?" He tousled my hair. Smiling Eddie was back again. In fact, the whole family was smiling once again, relieved to end the painful questions.

"Mama, can we show Eddie our pictures?" I didn't want him to think I looked strange when I was a baby.

Mama rose from the table. "We will clear the table first. Then we will all meet in the parlour to show Eddie the few pictures we do have." Eddie was helping to clear the table. He was about to follow Mama into the kitchen, his hands full of dishes. "No! Eddie, no!" Alarm rang from Mama's voice. "You go ahead to the parlour with Papa. We will join you in a few minutes. We will take our refreshment in the parlour." Mama looked over her shoulder at Eddie as she continued on to the kitchen. "Would you like some tea, Eddie? We are all out of coffee for now." Eddie hesitated and looked at me as if for guidance.

Karla explained to Eddie, "The ladies will just put the dishes in the sink. We will do them later." I smiled at Eddie to reassure him. Karla continued, "They will join us as soon as the tea is made." Eddie was confused by Mama's reaction once again. He was the only one who didn't understand that if he went to the kitchen sink with his handful of dishes, he would have a full view of the dreaded shelter in the back yard through the window. I think Eddie was feeling as confused around my family just now as I had felt earlier in the company of the Canadian soldiers.

Eddie reached into his pocket and pulled out a small package. "Perhaps these would go nicely with a cup of tea, Frau Schmidt." He solemnly held the package out to Mama.

"What do we have here?" asked my puzzled Mama. Her hands remained at her side.

"They're cookies I bought in England just before we came to Leer. I held onto them in case I had a special occasion to eat them. This is a very special evening for me so I'd like to share my treat with all of you."

"But you have done so much for us already, Eddie. We cannot eat your cookies. They are for you."

Eddie took Mama's hand and placed the package in it. "What good is a treat if you have no one to share it with? Please allow me the privilege of sharing them with you." Eddie closed Mama's hand over the cookies and turned to me. He tousled my hair, closed one eye, and made that clicking sound with his tongue.

I must remember to ask Eddie what that strange gesture means sometime, I thought, but right now the notion of having a cookie for the first time in months took precedence over any other thoughts going on in my mind.

"I'll bet Johann here would enjoy a cookie just about now. Am I right about that, Johann?" asked Eddie as he gave me a playful jab in the side. I giggled and found my head bobbing up and down in whole-hearted agreement. Eddie adopted a British mannerism to declare, "That settles it then. We shall have cookies with our tea this evening."

"Come, Eddie," said my subdued Papa. "I would like to show you . . ." Papa gulped. "Show you my stamp collection." I followed Papa and Eddie into the parlour while two of the girls helped Mama in the kitchen. Of course, Karla needed to stay with Eddie so she could interpret.

The four of us moved into the parlour. Papa turned to Eddie and appeared to want to say something. He shook his head and, instead of speaking, he walked over to the shelf that housed his cherished stamp collection. Eddie looked confused as he stood by the armchair. He looked at me, then at Karla. "Karla, did I upset your father? He seems to be somewhat agitated."

Karla took Eddie's hands in hers and looked into his worried eyes. "Papa is not upset with you, Eddie. He is moved by your kindness. I think he would like to say so to you but it

is difficult for him to express his feelings in words sometimes." Eddie just slowly nodded his head.

Eddie stepped towards the armchair. He was about to sit
down when Papa motioned for him to sit on the sofa instead.
Eddie looked at me and pointed to the sofa with a questioning look. "Yes, Eddie," I said in English, "sit there." I had
heard so much English being spoken tonight that I was feeling much more comfortable using this new language myself.

Papa brought the oldest stamp album over to the sofa.
He sat down beside Eddie. "This album is over one hundred
years old. It was started five generations ago by my great-great-
great grandfather. It was given to the oldest boy in each family: I am the oldest in my family and that is how I came to
have it. My son Arthur will receive the collection some day."
Papa opened the ancient book gingerly. He pointed to the
first stamp in the collection.

"This very first stamp was placed in this album by my
great-great-great grandfather. It was on a parcel received when
his first child was born." Papa heaved a deep sigh while Karla
translated his words for Eddie. When she was done he continued. "That son was my great-great grandfather. The original
stamp was on a parcel sent by his grandparents. Anyway, the
stamp, as you can see, was unusual, so my great-great-great
grandfather became interested in it and decided to start a collection of unusual stamps. Shortly after he began his collection,
he died from consumption. It is my understanding that this first
page, which we can see has empty spaces, was his contribution.
His son, who of course was an infant when he died, never com-
pleted the page. He decided to carry on his father's collection
but he left that first page incomplete. The story goes that he felt
the unfinished page represented his own feeling of incomplete-
ness. He never knew his own father and that left him feeling a
little less than whole, or so the story goes." Karla had no prob-

lem remembering all that Papa said because she had grown up hearing this same story.

Papa had told us that he honoured those feelings and he instructed us to never fill the empty spaces on the page. The widow later collected the missing stamps. They were in the cigar box that was still sitting on the shelf. They were safely stored in a small envelope inside the old box. We were told to leave them there in honour of the originator of the collection. Through Karla, Papa relayed this information to Eddie.

"How sad it must be for a father never to see his son grow up," commented Eddie. "And for the son, I can't imagine what it would be like to grow up without a father."

Papa and Eddie had both become so sombre. I wanted to lighten the moment so I said in my halting English, "Eddie, Johann tell you something." That got his attention and a smile. "Arthur collecting stamps too."

Papa looked inquisitively at Karla. She relayed my declaration and Papa nodded his head. "Yah, yah," he said. Then in German he went on to explain that the other stamps in the cigar box were the ones Arthur began collecting when he went away to war. It seemed that the only thing Arthur enjoyed about the army was that he had an opportunity to add quite a number of stamps to the family album. Every time mail came to Arthur's battalion he would go around and ask the other soldiers for their stamps. The one and only time he had been permitted to come home on a leave he almost filled the cigar box with his collection.

"They must be left there," Papa continued, "until Arthur returns to place them in the album himself." That way, Karla took it upon herself to explain to Eddie, Arthur must return from the war. She told Eddie that Papa had been spending a great deal of time with his stamp collection since

Arthur was sent away. She said she thought it made Papa feel closer to his missing son.

I never knew this thing about Papa poring over his stamp collection so he could feel closer to Arthur. *I don't think that would make me feel closer to Arthur,* I thought. Then I realized that I'd read and reread the book Arthur gave me just before he left for the war. In fact I'd read it so many times that I almost had it memorized. Yet I'd find myself reading it again. *Is that my way of trying to feel closer to my big brother?*

"Would you like to collect Canadian stamps as well? I could easily collect stamps from any parcels I receive. In fact," said Eddie as he sat on the edge of the sofa, visibly excited by the prospect, "I'm sure my buddies would add any stamps they receive to the collection as well. Would you like that, Mr. Schmidt?"

"That is a fine idea. We could begin a brand new collection in honour of our friendship with you, Eddie," declared Papa with a broad smile.

"I must warn you, Mr. Schmidt," replied Eddie," that any collection I could undertake would pale in comparison to your fine treasury of stamps. We don't really get that much mail, I'm afraid. However, I'm very willing to see what I can do."

"Maybe so," said Papa, "but it could be a unique collection of Canadian stamps. It would seem appropriate that such a collection should be started for my second son, do you not think, Eddie?"

"For me, Papa? Really? A stamp collection just for me?" I didn't think I could trust my ears. I had never dreamed that one day I too would have a stamp collection of my very own. Of course I realized that anyone can start his own collection but that is just not the same as one someone else started just for you.

"Why not?" asked Papa. "You are the one who brought

Eddie to us. This new collection would serve as a reminder to all the generations that follow of our good friend from Canada, named Eddie."

Karla's interpretation of this last exchange between Papa and me brought a vast smile to Eddie's face. He looked up at me and said, "Would you like a Canadian stamp collection for your very own, Johann?"

"Canada stamps for me, Eddie?" I just could not believe my good fortune. My eyes felt like they were about to burst from their sockets. "I keep stamps for my family when I am big. Yes, Eddie?"

"That sounds great to me." He turned to Papa and Karla and asked, "What do the two of you think?"

Papa simply nodded his head. Karla smiled. "Eddie, I have observed Johann as he sat with Papa many times looking at the albums. He never said so but I believe he secretly hoped to have his own collection some day." Karla stood up and moved over to the sofa. She knelt down in front of Eddie and put her hand on Eddie's shoulder. She said in a soft voice, "You have made my little brother very happy. Thank you."

Eddie looked over Karla's head at Papa. Papa put his hand on Eddie's other shoulder and patted it to assure Eddie that everything was okay. No one noticed that Mama and my sisters had entered the room laden with the tea service and cookies. When Papa saw them standing at the side table he explained what had just transpired. Mama broke into an expansive grin and came over to hug me. Marlene's eyes sparkled as she said, "*Danke*, Eddie."

Mama served Eddie first. "I'm sorry we don't have any cream, sugar or lemon for your tea, Eddie. We do not have any more food cards for milk or cream left for this month and we never get food cards for luxuries like lemons."

"I like my tea black anyway, *danke*." Eddie accepted the

dainty china teacup. "So are you able to buy food with money here?" he inquired.

"We no longer have currency here in Germany. The only way you could get cream, meat, and vegetables is if you had something to barter with the farmers. Otherwise, you have to do like us and only use food cards," explained Mama.

Papa's face was lowered. I knew that he felt it was a man's job to provide for his family but it had been very difficult for Papa to get work in the war years. The fact that Arthur served in the army did put our family in some people's favour so he did have odd jobs. The income was so scarce that he was not able to support his family. We were barely able to procure enough food to keep us alive. Hitler had allocated most of Germany's funds to the war effort, leaving only enough to provide our people with the bare necessities of life. Marlene was fortunate to be able to have steady work at the railroad station. Her earnings were meagre and Papa insisted that she save some of it for her upcoming marriage to Otto. They were not formally engaged yet but that would happen as soon as Otto returned from the army. Diane was already married and therefore she had trouble finding work. Married women were the last to get hired. She got her odd jobs just like Papa because, in her case, it was her husband who was away in the army.

"Food is rationed back home, too," said Eddie, "and most of the men are not able to support their families very well either."

"Does your wife have food cards too?" asked Marlene.

"She has much the same thing but we call them food stamps."

"We are only able to get fifty to one hundred grams of butter per person weekly. I do have some flour but I cannot bake much without butter or lard," apologized Mama. "We have not had a cookie for many months. Sometimes we will save up our small portions of butter until we have enough for a small batch." Mama sighed heavily. "But most of the time we use it up for our daily needs."

Diane was carrying the dessert plate. I was relieved when I counted nine cookies and there were only seven people in the room. They were so tiny that one large bite would pretty much consume a whole one. Diane offered the cookies to Eddie. He shook his head no, insisting that he was too full for dessert.

Mama was done serving tea by this time. She put her hands on her hips and turned to Eddie. "No one in this family will touch one bite if you do not join us. You said you wanted to share these treats, did you not?"

"Yes, that's what I said all right, Frau Schmidt." Eddie looked a little bewildered at her tone of voice.

"Sharing implies that we all do the same, do you not agree?" asked Mama as she placed a cookie on a saucer for Eddie. She handed Eddie the saucer and this time he accepted it.

"Your Mama sure drives a hard bargain," Eddie stated to Karla. "Please tell her I said so."

Papa reacted to that remark with a knee-slapping laugh. "Yah, Eddie, yah." Everyone in the room burst into laughter, including Mama.

Once the laughter subsided the room became quiet except for the sound of people nibbling on their treats. That one little cookie per person was savoured by each of us. It amazed me how long one could take to eat what was essentially only one mouthful. I stole a glance at Eddie. He had his eyes closed and was chewing the morsel ever so slowly. Mama noticed too. She reached over to touch Papa's arm and pointed her finger at Eddie. Papa blissfully nodded to her.

This silent message was received and understood by all the members of my family. At that moment we all realized that Eddie didn't get treats like this much more often than we did. Diane's face softened and she gave me a small smile as her eyes darted from Eddie to me.

Karla and I did not really like the taste of black tea. It tasted so strong to us. We thought it would taste better if it were white with milk and sweet with sugar. This evening, as usual, we had none of either. We were accustomed to not having the extras so we just drank our bitter beverage without complaint. Eddie, however, seemed to be enjoying his tea. He was holding the dainty cup with his little finger raised in the air. He tipped up his nose and imitated British mannerisms. "My, what delicious tea you serve, Madam. May I ask what your secret is?"

Mama took her cue and pretended to be snobbish. Karla giggled as she translated, "Really, my dear, how can you ask a lady for her secret recipes? This recipe has been served to the royal family, I will have you know. It is not a secret I will ever reveal to anyone outside my own family. Humph." She indignantly threw her head back, nose aimed at the ceiling.

Marlene joined in the fun. "Tell us, Sir Eddie, what are your plans now that you have returned from the city?" Karla's eyes danced as she struggled to do the translations justice.

"Oh, I thought I'd play a little polo. Perhaps I'll participate in a foxhunt as well." Eddie turned stiffly in his chair to face Papa. "What do you say, old sport, would you and Johann care to join me in a little fox chase?" He took a dainty sip of his tea and raised his eyebrows at Papa. Diane and Papa sat together on the sofa, tears streaming down their cheeks. Papa was unable to answer with anything but laughter. Diane stopped wringing her hands and sat back on the sofa.

Marlene balanced her teacup on her knee and, with a

straight face, she inquired, "Tell me, Sir Eddie, just when is Lady Eddie planning to join you here in the country? I shall throw a party in her honour when she returns."

"How very kind of you, Lady Marlene. I believe she should be here by this weekend. She's still in Paris acquiring a new wardrobe, I believe. I'm quite sure she would look forward to a party upon her arrival to show off her new acquisitions."

"Then it is settled." Marlene turned to Mama and Diane. "We shall have to make plans immediately for Lady Eddie's party." Karla was trying to stop laughing long enough to translate. Everyone in the room, except for Marlene, was in various stages of hilarity. Marlene kept her composure and with only a brief smile she continued, "Mama, shall we have the party in the garden? The gardener has done a splendid job this year, do you not think, Sir Eddie?" Karla was giggling almost uncontrollably. She stood up and walked over to the side table to set her teacup down. She took a moment to regain her composure so that she could continue with her translations.

Marlene remained in character, but everyone else, including Diane, was wiping tears of laughter from their eyes. Eddie's laughter subsided just enough to allow him to respond. This time he spoke in his own accent. "You really should have been an actress, Marlene." Seriously he added, "I think you really have a talent there."

With sadness in her eyes Marlene proclaimed, "Perhaps, in America, people have opportunities to become whatever they desire, but things are very different here in Germany. Our mission here is simple survival." Marlene placed her teacup on the side table. She looked at Eddie with a shy smile and added, "Thank you for making my family laugh. Your presence has enriched our days and for that I am thankful."

The others sat quietly nodding their heads in agreement. She turned to Diane and together they said in English, "Thank you, Eddie."

Chapter 9

I was so busy with English lessons all week that I didn't see Eddie until the following Sunday. I decided to pay him a visit at his barracks later that sunny afternoon. I found him sitting on a bench outside the railway cars the Canadians now called home. He had his rifle apart and was carefully cleaning it. It's a good thing it was apart because he pointed the barrel right at me before he knew I was there. Even though I knew the rifle could not fire, I jumped at the sight of the barrel levelled at my head. Memories of the Polish soldiers who had occupied our home a few years ago flashed through my mind. A nervous giggle escaped from my trembling lips.

"Oh, Johann, I'm so sorry," said Eddie as he dropped his rifle to the ground and jumped to his feet. He squatted down to look me in the eye and he put both of his hands on my quivering shoulders, saying, "I didn't mean to scare you, Little One. Please, come and sit down beside me." My shaky knees caused me to stumble as I made my way to the bench. Eddie caught me and, with a sadness in his eyes, he said, "You must have seen some terrible things in your short life, Johann. I can't even begin to imagine what you've been through." Eddie hugged me.

I couldn't understand all of the words but I knew this man would never hurt me. It seemed like I had known him all of my life, yet we had just met.

I sat quietly on the bench beside Eddie as he re-assembled his rifle. "I really hate these things," Eddie whispered. "They're so violent. I had never touched a gun of any kind until I joined the army. Thankfully, I've never had to use this thing except in training exercises. You don't have a choice when you join the army, Johann. Every soldier is issued a gun whether they like it or not. I don't think I'll ever understand how it's possible to take another person's life." Eddie let out a deep sigh as he pondered the thoughts he had just expressed. Eddie was looking at me with those melancholy eyes again, shaking his head.

"You're just a child, Johann, so why am I baring my soul to you? I've never told anyone how I really feel about guns and war except for my wife. But she's so far away and I can't say anything confidential in my letters because they're usually censored before she ever receives them. It's so nice to have someone to talk to even if he doesn't understand everything I say to him." Eddie closed one eye tight while making a clucking sound with his tongue. I had never seen anyone do that before Eddie, but when he smiled at me once again I knew it was a gesture meant to comfort me.

He gave my shoulder a little squeeze and said, "How would you like to take a walk? I understand that the canal just behind our barracks . . . oh, that's right, we can't be seen together in public just yet, can we? Freedom is a wonderful thing, Johann. I'm sure that you'll appreciate it much more than we North Americans do. We've taken our freedom for granted, I'm afraid." Eddie's low voice was silenced by the sound of approaching footsteps. A short man with blond hair, small eyes, and a pouting mouth appeared from around the corner. It was the same man who seemed so upset when Eddie gave me the potatoes. I shrank into Eddie's side. Eddie sensed my fear. He put a reassuring arm around my shoulders.

"Hi there, Shorty. What are you up to?" asked Eddie.

"Well, I'm not sitting around making friends with no Nazis, that's for sure." The scowl on his face and the glare in his dark eyes as he looked at me made me nestle closer to Eddie. "You seem to have forgotten that these Nazis are our enemies, Ed. We came overseas to fight against them, remember? How can you make friends with these despicable, no-good Nazis?"

"You know, I've never actually met a Nazi, Shorty. This young fella is German, it's true, but that doesn't make him a Nazi. The way I hear it not all Germans were on Hitler's side. I believe this young man and his family hate Nazis as much as we do." Eddie didn't raise his voice yet his message was delivered in a strong and firm tone.

"Germans, Nazis. They're all the same as far as I'm concerned," asserted Shorty, the scowl etched deeply into his face.

"The war is over now, Shorty. It's time for all of us to get along and try to be happy again." Eddie gave my trembling shoulder another reassuring squeeze.

"I'll never be happy as long as I'm living with Nazis as my neighbours," Shorty grunted and spat on the ground. With fire in his eyes, he continued, "I think you're nuts to hang around with Nazis, Ed. Nuts is what I say." And with that he spun on his heel and walked back to the barracks. I felt the tension go out of my body. I felt Eddie's arm relax and realized that Eddie was just as upset by Shorty's angry tirade as I was.

"I haven't known Shorty all that long but I think he's a good enough fella. He just doesn't understand that the war is not your fault or even the fault of the German people. Maybe in time he'll get to know you and understand that we're all just ordinary people who are simply trying to survive in these rough times. It seems to me that we can make life better for everyone if we try to help each other." Eddie took my chin in his hand and looked into my eyes. "Shorty, or for that matter no one, can stop me from being your friend, Johann. Eddie, Johann, friends. Do you understand?"

"Eddie, Johann, friends," I agreed as I felt a smile spread across my face. I rose from the bench and gave Eddie a hug. I said, "War over. We be happy now, right Eddie?" Eddie nodded his head and gave me a reassuring smile. "Time I go home now, Eddie. See you later. Remember Mama ask you for supper? Six o'clock."

Eddie nodded and returned my hug. Smiling, he said something really strange about alligators. "See you later, alligator." Eddie waved goodbye as he picked up his rifle and headed for the barracks.

I sprinted all the way home with the word "alligator" resounding inside my head. Karla had been teaching me some of the words that were the same in German as in English and alligator was one of them. Eddie would be coming for supper tonight so Karla could ask him about the puzzling message. Her English was much better than mine but I was learning fast. Alligator . . . alligator. Hmm.

Chapter 10

Karla met me at the door. "Johann, where have you been? I wanted to teach you some more English before Eddie gets here. We only have a couple of hours, Johann. Let's go. Come on."

"Karla, what is alligator? Is it animal?" I asked in English.

Mama stopped humming and turned me around so she could see my face. "Alligator? Johann, what made you think of an alligator?" asked my concerned Mama.

Karla looked confused too. "An alligator is an animal. But why do you want to know what an alligator is? Eddie will be here soon and he certainly will not be talking about alligators, Johann. Now let's just go and study our English." Karla had that no-nonsense air about her again.

For once my sister was wrong. "Eddie called me an alligator when I said goodbye to him this afternoon. What does that mean?"

Karla mused over the question for a moment. Frowning, she shook her head. "I am not at all sure, Johann. An alligator is a big lizard, I believe. We will look it up in the dictionary later. Now can we just go and get started?"

"Why don't we ask Eddie about what he meant," suggested Mama. "I do not really think he called you a lizard, Johann. Sometimes when we speak a different language we find that ordinary words can have some strange meanings. We will straighten this out with Eddie tonight. Yes? Now go with your sister and practise your English. Papa, your older sisters, and I will need all the help we can get with this English language."

I was more confused than ever when we read the meaning of the word alligator. The dictionary defined an alligator as a large lizard of the crocodile group, found in the tropical rivers and marshes of the United States and China. Its snout is shorter and blunter than the crocodile's.

Did Eddie think I look like a large lizard with a short, blunt snout? I wondered. Out loud I asked, "Karla, what do you think Eddie meant when he said, 'See you later, alligator'? Do you think I look like an alligator?"

"Of course not, silly. It is probably just an expression. I will ask Eddie tonight what this expression means. We have to continue to work hard to translate for Eddie. This was not easy for me the other night, Johann."

"I don't always understand all of the words but I usually understand what Eddie is saying to me. Karla, I think Eddie is very sad."

"You would be too if you had to live thousands of miles from your family. Maybe we can be his German family while he is here."

"I think Eddie will want a German family. He is very lonely. He likes it when I go to visit him. He smiles at me a lot."

Karla glanced at me over the edge of her textbook. "He is very lonely for his family. Anyone can see that. Now let's get to work so that we can make his evening visit a pleasant one. Eddie deserves our best efforts."

I could hardly argue that point so I tried to focus on the lessons. The image of that rifle pointed at my face kept surfacing and interfering with the lesson.

Finally Eddie arrived for the evening meal and rescued me from the dry English lessons. I escorted him to the dining room. Mama was much more relaxed this Sunday. She rushed over to Eddie and shook his hand as she said with ease, "How do you do?"

Eddie chuckled. "Your English has improved dramatically since last Sunday, Frau Schmidt. I'm afraid the only German word I've learned since we arrived is *Danke*. You put me to shame."

Mama looked confused. "Shame, Eddie, are you ashamed of something?"

Eddie's brow furrowed as he shook his head. "No, no. That's just one of those expressions we have in all languages. I mean that you are doing so much better at learning another language than I am."

Mama nodded her understanding. I saw this as my opportunity to find out about the alligator thing. Eddie burst out laughing when he realized that I thought he was calling me a lizard. "We have some pretty funny sayings in our country. I have no idea why we even say some of them. 'See you later alligator' is just something we say to special people, usually children, in Canada." Eddie tapped his fingers on the table. "I think they say that in the States too, come to think of it." He looked at my parents and added, "The person responds with 'In a while crocodile.' It's just a happy way of saying so long to someone you care about. Do you say such things in German?"

Karla looked at the others for a response but they were all shaking their heads. "I think," she speculated, "that people in Canada must not be quite as serious as we Germans are."

Eddie solemnly nodded his head. "I suppose you're probably right about that. We've had our tough times too, but I dare say they're minor in comparison to those here in Germany. We think the Dirty Thirties were the worst times a person could endure, but I can see that the lack of food for us was not nearly as grim as your wartime experiences have been for you."

We retired to the parlour for our evening refreshment. As we sipped our tea Eddie asked Papa, "Do you think it's all right for my army buddies to know that I have come here for a visit? Would you be in any danger if that knowledge became known in the community?"

Papa rubbed his chin with his thumb and forefinger while he mulled the question over. "We are not yet certain what to expect these days. I wonder if it would be a good idea to continue to keep our friendship to ourselves for now. What do you think, Mama?"

Mama slowly stirred her tea with her spoon. She looked up and said, "Could we discuss this further the next time you come for supper, Eddie? Say next Sunday? Until then we will keep our friendship between us. Does everyone agree?" Heads nodded around the room.

"It's not necessary to invite me back so soon, Frau Schmidt," said Eddie, as he took another sip of his tea. Eddie seemed to be having trouble handling the delicate teacup. It slipped from his hand and landed empty on his lap. Eddie's sparkling white shirt now sported a dark brown stain right over the pocket. "I'm so sorry. Thank goodness I didn't break your teacup. I guess I'm not used to handling delicate china any more. My regiment is fresh out of china teacups at the moment," said Eddie with a screwed-up face and upturned nose. He was using his British mannerism. It's a wonder more teacups didn't tumble as everyone vibrated with laughter. Marlene had a mouthful of tea when Eddie started his antics. She sputtered and almost choked on it.

"I've seen their teacups," I declared. "They're about the size of an army truck. China, are they?" On the last three words I imitated Eddie's turned-up nose and tried to speak like the British.

"Eddie, would you please leave your shirt here for me to clean?" Mama requested. "That is the least I can do for you."

"No thanks, Frau Schmidt. I'm used to doing my own laundry. I'll just rinse it out when I get back to the barracks. Thanks anyway." Eddie was so busy inspecting the stain that I don't think he realized Mama had gotten up from her chair and was standing in front of him. Her hands were on her hips again.

"I will not take no for an answer, Eddie. I am doing laundry tomorrow morning. If you care to leave the shirt with me I will soak it overnight. Tea stains do not come out so easily." Mama turned to Marlene. "Do you remember that white shirt Arthur had in his room, Marlene? Did he take it with him or is it still in his drawer?"

"I believe it is still there, Mama." Marlene rose from her chair. "Would you like me to fetch it?"

Papa nodded his approval. Mama replied, "Yes, dear. I would appreciate that."

"You can change your shirt in the next room, Eddie. I would like to soak yours immediately. Water is something we do have lots of, thank goodness for that," said Mama with a chuckle.

Marlene returned with the fresh white shirt. It looked almost the same as Eddie's. He left the room to change.

I went over to the sideboard and took out Arthur's picture. The thought of Arthur's clothes sitting in our room awaiting his return saddened all of us. Seeing his white shirt brought back the feelings that were so carefully locked up in our hearts. We were trying to be patient but as the days went by with no word of our boys, we became more and more anxious about their safety. Mama and my sisters wept quietly as I put Arthur's picture back in its safe spot in the sideboard. Papa sat stiffly upright in his chair. "I wonder," he said out loud, "if Eddie or his superiors could give us any information on the whereabouts of our boys' battalions." Looking at Mama, he asked, "Do you think we could inquire if he could help us in this regard?"

Mama clasped her hands together loosely and looked solemnly at each of us. "He seems like such a fine young man, our Eddie. I really think he would help us if there were any way he could. However, I think it is a lot to ask of him. Perhaps we should wait a while yet. We may hear something any day now."

Eddie must have wondered what on earth had transpired in his absence as he entered the parlour dressed in Arthur's shirt. He looked at Papa and asked, "Is everything all right?" He didn't wait for a translation. Instead he turned to his translator and asked with an anxious voice, "Karla, is there something wrong? Is it okay that I am wearing your absent brother's shirt? I don't need to be wearing it." Eddie glanced from Papa to Mama and back to Karla with wide worried eyes.

"Nothing is wrong with you wearing Arthur's shirt, Eddie. We were just having a serious family discussion on another matter. We may be asking your advice about this matter next week. Would you mind very much if we did that?"

"I'd be happy to assist you if I can." Eddie directed his response to Papa, then Mama. Then he looked around the room at the rest of the family and he stated, "I'll do anything I can to help this family. You just need to let me know how I can be of service to you."

Mama looked into Eddie's eyes. "We feel that we've known you for years instead of just days, Eddie. We have so much to thank you for already, but we may just require some advice from you next Sunday. Until then we cannot reveal any details, yes?"

Mama's questioning look was met with a smile. "That's just fine. It feels wonderful to have some friends in this new land. It's I who am in debt to you for your friendship." Eddie ruffled my hair and he looked into my upturned face. "And I owe it all to you, little pal." My broad smile was short-lived as he went on to say, "I really must get back to the barracks now. As it is, I'll have a difficult time explaining my absence. Shorty will be drilling me with questions as to my evening's activities."

Mama was holding out the almost empty package of cookies that Eddie had left behind last week. "Eddie, there are still two left from your last visit for you to enjoy. We are grateful that you shared your treat with us. They were delicious. Thank you."

"I rather think that someone else I know could make short work of finishing the package." Eddie was not reaching for the cookies. Instead he was looking at me." Johann, why don't you and Karla have the last two?"

I got up and stood next to Mama. I put my arms around her waist as I fixed my eyes on Eddie. "There may be six of us and only two cookies, Eddie, but we'll all share them. That is what this family does."

Chapter 11

Eddie was on my mind a lot all week but I didn't actually get to see him until Saturday. Every time I tried to visit him he was away from the barracks. I tried to see him on Monday evening before nightfall. Just as I approached the railway cars, Shorty came out of the supply car. He intercepted me before I could reach Eddie's car. "Well, well, well. Who do we have here?" Just the sound of his sneering voice raised the hair on the nape of my neck. I knew who was speaking even before I turned around to face him. I remembered what Eddie told us about Shorty. "He spends a lot of his time scowling and grumbling." However, Eddie also told us that Shorty is a very funny man sometimes. The memory of Eddie re-enacting Shorty's antics brought a smile to my face. I think I took Shorty off guard with that smile.

He countered with a fiercely mean look. "So, what does the little Nazi want today? You won't be getting no more food from nobody around here, that I can promise you." The clipped words were delivered with blazing eyes. Shorty crossed his arms firmly over his chest as he tried to look down at me. This tactic didn't quite work for him. He was only an inch or so taller than me. I could look him straight in the eye. I was just about to ask him where Eddie was when the cook popped his head out of the cook car.

"Hello, Johann." He enunciated each word carefully. "How are you today?" The jolly man was grinning as he approached Shorty. "Don't let old Shorty here scare you," he said as he put his arm around the short man. "He's not half as scary as he looks, are you Shorty?" The big cook gave Shorty a playful slap on the back.

Shorty shook the cook's arm off his shoulders and stomped his foot. "Why don't you leave me alone? And get rid of this kid while you're at it. I'm not going without no more food for these Nazis. I don't care what anybody says." Shorty stomped off to the sound of the cook's laughter.

"Are you looking for Ed?" Cook asked.

"Where Eddie is?" I inquired in halting English.

"Eddie's not here. He'll be back later," the cook informed me. "Come back tomorrow, okay?"

"Tell Eddie I see him Saturday." I searched the cook's eyes to see if he understood my words.

"Eddie should be here Saturday. I'll tell him you're coming back then, okay?"

I nodded my head in agreement. "Goodbye, Mr. Cook."

The cook threw his arms out in front of him and clapped his hands together. "Mr. Cook, that's a good one." He bent over with convulsions of laughter that followed me almost all the way home. As I sauntered home I recalled Eddie's first visit with my family. I had been surprised at how much of the English I understood. I was able to comprehend most of the conversation I had just experienced with the cook and Shorty. As I recalled Shorty's disparaging remarks I realized that learning this new language might not always be so much fun.

When I returned to the barracks on Saturday I was pleasantly surprised to see Eddie sitting outside on the wooden bench. This time he was polishing his boots. "No rifle, Eddie?" I chided him.

With a chuckle he replied, "I can't shoot you today, Johann. These boots might kill a person with their smell though." He held the boot up to my nose to prove his point.

"Boot smells bad," I agreed. "Why boot smells bad?"

"We spent most of this week on parade. We had to march for miles, usually fifteen to twenty miles each day. After a while your feet sweat. These boots don't have any ventilation. No holes, see?" He held the boot up to the sky. I sat down beside Eddie and we peered at the skyward boot together.

"No holes," I agreed.

Eddie began polishing again as he spoke. "I hear you ran into Shorty the other day. Does he still scare you?"

"Not scared any more. I almost as tall as Shorty."

"I believe you're right about that, Johann. You're probably about the same height all right." Eddie looked around, then he lowered his voice to a whisper. "Don't tell him I said so, but Shorty's a little sensitive about his height, you know."

Just then a truck drove into the unloading area to the east of the train. I heard someone shout, "Mail! Boys, the mail truck's here." Suddenly men were flying out of the boxcars. They congregated around the mail truck.

"It looks like we may get some of those stamps we've been looking for to start your collection." Eddie jumped up from the bench and beckoned me to join him as he approached the truck. The driver of the truck called names as he handed out letters and packages. Some people got two or three letters. Some even got more than one parcel. Eddie and I stood silently by, watching as the others celebrated their good fortune. Men were ripping the letters and parcels open. Some of them moved off to the side so they could read their mail in private. Finally, the man on the truck stopped reading out names. He jumped off the truck and went inside the dining car. Eddie's shoulders were sagging. "I guess there's no mail for me today. That's okay though; the others will save their stamps for us." Eddie's eyes reflected his disappointment as we walked slowly back to the bench. He sat down heavily and began polishing his boots again. "My parents have three sons away because of the war. They can't send letters every time. I sometimes get more than one letter at a time, usually from my wife. But then she's raising our three sons by herself. She's a very busy lady, you know," he added wistfully.

Just then I remembered that I had brought my art project to give to my new friend. "I have mail for Eddie," I said sheepishly. "I almost forgot. I made this for you in art class." With a flourish I reached inside my pocket and pulled out a folded piece of paper. As I handed it to Eddie I added, "no stamps on it."

Eddie tweaked my nose and gave me a smile. "So I really did get mail today, did I? I guess it's not such a bad day after all." Eddie unfolded the paper carefully. He gently flattened it on the bench beside him. In a hushed voice he said, "This is beautiful, Johann. Did you draw it?"

Nodding my head I replied, "I draw horse for Eddie to make him happy."

"You drew a beautiful horse, Johann. I love to draw too and horses are my favourite subjects." Eddie carefully examined the drawing. "Did you draw it from a picture, or," he queried with a twinkle in his eye, "did you have a real horse modelling for you in your classroom?" We burst out laughing at the thought of a horse inside my classroom.

"Yes," I kidded right back, "horse model in classroom . . . but horse not stand still!"

"Really? Did he trot around your classroom; did he nuzzle you with his nose? Did he buck your teacher off his back; did he smell up all your clothes?" We were both giggling as Eddie acted out each line. We were so wrapped up in our horseplay that we didn't hear Shorty approaching. He planted his feet firmly in front of Eddie and me, his arms folded stiffly across his chest. He wore a self-satisfied smirk on his face.

"Having fun, are we? Really, Ed, I can't figure out why you bother with these people! Ever since I joined the army and met you I've been puzzled by your constant need to give both your attention and your worldly goods to total strangers. I think you're just plain nuts sometimes." Shorty shook his head in wonder. "You know I told Cook to get rid of this Nazi brat and here he is again."

Eddie squared his shoulders and glared right back at Shorty. "That's what I heard, Shorty. I don't understand why you have to be so rude. He's only a little boy. Why can't you just leave him alone?"

"That would be easy if he didn't insist on hanging around here all the time. He has no business bothering us." Shorty returned Eddie's glare, his tense body giving up no ground. "It's all your fault too, Ed. These people are no good. They don't do nothing for nobody is what I say."

Eddie put his arm around my trembling shoulders as if to protect me from Shorty's bad temper. "That's where you're very wrong, Shorty, my man. Sit down. I want to share something with you." Shorty turned as if to leave. "Shorty, please just sit down and hear me out."

"It won't matter what you tell me, Ed, I'll never change my mind about these Nazis. They're our enemies, remember? As far as I'm concerned they're all the same. They're selfish, hateful excuses for human beings, is what I say. I hate Nazis." Shorty spat on the ground as he glared at me.

Eddie took Shorty by the arm and sat him down on the bench. "Do you remember last Sunday evening when you asked me where I was all evening and I told you that I would tell you later? This is later," said Eddie firmly.

"I thought maybe you'd gone for one of your walks," replied a subdued Shorty.

"Well, you're wrong," Eddie informed Shorty as he sat down beside him. He looked him straight in the eye. "I was at Johann's home. They invited me to share their supper with them. Do you have any idea how these people's lives have been affected by this war?"

"But, but . . . " Shorty tried to interrupt. He glanced sideways at me.

Eddie pointed his finger right in Shorty's face. As he continued his voice rose: "They didn't ask for the war any more than we did, you know. When I saw the portions of food they have to live on it amazed me that they haven't starved to death by now." Shorty looked away from Eddie. His gaze was on me. "Go ahead, Shorty, take a good look at Johann. Did you not notice how terribly skinny he is? Did you not stop to wonder why he's so thin?" Shorty shook his head but he remained silent. Eddie's voice softened again. "We eat more food in one day than they have for a whole week. And we think we go to bed hungry! In spite of all this they chose to share their meagre meal with me, an enemy soldier." Eddie glanced over at me with a reassuring smile. He returned his attention to Shorty. "You just think about that, Shorty. These people are generous and, by the way, they do want to help others. For example, I spilled my tea on my good white shirt. Immediately, Johann's Mama offered to clean it for me. They gave me another shirt to wear while she washes mine for me. Then they invited me to go back for supper again tomorrow night. Frau Schmidt will have my shirt all washed and pressed for me to pick up. I, on the other hand, will have to return their shirt unwashed. I don't have any soap. Unless you do, Shorty?" Shorty shook his head. "No, I didn't think so. That means it'll have to go back soiled. I did rinse it out but that's not the same, as we both know, right, my friend?"

"You got that right," murmured Shorty. Suddenly his

eyes lit up. "As a matter of fact, that's why I came to talk to you in the first place. I was hoping you still had some soap for me to borrow." Shorty glanced over at me. This time I could read no resentment in his face. "Then I saw the little boy and forgot all about the soap. How could I be thinking of soap in the midst of that lecture, Ed?" Shorty's demeanour was much calmer than before. His shoulders were relaxed and his glowering face had softened.

"Sorry I couldn't help you out, old buddy," apologized Eddie, "but I haven't had any soap for a couple of weeks now."

"I've asked most of the boys already. It seems there's a real shortage of soap around here." I thought I saw resigna-tion replace the anger I had come to associate with Shorty. "I don't know what they expect us to do. They send us to this God-forsaken country and don't even send the bare necessi-ties along with us." The fire was back in Shorty's eyes but somehow I knew that this time I was not the source of his anger. "I got a chit quite a while ago. That means I'm sup-posed to get a package soon. You got one too, didn't you, Ed?" Eddie nodded. "What good is a chit if the promised package never arrives? We haven't had a Red Cross package for months either. I wonder what's going on." The two men sat side by side shaking their heads. Shorty continued, "I can't remember the last time I had clean clothes to wear. I'm sick of wearing dirty clothes. My socks are so filthy they can practically stand up by themselves. Just look at this." Shorty removed one boot.

"Pew!" responded Eddie. "Remember, Johann, what I said to you earlier about deadly socks? I think Shorty's here are worse than mine. What do you think?"

"Smell bad," I whispered as Shorty proceeded to remove his sock. He stood his sock on the ground. Sure enough, it was stiff as a board. The sock stood upright without aid. I'd never seen a sock do that before.

"Just look at my ankles and the soles of my feet." Eddie and I held our noses and our breath as we examined Shorty's feet. They had been rubbed raw. "They put us on parade and make us march for miles with feet like this! We marched fifteen miles again yesterday! This army likes to see us suffer, is what I say. I went to see the medic about these sores but he's out of cream again. The officers who give these orders to make us march all day couldn't do it themselves, not even with good feet and in clean socks. Yet they don't think twice about making us walk all day and they don't even care that we have no soap to keep our clothes half decently clean."

"Yes, I know," replied Eddie absently as he rubbed his chin.

"Clean socks are all I want. Now, is that too much to ask for?"

"I wonder, would you be willing to pay somebody to do your laundry," asked Eddie. "If I could find someone to do it, that is," he added quickly.

Shorty put his sock and boot back on. "Yeah, right. Where are you going to find anybody in Naziville who'd do anything for us, even for pay? You find somebody to clean my clothes, Ed, and I'll pay. You bet I will." He walked away scowling and grumbling, just like his usual self, I thought.

Once Shorty was out of sight, Eddie and I burst into giggles. "He's quite the character, don't you think?" Eddie chuckled.

"I think Shorty sad, too," I observed sombrely.

"I think you're absolutely right, my friend." Eddie patted me on the shoulder.

"By the way, you don't have to worry about Shorty telling

anybody about me going to your house for supper last Sunday. He'll keep that quiet until I tell them myself." Eddie followed Shorty's retreat with his eyes. "Like I told you before, Johann, he's really not such a bad fella."

Chapter 12

Eddie wasn't at church the next morning. He had said he
would see me at church. What could have happened to him?
I broke away from my family without a word after the service
and I bolted for home. I checked the brush in the field to see
if Andreas wanted to meet me but there were no stones set
out. That was strange. I hadn't met with him since he
received the news about his father. I hadn't seen him in
church today either. Had something happened to him? What
if he's been taken away just like his father? Who could I ask?
Nobody. No one knew of our friendship, except possibly Frau
Berg. She may have seen us down by the canal one day when
she was walking to our house, but I couldn't be sure if she
could see us well enough to identify us. If anybody knew what
was going on in Leer, it would be Frau Berg. I didn't want to
risk asking her so I would just have to wait until Andreas con-
tacted me. I had no choice.

I hurried to the house to change out of my good clothes.
Then I raced over to the barracks. No one was there except
for a couple of guards posted at either end of the railway cars.
I had never seen guards posted at the barracks before today.
I knocked on the door of Eddie's car, but no one answered.
One of the guards was quickly approaching me. I was relieved
that he didn't point the rifle at me. He held it skyward as he
asked brusquely, "Hey, kid, what do you want?"

I was so afraid of what might have happened to Eddie
that I stayed my ground and stammered, "Where is Eddie?"

"Oh, are you the kid I've heard Cook talk about?" he asked with a softer voice.

"Eddie is my friend," I answered with a pounding heart. "Where is Eddie? Is Eddie gone?" I held my breath as I awaited his reply.

"Eddie? Oh, you mean Ed. Yes, Eddie's gone," the guard confirmed.

"Gone? Gone away?" I asked as I fought off tears.

The guard was regarding me with a very serious look. "Oh, no. No, no. He's only gone for the day. The men are on parade all day. They had a church service out at the compound this morning, too."

"Eddie come back?" I asked hopefully.

"Oh, yes, he'll be back before supper."

Relief washed over me. *"Danke,"* I said as I backed away. "Thank you," I repeated as I turned and darted for home.

Karla met me at the door. We were entering the dining room when I told her Eddie was gone. Mama had just entered the room and thought I said Eddie had gone away. "Is Eddie gone?" she asked incredulously as she put her arms around me and looked down at me.

"No, Mama, no." I hugged her back. "The soldiers had to go to the compound this morning for a church service; then they have to spend the rest of the day on parade."

"Just how do you know all this?" Mama asked as she held me close.

"That's where I ran to after church. The guard told me Eddie would be back by supper time. He will still come for supper tonight, Mama. I know he will. He told me so yesterday."

"You have really become fond of Eddie, haven't you, my son?" Mama asked softly.

"He's my best friend in the whole wide world," I proclaimed.

Eddie arrived for supper at ten minutes after six o'clock. He was all out of breath as he stood on our doorstep carrying a paper bag. Karla and I had answered the door. "I'm so sorry I'm late," he apologized as we led him to the parlour. "We didn't get back from parade until ten minutes ago. I quickly cleaned up and I even remembered to bring Arthur's shirt back." He reached inside the bag and pulled out the white shirt. He held it out and Marlene took it from him. She placed it on the side table. Eddie looked at me and added, "By the way, Shorty said to say hi to you, Johann."

Diane had gone to fetch Eddie's shirt for him. She handed the shirt to Eddie and said in English, "Shirt clean."

Eddie's face broke out into an enormous smile. "*Danke*," he said simply. "I'm sorry that I couldn't wash Arthur's shirt for you. I did rinse it but we don't have any soap at the barracks for washing clothes. I'm really sorry about that," Eddie apologized.

"That's fine, Eddie," Mama assured him. "I will just wash it with the others tomorrow. It will not be a problem. What can you do if you have no soap? That is not your fault." Mama patted Eddie on the back. "We did get your shirt clean. The stain came right out. See?" she said as she held the shirt with the pocket side up for him to examine.

"You have no idea what a pleasure it will be to wear clean clothing, right Johann?" The two of us shared a chuckle at the memory of our encounter with Shorty yesterday.

"You always have to do your own laundry?" asked Mama.

"Yes, I'm afraid we do. The maid is off work for the time being," he said with a grin.

Mama looked at Papa. He nodded in agreement at her silent question. "I could do your laundry for you, Eddie. What are a few more pieces of clothing on laundry day? I trust you don't have an extensive wardrobe?" she asked, eyebrows raised and eyes twinkling.

"I'm afraid I had to leave most of my wardrobe at home." There was that British mannerism and nose in the air again. Everyone giggled.

"You should have seen Shorty's socks," I said. "They were so hard they stood up by themselves, didn't they, Eddie?" Eddie answered with a slap on his knee and more laughter.

When the laughter subsided, Mama asked, "Do the other soldiers have to do their own laundry as well? Do you have others with stand-up socks too?" she added with a chuckle.

"I wanted to discuss that with you, as a matter of fact," said Eddie seriously.

"Very well. Let's have this discussion at the dinner table, shall we?" Mama stood up and offered her arm to Eddie. He placed her arm through his and escorted her to the dining room table.

Once everyone was settled at the table and the meal was progressing to Mama's satisfaction, she turned to Eddie and inquired, "Just what was it that you wanted to discuss with me, Eddie?"

"I was wondering if you would be interested in doing laundry for some of the men in my barracks. They would pay you, of course. However," he rushed on to explain, "they may not be able to pay you with money. It's more likely that they could pay with cigarettes and chocolate bars. Is that something that would be of interest to you?"

"I believe I could handle that," replied Mama.

"I can help you in the evenings and on my days off," offered Marlene.

"Me too, Mama," said Diane. "I never know when I am working but I can certainly help you when I am free."

"What do you think about this, Papa?" inquired Mama.

"Is this something you really want to do, Mama?"

"I have the time, the supplies, and, it appears, the assistance to do the job. I think it would be a good opportunity for our family, Papa."

"I have already spoken to six of the boys and they're all interested. Would that be too many for you to handle, do you think?" asked Eddie.

"That shouldn't be a problem. Papa, what do you think?"

Papa looked around the table. He nodded his head. "Then it is settled. The rest of us can help with the washing, folding, and ironing when we have time. If we all pitch in it should not be too much for us to handle." Papa turned to Eddie. "You may tell your friends that we would be happy to do their laundry chores for them."

"We discussed payment earlier." Eddie's lips were pursed. "They could pay with cigarettes and chocolate bars mostly. Would that be all right with you?" He looked from Mama to Papa. They both nodded in agreement. Eddie went on to explain, "We don't always have cigarettes or candy bars on hand. I would keep track of each person's laundry and how much they owe you, if that would be okay with you? Then you would get paid as the supplies come in. That way you would not have to collect from the men. I would do that for you. These are good honest men so I'm not worried about them not paying."

Papa glanced at Mama. She nodded. "How much is a week's worth of laundry worth in cigarettes or candy bars, do you suppose?" Papa asked Eddie.

Eddie shook his head. "I really don't know. I think you'd

have to figure out a monetary amount you should charge for the laundry. Then find out how much cigarettes and candy bars are worth on the black market here. Then we could translate the value of the goods in terms of their monetary value. Each person's laundry would be worth two candy bars or one package of cigarettes or whatever you consider to be fair. It's really up to you. I will present your proposal to the boys once you make a decision."

Papa was rubbing his chin as he pondered the worth of a person's weekly laundry. Mama suggested, "Why don't we give it a try and see what happens? If it does not suit either the men or ourselves we will just stop doing their laundry. In either case, Eddie, I will continue to do your laundry for you." Mama rose from the table. "I think it is time we moved into the parlour to have some tea. Why don't the rest of you go ahead. I will join you as soon as I put the kettle on." Mama picked up some dishes and started heading towards the kitchen. She stopped and turned around to see Eddie, his hands loaded with dishes, following her.

"Eddie, you do not have to do dishes here. You are our guest. Please go ahead and join Papa in the parlour."

"I thought I could help you make the coffee first," Eddie replied with a grin on his face.

Mama shook her head in dismay. "I am sorry, Eddie, but we have no coffee. I wish I could make coffee for you but I cannot. I have none to make. I really am sorry," she said, returning Eddie's smile with a troubled look. She looked into his eyes and asked hopefully, "Would tea be all right with you? Unless you don't like our tea?"

"Of course I like your tea," he assured her. Then Eddie set the dishes he was carrying back down on the table. He reached into his paper bag. "Are you looking for coffee like this?" he asked as he produced a can from the bag he'd set on the floor by his place at the table. He removed the lid from the can and held it to Mama's nose.

My Mama closed her eyes and inhaled deeply. "But where did you get coffee from? We have not been able to get coffee from the market for months!" She held the coffee out to me to smell.

Eddie just smiled at Mama. "I did some fancy talking to Cook and he let me have a can of coffee."

Mama's hands were trembling. She set the dishes back down on the table and asked in a hushed tone, "You will not get into any trouble for this, will you, Eddie? I mean, is it okay for the cook to give you coffee? Did you have to pay something for it?"

Eddie smiled at me, then he put his hands on Mama's shoulders and looked into her worried eyes. "Frau Schmidt, it's okay. I didn't steal the coffee. I just found a way to negotiate with Cook to get the coffee. It's all right, really it is." Mama looked away from Eddie. She was close to tears. Eddie was confused. He turned to Karla and me. "What is wrong? Have I done something I shouldn't have done?" Eddie's eyes pleaded with us to help him understand what had gone wrong.

"You have to understand, Eddie," explained Karla, "that here in Germany people have died for lesser reasons than stealing food. Mama is afraid that you will be hurt or even killed if you did not come by this coffee honestly. I think she is fearful that you may have compromised your own safety for us. Could you just please explain how you got it?"

Eddie's cheeks flushed. He looked down at me and patted my shoulder. He looked somewhat embarrassed. He hesitated, then Eddie turned his serious eyes back to Mama as he gently massaged her shoulders with his hands. "I didn't want to tell you this, but I gave up drinking coffee last Sunday when I saw how much the coffee that we take so much for granted meant to you. I couldn't enjoy drinking coffee three times a day knowing that you folks hadn't had coffee for months. I decided to take my share of coffee and bring it over here. That way I can enjoy a cup of coffee here." Eddie's eyes were twinkling again. "That is, if you will allow me a cup of your coffee."

"Oh, Eddie." Mama reached up and gave Eddie a fierce hug. "You are truly an angel."

"That's what the nuns used to tell me when they hauled me into the principal's office at school. Or," he screwed up his face, "did they say you're *no* angel?" He scratched his head. "I can't remember which it was now." The tension was broken. Eddie handed Mama the coffee can. "Now, what do you say? Can we brew a pot of coffee or must I go back to the barracks dying of thirst?" Eddie put his arm around my shoulder. "What do you think, Johann? Would you like a cup of good Canadian coffee?"

I smacked my lips and made slurping sounds as I pretended to drink coffee. "Mmm, good."

Papa went to the larder in the corner of the kitchen. He came back carrying an old bottle. When Mama saw the bottle she threw her arms around Papa. "What a good idea you have, Papa."

"We haven't had much to celebrate in several years, not since the war began. Diane was married just before the war started and Marlene is not yet formally engaged" — Papa gave Marlene a sideways glance — "although we expect that to change when Otto gets home."

"Do you expect Otto home soon?" Eddie asked Marlene.

Marlene looked at Eddie with solemn eyes. "We are not sure where any of our men are at the present time. It is true that when Otto returns we are planning to get married as soon as possible. We just did not want to start our lives out together with so much uncertainty in our futures."

"So you won't have a long engagement then?" Eddie asked.

"No, we plan to get married fairly soon after his return." I wrapped my arms around Marlene's waist and she gave me a squeeze.

"My wife always says that our two-year engagement was far too long," Eddie said. "We met in 1934. I fell in love with her the first time I saw her. We didn't get married until October 1939. I joined the army in 1943 and have been gone ever since except for a couple of short leaves. That means I've been gone almost half of our married lives. I think perhaps my wife was right. She would approve of your plan for a short engagement." I sensed Eddie's melancholy so I reached over and took his hand in mine and squeezed it.

Papa handed the bottle to Eddie, saying, "Son, I have been saving this bottle since 1939. That's six years ago now." Eddie turned the bottle over and over as he tried to read the label. "We only serve brandy in our coffee when we have something very special to celebrate."

Eddie shifted his weight from one foot to the other. He looked down at me. Then he stood steadily on his two feet and he looked at Papa. "Would it be a good idea to save it for Marlene and Otto's upcoming celebrations?"

"Ah, Marlene and Otto's celebrations. You have a good point there, my friend." Eddie tried to hand the bottle back to Papa. Papa shook his head. "I have two special bottles in safe storage at my parents' home in Lingen. They will travel here when the engagement and then the marriage are celebrated. They will bring the bottles with them. In the meantime, however, this family has received a special blessing. Eddie, would you do us the honour of opening this bottle of brandy?"

Edmond Joseph Donais

Known as Eddie to the German family, he was my father. He and Mom, Frances Peters, were married October 7, 1939, in Alida, Saskatchewan. They had three sons born during the Second World War. Though Europe was on the other side of the world from Canada in what was referred to as "overseas," Dad volunteered to enlist. He registered with the army in 1942. He served in the RCEME—Royal Canadian Electrical Mechanical Engineers from 1943—1946. He trained in Canada then was sent overseas to London, England, in early 1945. His discharge papers state that he served 1036 days of which 462 days were served overseas. He spent approximately one year of that time in the role of peacekeeping in Germany immediately following the end of the Second World War. He met 10-year old Johann immediately upon his arrival and quickly became an integral part of the German family.

Karla and Johann are seen here with their parents and grand-parents. Johann was ten years old when the Canadian soldiers came to his hometown of Leer, Germany. He met Eddie imme-diately after the Canadians arrived. Eddie and Johann became fast friends. It didn't take long for Johann and his family to "adopt" Eddie. Johann helped to fill the gap left in Eddie's heart due to the separation from the three little sons left back in Saskatchewan. The rest of Johann's family provided Eddie with the one thing he missed most while serving in the Cana-dian army: a family way of life.

RCEME Compound, Leer, Germany

Eddie in the middle with his arms around each of the boys in front of the RCEME Compound. This is where Eddie and his regiment spent most of their time while in Germany. Here, they worked on the trucks, motorcycles, etc. that were rendered inoperable during the devastating days of the Second World War. These mechanical engineers also served as peacekeepers during their year long stay in Germany. Not only was the machinery broken but so, too, was the spirit and the economy of this country. Many, if not most, of the common German folk were not on Hitler's side but they were powerless to stop him.

Eddie and his army buddies. Eddie (back row on the left)

This photo illustrates how the boys were a tight-knit group. Note that the men in the back row are arm in arm, forming a protective wall for the two men in the front. Soldiers who serve long periods of time together tend to become close friends. Each of them has left their families behind. They find themselves in situations not of their own choosing. They go to bed hungry at night, follow orders whether they like them or not and, ultimately, they hope to make a difference. History has proven that the men in this photo did make a difference for all of us. Eddie made a life-saving difference for a German family, thereby modelling the true spirit of a peacekeeper.

German soldiers marching home

Tens of thousands of German soldiers marched back to their homeland. These thousands of Germans were accompanied by only a handful of Allied soldiers in the cars you see in this photo. The German people were forced to serve their country in a war which most of them did not support. Therefore, the soldiers did not try to escape. They walked, with heavy hearts, through country after country to return to their loved ones.

Chapter 13

Eddie was fast becoming my family's beacon of light after more than a decade of darkness. I enjoyed every minute I spent with him. However, he was here with the Canadian army and he had very little recreational time. Sometimes he had free time on the weekends, so I walked over to the barracks the following Saturday. It was nearing the end of July already and the weather was finally beginning to feel like summer. One of the guards saw me approaching and said, "Eddie's not here." He took my hand and led me around the back of the barracks. He pointed to two figures in a canoe on the eastern end of the canal. "Eddie's over there," he told me.

I nodded my head and said, "Thank you." The guard nodded and went back to his duties. I stood on the shore and watched the two men in the canoe. Shorty was in the steering position at the back of the canoe. Eddie was in the front. They were intent on trying to row the canoe in a straight line and didn't even notice me standing on the shore. They would get the canoe going straight, then it would veer to the left. The next thing I knew it was veering to the right. Left, right, straight, left, right, and so it went. Canoes were commonplace in our community because of the canals but I'd never been in one. I'd never seen one going in circles before either. I giggled to myself. I tried to get their attention but they couldn't hear my screams. After a while I just enjoyed standing with the sun beating down on me. It felt so good after the cold spell we'd just experienced. I decided to just enjoy the sun while I waited. I sat down and listened to the sound of the paddles as they pushed water away from the canoe with each stroke. I closed my eyes and concentrated on the sounds around me. I could hear birds landing in the water. There hadn't been any fish for years in the canals, according to the townsfolk. They said that the return of the water birds meant that one could expect to find fish in the waters again in time. I had no idea about these things, and right now, with the sun warming my face, I didn't much care about such things either. I lay back with my arms behind my head and my eyes closed. I knew the canoe wasn't far away by the sounds of the paddles and the water lapping against the bank of the canal. I dozed off as I listened to the calming sounds and enjoyed the sun.

I was brought back to reality with the feeling of cold water on my face. Eddie and Shorty had rowed to shore and Eddie was holding his dripping paddle over me. I jumped to my feet with a squeal. The water felt like ice on my warm skin.

"So this is what you do with your Saturday mornings, is it?" Eddie asked as he laid his paddle on the ground beside me. He reached down and filled his hands with water. The next thing I knew water was flying at me. Eddie and I tossed handfuls of water at each other. We danced around as we tried to dodge the icy shower. We were both hopping around giggling like school children as we thoroughly enjoyed our water play.

Shorty was trying to push the canoe out of the water by himself. He stopped and watched our water play for a moment, then he shook his head and mumbled something inaudible. Shorty plunked himself down on the shore. Eddie turned around and splashed water at Shorty. "Ed, what do you think you're doing? You're going to get me all wet." Shorty was frowning in his typical fashion.

"That's the idea, Shorty," he said as he tossed another handful of water at his friend.

"Stop this nonsense." More water was thrown into Shorty's face. "I said stop it right now!"

Eddie stopped his water play and placed his hands on his hips as he faced Shorty. "Shorty, don't you ever want to just have some fun in life? Loosen up, old buddy," and with that Eddie threw another handful of water at Shorty's face.

Shorty jumped up and said, "So, you want to have some fun in life, do you? I'll show you fun." Shorty grabbed Eddie and tried to throw him into the canal. Up until now I had been afraid of Shorty, but when he tried to push Eddie into the brink I was sure he was going to hurt Eddie, so I jumped onto Shorty's back. He was so short that my legs almost touched the ground. I wrestled him down. We fell backwards and rolled towards the edge of the shore. Eddie sprang into action. He leaped ahead of us and knelt down to stop our rolling bodies from landing in the water. The three of us lay there breathless, our chests heaving from the horseplay. After a while Shorty said, "I guess I didn't learn much about having fun as I was growing up. I didn't have no brothers or sisters to play with and we lived out on a farm." He rolled over on his elbow and looked at Eddie. "You must have had a lot of fun when you were a kid. You still act like a kid lots of the time. You're a lucky man, Ed." Shorty sighed and rolled over onto his back.

"I had lots of siblings to play with when I was a kid, it's true, but I think people can learn to enjoy life even when they're an old man like you, Shorty." Eddie jabbed Shorty in the ribs. "You must have a funny bone somewhere, Shorty. Everyone does, you know."

Shorty found himself giggling in spite of himself. Eddie kept jabbing Shorty in the ribs. Shorty would cover one target, leaving another one exposed. Pretty soon Shorty was laughing uncontrollably. It turns out that Shorty had a high-pitched laugh that sounded like a donkey.

"Maybe," giggled Shorty, "we could all go for a swim together."

Eddie looked at me and winked. "There is just one problem with that plan, Shorty." *What does Eddie mean when he winks like that? Maybe I will ask him when Shorty is not with us.*

"What could be wrong with my plan?"

"I can't swim," declared Eddie.

"I guess you'll just have to learn then," said Shorty as he jabbed Eddie in the ribs. "We could just throw you in the canal and you'd learn soon enough, I wager."

"I can't see it happening, Shorty. I'm afraid I'm hopeless in the water. You see, I didn't have any water to play with when I was growing up." Eddie and I howled at the little joke. I sneaked a peek at Shorty out of the corner of my eye. He had a faint smile on his face.

Shorty finally stretched and stood up. "Well, boys, I think it's time we got on back to the barracks before they send a squadron out to look for us."

"Yeah, I guess you're right," Eddie agreed. "Johann, do you want to help us take the canoe back to the compound? Shorty here needs help holding up his end of the canoe." Eddie snickered at his own joke.

Shorty ignored the wisecrack and tried to pick up the back of the canoe. I went to the other end but Eddie motioned for me to help Shorty. Eddie picked up the front and off we went. After we placed the canoe back into the army's storage compound, we walked back to the barracks.

As we approached the railway cars, we could see a large truck parked near the rear car. Shorty turned to face us with a grin on his face. "Ed, look! The Red Cross truck is here. Maybe we've got packages at last. We both received chits so maybe we both have parcels too." Shorty hurried on ahead of us.

"What is a chit, Eddie?" I remembered Shorty mentioning this strange word the day I saw his socks standing up on their own.

"A chit is like a note or a memo. We get chits to tell us we're going to receive a parcel that's addressed to us personally. When we get Red Cross packages, we all get Red Cross packages, so we don't get chits for that. Does this explanation make sense to you?"

"Yes, I think so. Do you get lots of chits, Eddie?"

"Not nearly as many as some of the boys do, but I get as many as my family can muster. That's all a guy can ask for, don't you think?"

"Yes, I understand. We not have much to send to Arthur. I not think he received a chit either for a long time." I lowered my voice so that only Eddie could hear me. "Eddie, can you keep secret?"

"I believe I can." Eddie replied seriously.

"Once Marlene took some goods she earns at railway station, she get paid sometimes, you know. She found someone who sells woollen socks. She traded all goods and bought socks for our boys. She send them to Arthur, Otto, and even to husband of Diane. She supposed to save earnings for her wedding. Mama and Papa don't know this secret." I searched Eddie's eyes for reassurance that he would keep the secret. Eddie's lips trembled as he nodded and tousled my hair. Shorty had stopped up ahead and was waiting for us to catch up to him.

"Did you remember to order our cigarettes and chocolate bars?" Eddie looked at Shorty with hope. "Or did you forget again like the last time?"

"I remembered," Shorty said. He looked at Eddie with serious eyes. "I did, I tell you. I didn't forget this time," he said as he shook his head.

"Okay, then," Eddie said, "let's race to the truck. Should I give you a head start, my friend?" With that Eddie took off like a bolt of lightning. Shorty and I couldn't possibly catch the sprinter already so far ahead of us. We did our best though, and by the time we arrived, Eddie already had the two parcels that had been left for him and Shorty. "I didn't check on the cigarettes because they were ordered in your name so you'll have to pick them up. Do you want to do that before we open this care package?"

"Did you see the Red Cross driver?"

"I'd check the dining car if I were you. He's probably having a bite to eat before he heads off to . . ." Shorty was on his way before Eddie finished his sentence. Eddie and I sat down on the bench to wait for Shorty's return. "I sure hope there's some shaving cream in here. I ran out of that stuff two weeks ago. It's not much fun trying to shave without shaving cream, Johann. Not much fun at all."

"Papa uses soap. Why doesn't Eddie use soap, too?" The solution seemed simple enough to me.

Eddie looked wistfully at me. He patted my arm and said, "That would work just fine if I had any soap but I don't have any of that either." Eddie leaned back on the bench and sighed.

"Papa lend you soap, Eddie. I will ask him tonight."

"That's all right, Johann. I'm really hoping there's some in this package." Eddie glanced in the direction of the dining car. "Now where do you suppose that Shorty went anyway? If he doesn't hurry up, I'm going to have to open my parcel without him."

"Is parcel just for you, Eddie?"

"Yes, it is." He picked up the other parcel. "And this one is for Shorty."

"Why you not open your parcel by yourself?"

"Ever since we crossed the ocean together, Shorty and I have opened our Red Cross packages and other parcels together. I think we both just want someone to share our excitement with. I have you and your family now, but Shorty has just me, so I'll wait for him. Is that okay with you, little pal?" Eddie tousled my hair.

"Does Shorty not have any other friends here?" I looked up at Eddie.

"You know how much he seems to be a grump," Eddie explained. "Most of the boys don't appreciate his moods. They think he's mad all the time. In the army it's hard enough to keep your spirits up without spending a great deal of time being around a grump."

"Then why you want to be his friend, Eddie?"

"Shorty has a lot of good qualities in him once you get past the grumpy face he puts on. He's fair-minded." Eddie looked at my unconvinced face as I remembered Shorty talking about Nazis and Naziville. "Well, most of the time he is. I think he's beginning to like you too, Johann."

"Did Shorty send laundry over to Mama for cleaning?"

"He was the first one of the boys to decide to do just that. In fact, I overheard him talking to Earl about it and the next thing I knew Earl had his laundry ready to go as well."

Suddenly I remembered the purpose of my visit with Eddie today. I thumped my forehead with the heel of my hand. "I almost forget to tell you, laundry will be ready to pick up tomorrow when you come for supper."

"Am I coming for supper again? Isn't that a bit too much for your mother? I don't have to eat with your family every Sunday, you know."

I began to wonder if Eddie was getting tired of coming for meals with a family who had so little food to offer. Surely he must have better meals here at the barracks. The startled look on my face must have betrayed my thoughts because Eddie sat his parcel down and took my chin in his hand. He tilted my head up so that I would look straight into his eyes. "Johann, I would be honoured to have supper with you and your family. You have no idea how much your friendship means to me. I am a very long way from home but I'm the lucky guy in this camp because I . . . have . . . you." Eddie gave me a jab in the ribs on each of the last three words, making me giggle.

Shorty came sashaying out of the dining car, his hands full of packages. "So, I forgot to order the cigarettes and candy bars, eh? Then I guess these must be just for me. Ha!"

Eddie's eyes lit up. "Did the other boys get packages today too?"

"Apparently the truck delivered a huge shipment here today, so I expect they did."

"Great. Then I can collect for the laundry and pay Frau Schmidt tomorrow when I go there for supper."

Shorty looked at Eddie with dismay. "I can never figure you out, Ed. You're always giving away your meagre supplies to anyone who needs them. Don't you ever think of yourself before others?"

Eddie's cheeks turned red. "Let's take a look at what you have there, Shorty."

"I ordered four cartons of cigarettes and two cartons of candy bars, remember? Half for you and half for me."

"Do you want me to pay you now or is after supper okay?"

Shorty nodded. "Tonight is fine," he said. He set the packages on the ground beside the bench. I could smell the chocolate bars even through the wrapping. My mouth started to water at the memory of the only other chocolate bar I had ever tasted. I closed my eyes and inhaled deeply.

"Would you like me to send a candy bar home with you for supper tonight?" Shorty's voice broke into my reverie. "That could be a down payment on the laundry your Mama has done for me." I was stunned. I wasn't sure what to say. I didn't think I should take anything for payment. That was between Eddie and Mama, I thought.

Eddie read the confusion on my face. "What do you think, Johann? You could tell your Mama that the candy bar is a partial payment from Shorty. I'll make a note of the payment. Then I'll bring the remainder of the boys' payments with me tomorrow evening when I come for supper. Would that be okay?"

I nodded enthusiastically as the scent of chocolate floated in my head. Mama wouldn't mind if Eddie said it would be all right.

"Please mention to your Mama also that I will be bringing another sack of laundry tomorrow evening. The boys think they'd like to make this a regular event. If she doesn't agree, I'll simply bring the soiled laundry back with me when I return after supper. Okay?"

Shorty had opened his carton of candy bars and held it out to me to choose one. These were the same as the one Eddie gave me a few weeks ago. I stood up and gingerly picked one up with my thumb and forefinger. I placed it carefully in my pants pocket. I remained standing with my hand guarding my pocket as if I expected something to sweep down from the sky and pluck it out of my hiding place.

"Well, my friend, what do you say?" Shorty asked. "Are

you ready to check out your parcel yet? Or," he pretended to scowl at me as he pursed his lips tightly and shook his finger in my face, "do I have to wait all day while we sit here and gawk at Johann here?"

"Why don't you go first?" Eddie offered. "Who is your parcel from?"

"It's from my folks back home. What about yours?"

"Mine says the Ladies Auxiliary," Eddie replied as he examined the return address.

Shorty carefully tore away the paper with the stamps on it. "Here you go, Johann. I understand you've started a stamp collection. Right?" I nodded my head. He carefully handed the torn section over to me.

"Thanks, Shorty," I said as I gently placed the paper with stamps in my other pocket.

Shorty folded back the paper to reveal a brown cardboard box. He untied the string holding the parcel together. It was also taped shut so he carefully slid his fingernail along the tapeline to release the bond. He lifted the flaps one at a time, taking care not to disturb the contents. The very first thing we saw was a pair of woollen socks. We all burst out laughing at the sight of these brand new socks. "Maybe someone back home heard about your stand-alone socks, Shorty," Eddie chuckled as Shorty lifted them out of the box.

"It's about time I got some new ones. My socks are wearing so thin they're almost invisible."

"Really, Shorty?" teased Eddie as he winked at me. "Is that why you keep a thick layer of dirt on them? That way you can always find them even if they're invisible." Eddie held his thumb and forefinger over his nose. He looked over his hand at me. "You do remember the smell of Shorty's socks, don't you Johann? Pee-u-wie!" Eddie and I were laughing so hard that we had to hold our aching sides.

Shorty placed the socks beside him on the bench. He closed the flaps leaving the remaining contents hidden from view so that Eddie could open his. Apparently they took turns unwrapping each item. "Okay, smart guy, let's see what you have in your parcel." Eddie was still laughing and holding his sides. "Come on, come on, I don't have all day," Shorty urged.

Eddie followed the same steps to open his parcel as Shorty had. He used just as much caution, too. The first item to be revealed was a tube of shaving cream. Eddie rubbed his stubbly chin and said, "Yahoo! This is just what I needed. Finally I can have a clean shave without all of the cut marks I've been sporting lately. Wow! What a treat." Eddie's eyes were sparkling.

"Okay, my turn," said Shorty impatiently. He opened the box's flaps. He peeked his nose inside, reached in, and pulled out a pen and some blue ink.

"Is that a hint for you to write more often?" Eddie chuckled.

Eddie reached into his box and this time he pulled out a bar of soap wrapped in a face cloth. "Isn't that just what you wanted too?" I asked. "Do you send order to someone for things you need?"

Eddie was holding the soap to his nose. "Just smell that, Johann. I sure hope Shorty gets one of these in his package or I'll have to lend him mine again. That's why I'm forever out of soap, isn't it, Shorty? You've always got mine. I'll tell you one thing though, Shorty, you ain't getting my face cloth. That, my friend, is for my use only." Eddie poked Shorty in the side with his elbow.

"Humph!" grunted Shorty.

"To answer your question, Johann," said Eddie, "some-times we write to our families and tell them things we need, but this parcel is from the Ladies Auxiliary back home. These ladies make up parcels for the men from their community. They just put things in the parcels that they have available at the time and that they know we need. I'm just grateful they realize that we're in dire need of personal hygiene items."

Shorty was rummaging in his box again. He pulled out two bars of soap. Eddie made a grab for one of the bars. "Don't you owe me a few bars of soap by now?" Eddie yanked one bar away from Shorty. Shorty grabbed back and the fight was on. They wrestled back and forth for a few minutes, then Eddie conceded defeat. "Okay, Shorty, you can have it, but don't you come around and ask me to lend you any more soap." Eddie winked at me. "At least not in the next little while anyway."

Eddie took his turn and pulled out a tube of toothpaste. Shorty wisecracked, "Aren't you going to smell pretty now? Shaving cream, soap, and now toothpaste. You'll smell so good you'll attract the flies now, my boy." Shorty was already reaching into his box for the next item. It was a package of homemade cookies. "Smell that and weep," he said to Eddie as he held the cookies up to Eddie's nose.

Eddie took a long whiff. "I think I can remember eating homemade cookies once, a long time ago. It seems like a lifetime ago since I was home and had cookies like this. Cook keeps promising us some but he doesn't have enough flour yet to make any. Hopefully, he'll get a good supply with the next shipment of food." Eddie reached into his box hoping, I think, for some cookies too. Instead he found a smaller package inside the box. It was wrapped in brown paper. Eddie opened it to reveal a letter.

"You get letters in parcels too?" I asked.

"Yes, sometimes," said Eddie as he peeked at the letter. "This one is from Mrs. Stoppel. She and her husband are good people, Johann. When my wife and I were getting married our church was five miles from the town we lived in. I didn't have a decent car to drive on my wedding day so they lent me their car to drive my new bride home in. I've never forgotten their kindness." He turned the letter over and over in his hands. Then he set it back in the box carefully. "I'll just read my letter later." He proceeded to empty his box. He found some food items. There were two cans with pictures of fish on them, a hunk of cheese, and a small tin of milk. "This is even better than I'd hoped for," Eddie whispered. "It feels like Christmas back home."

"Do you really get this many presents at Christmas time, Eddie?" I asked, astonished at the possibility.

Shorty reached to the bottom of his box and pulled out the final items. He had four of the cans that looked like Eddie's, the ones with fish on them. "Ooh, yuck! I thought my mother knew I hate sardines. Ed, I'll trade you the sardines for the milk, what do you say?"

"Oh, I don't know . . ." Eddie winked at me again. "I'll have to give that some serious thought."

"Yeah, I'm sure." Shorty grabbed at the milk.

"Let me get this straight. Are you giving me four cans of sardines for one measly can of milk?" asked Eddie in disbelief.

"If I know you," retorted Shorty, "you're just going to share them with Johann's family anyway." Shorty faced Eddie. "Aren't you?"

"Do you like sardines, Johann?" Eddie inquired.

"What are sardines?" I asked.

Shorty screwed up his face and said, "They're ugly little fish and they taste really awful. Yuck!"

"I never seen sardines." I turned to Eddie. "Is it true they really are little fish you can eat?" I whispered, not sure if I should believe Shorty.

"They sure are, and I, unlike my friend here, love them. Do you think you'd like to try this new food, Johann? Do you think you'd like it?"

I looked at Eddie with wide eyes. "Sardine is food. What not to like about food, Eddie?"

Chapter 14

We had a banquet for our Sunday evening meal. Eddie had brought along the six cans of sardines and his cheese to add to our usual fare. Mama still had potatoes to serve. We only had potatoes when Eddie shared a meal with us. We especially enjoyed this evening because we knew the potato supply was now depleted.

"Did you bring another bag of laundry for me to do this week, Eddie?" inquired Mama.

"I did, indeed. I wasn't sure if you were interested in continuing the laundry chores but I brought two bags along just in case."

"Everyone pitched in and helped, so it actually went very well."

Eddie blushed a little. "I hope you don't mind, but four more of the boys begged me to bring theirs along when they found out about your services."

Mama got a glint in her eye. "You did, now did you? The next thing I know you'll have to quit the army so you can come and help me with all this laundry." Happiness washed over me as I observed Mama's light mood. Eddie had that effect on my family.

"That may be an offer too tempting to refuse. However, I think my Sarge may have something to say about that. And then there's my wife. If I'm going to quit the army I'll be making a beeline for home to see my wife and sons."

My heart stopped. "You leave us, Eddie?" I choked back tears. "Are you, Eddie?"

Eddie sighed. "Sorry, Johann, I didn't mean to sadden you. It's just that sometimes I miss my family so much . . ."

Mama rose from her chair and went over to Eddie. He stood up as she approached him. Mama put her arms around him and silently hugged him. Eyes were lowered at each place of our Sunday evening table.

Mama stepped back from Eddie and looked into his eyes. "We cannot take the place of your family, Eddie. No one can. Perhaps, though, we can be your German family. Would you like that?" Eddie nodded and gave Mama a weak smile. I reached over to hug Eddie.

Papa cleared his throat. "Eddie, I would like to call you son. I would consider that an honour. May I have permission to do so?" Eddie walked over to Papa's chair and embraced him.

Then Eddie looked into Papa's eyes. "Sir, the honour is all mine." Eddie smiled at Papa as he hugged him again.

Eddie picked up some dishes and headed towards the kitchen. Mama tried to stop him but he insisted, "Frau Schmidt, I have to do kitchen duty in the barracks from time to time. Come to think of it, I'm on KP duty tomorrow all day. Believe me, the few dishes generated in this house are a real treat after having cleaned up for the gang over there. It's my pleasure to help. Really."

When we were ready to retire to the parlour for our coffee, I presented the chocolate bar that Shorty gave me the day before as partial payment on his laundry bill. We decided to enjoy the whole chocolate bar for dessert. Mama sectioned the pieces and placed them on a serving plate to be eaten with our coffee in the parlour. Diane poured the coffee while Marlene served out the dessert. We sat in silence for a while just enjoying the camaraderie and the food.

Eddie turned to Mama. "Did Johann tell you the Red Cross truck arrived yesterday?" he asked. Mama had a piece of chocolate in her mouth, so she shook her head in answer to the question. "Well, it did," Eddie went on to say. "That means that I have full payment for the first laundry bill."

Eddie got up and went over to a sack he'd set in the corner earlier in the evening. "It's all in here," he said as he unloaded the sack. "I hope you'll find the payment sufficient for your labour." Eddie pulled out 12 packages of cigarettes and 24 candy bars. "Each of the boys paid with two packages of cigarettes and four candy bars," he explained. "They realized that their first week's laundry was much larger than the subsequent loads will be, since we haven't been able to do laundry for weeks."

"But Shorty already gave candy bar yesterday. We just finished eating it," I reminded Eddie.

"It's funny you should mention that, Johann. I said the same thing to Shorty when he handed me four candy bars as payment. I tried to give one of them back to him. He wouldn't take it." Eddie screwed up his face, Shorty style, and imitated Shorty's gruff voice. "'Just never mind is what I say. Just do what I want and give it to the kid."

"'But, Shorty,' I protested, 'you've already given a candy bar as partial payment.' Shorty stomped his foot, as I'm sure you've seen him do, and said, 'Don't argue with me. Just do it!'"

Eddie looked slyly at me with his head tilted, and stated, "So I did." We burst into laughter.

The bounty lay displayed on the side table. Everyone gathered around the table in awe. It was as if we were looking into a treasure chest filled with precious gems. Finally Mama broke the silence. "We will trade these items on the black market. Each of us needs to think about what we would like to trade them for. We will make a list. Then we will give priority to the most important things on that list."

Diane was usually the quietest one in the family but this time she was the first to speak. "I think . . ." Diane looked around the room. She cleared her throat. "I think we should put one thing on the top of our list."

Everyone stared at her as Mama asked softly, "And what would that be, my dear?"

Diane cleared her throat again. "I think we should buy a new dress for Marlene to wear on her engagement day. Ten years ago I had a new dress to wear on my engagement day, and I think Marlene should have one too. That's the only thing I need to put on the list." That said, Diane moved away from the side table.

Marlene was looking at her with tears brimming on her lashes. "Diane, that is very kind of you. But I think there are more important things that the family needs than a new dress for my engagement." Marlene looked around the room for confirmation. Everyone seemed to be deep in thought. I wasn't sure what to say so I just gave her a weak smile and a shoulder shrug.

Papa finally broke the silence. "Does anyone have any idea how much a new dress costs these days?"

Mama chuckled. "No one has bought a new dress since before the war, Papa. Why don't we look into the matter and see what it would cost?"

Diane cleared her throat again. With her eyes lowered she responded, "I checked at the ladies' shop." She turned to Marlene. "Remember that pretty dress we saw in the shop window when we went for our walk yesterday?"

Karla spoke up. "Do you mean the navy one with the pretty red sash?"

"That is the one," Diane confirmed.

"Oh, that one," said Marlene. "That is a very pretty dress all right, but I am sure it would cost a great deal."

I picked up a handful of candy bars and turned to Marlene. "We're rich now, aren't we? We can afford a dress for you, can't we?"

Diane smiled. "I do believe we can, Johann. I went back later that afternoon and I asked the shopkeeper how much it was worth in terms of cigarettes. She looked me up and down. She tipped her nose in the air and said it did not really matter because it was not likely I would ever get my hands on cigarettes to trade anyway. I pressed her for an answer. She shrugged her shoulders and said that four packages of cigarettes could buy the dress. Then she walked away from me as if I did not really exist." Diane shrugged the memory away. "So, Papa, four packages of cigarettes would buy that dress; what do you think about that?"

Papa rubbed his chin. "I think we should give it some thought. It is only right that Marlene should receive some sort of benefit." He glanced sideways at Marlene with a sly grin. "Especially after what she did for Arthur and the others." My mouth fell open. Papa faced Marlene and looked straight into her eyes. "You didn't think I'd learn about this, did you?"

Marlene was horrified. "How did you find out, Papa?" Then she turned to Mama. "And do you know about it too?"

Mama just smiled with pride and nodded her head. Papa said, "Frau Berg was down at the post office one day when I went to check on the mail. She commented to me that she had also been there the day you sent parcels off to the boys. She said she thought that was an honourable thing for a young lady to be doing." Papa smiled and nodded his head. "I didn't ask her for any details. You know how that woman loves to talk." Then Papa informed Eddie, "Most of the time you can't believe a word she says, but I soon found out that this time she was right. A few months later we got that letter from Arthur thanking us for the woollen socks. I just put two and two together."

Eddie winked at me. We kept our knowledge of the incident to ourselves.

Marlene's eyes were wide with shock. She walked over to Papa's chair and knelt facing him. "Papa, I just knew that the boys needed good socks for all that walking they have to do. I understand that they are marching home as we speak. Can you imagine having to walk your way through complete countries? I don't know how they do it." She shook her head, then rushed on, "I thought the least I could do was buy them new socks. I saw some socks down at the market and I had enough goods to trade, so I just did it." She looked warily at Papa. "You do understand, don't you, Papa?" She looked over her shoulder. "Mama?"

Papa put his arms around Marlene and leaned over to kiss her on the forehead. "Of course we do. Since you spent your wedding money I think the least we can do is buy that dress for you, do you not think, Mama?"

"Papa," said Marlene, "let's just wait for a while until we decide what things we really need. Papa?" Papa didn't answer right away. "Papa, please?"

"If that is your wish, my dear, if that is your wish."

Marlene reached out to me and pulled me to her for a hug.

Diane spoke up. "Marlene, what have you heard about our boys coming home? Is it true that they will be home soon?" Diane's eyes shone at the prospect. Diane always shared any news she received from Friedel with our family. However, she hadn't heard from her husband for months now. Or was it years?

"They could be home any day now, according to my employer." Marlene replied. "He heard that some of the troops were making their way through Holland now. We are so close to Holland that it will not take them long if that is the case."

"It's not like Canada," I offered. "Right, Eddie? Canada is the second largest country in the whole world. It's a good thing our men don't have to walk across Canada."

"You're right about that, my boy," said Eddie as he tousled my hair. "How did you get so smart?"

"I asked my English teacher what he knew about Canada and that is what he said," I answered proudly. I turned to Marlene. "Do you think Arthur will be home this summer?"

"We are not sure where Arthur is at the moment," she replied, "but he will be home this year, I am sure of that."

"I am excited for you to meet my brother," I said to Eddie. "You will really like him."

"I'm looking forward to meeting him too," said Eddie with a smile. "I'm anxious to get to know the others as well. You know I heard, just like you did, Marlene, that many of the German soldiers were marching through Holland." Eddie looked thoughtfully at Diane and Marlene. "You and your men will have to get to know each other all over again, won't you? Do you think you'll feel a bit like strangers for a while?"

Diane nodded her head. "I have not seen much of Friedel these last seven years. I am sure he has been through a great deal in the war years, just as we have here at home." Diane placed her chin on her folded hands and sighed. "I suppose it will be like starting over, will it not?" She looked at Eddie. "I guess you will go through much the same thing when you get back home," Diane paused, "except that you even have children who do not know their own papa. That must be very difficult for you."

Eddie's head was lowered. He didn't get a chance to respond because a loud pounding was heard at the door.

Papa left the room and returned in just a few minutes with Frau Berg leading the way. Frau Berg was one of the few people I knew who always had ample food to eat. She had five brothers who had farms just outside of Leer. They shared their farm produce generously with her and she was able to trade any excess products on the black market for the extras in life that we had learned to live without. She had more clothes than any other person I knew. The variety of clothes didn't seem to help Frau Berg look any better than anyone else though. She was in her mid-fifties like Mama but she was not pretty like my Mama and my sisters. Her short legs and arms were pudgy. She had dimples on her elbows. Her ankles ballooned out from the tops of her shoes. She had more than one chin and her belly reminded me of the Cook's at the barracks. Her short dark curly hair framed an unusually large face with small bird-like eyes. Those eyes darted constantly as if afraid they might miss something.

Frau Berg's loud voice had preceded her into the room. Recognition of the voice even before she entered the room prompted my sisters and me to take action. We rushed over to the side table and stood in front of it in an attempt to block the bounty from her view. Frau Berg was immediately suspicious and headed straight for us. She elbowed me out of the way and surveyed the stacks of candy bars and cigarettes. Whirling around on those fat ankles, she faced Mama.

"Frau Schmidt, what is going on in this house?" She helped herself to a chair and plopped her heavy bottom on it. "Where did you get all these cigarettes and candy bars from? What secret are you hiding?" She looked at Mama, then at Eddie. "And just who might this young man be?"

Mama cleared her throat as she calmed herself down. "This is our friend, Eddie. Eddie, Frau Berg."

Frau Berg looked squarely at Eddie with those narrow little eyes and said, "Are you getting my friend here into some big trouble with all that merchandise?" Eddie was silent. He shifted his weight as he endured her unwavering stare. "You do not speak German, do you?" Her voice rose on the last two words. She turned back to Mama and emphatically declared, "Frau Schmidt, I heard that Diane, there,"—she wagged a crooked finger at my sister—"was looking at dresses and asking what their price would be in cigarettes and such. That made me wonder what was going on in this house. Now I see that you do indeed have a wealth of desired products right here in your parlour. Now, are you in some kind of trouble?" She leaned forward in her chair and patted Mama on the hand. "You know you can tell me anything, my dear."

Mama just stared at her blankly. Diane had stiffened in her chair and sat with her arms firmly folded over her chest. Her bottom lip trembled and she was close to tears. I sat down beside my sister and held her hand. Frau Berg was unaware of Diane's distress. She waited only a second for Mama to respond and when Mama remained silent she plunged on. "Now who is this young man? He does not speak German, I noticed. Is he one of those new Canadian soldiers? I do not care what nice things people say about those Canadians,"—she lowered her voice, leaned forward in her chair, looked Mama in the eye, and stated emphatically—"I would not trust them one little bit. You should not trust this young man either, Frau Schmidt. I am sorry if I have to tell you this, although," she said as she glanced at Eddie, "he is a pleasant enough looking young man, isn't he, with those big blue eyes." Frau Berg put her forefinger to her lips as she boldly appraised Eddie. "He really is a charmer, isn't he? Beautiful head of coal-black hair too. I always did admire a man with a full head of hair. I just cannot get over those beautiful blue eyes. They are the colour of bluebells . . ." Then she shook her head. "Humph, big blue eyes or not, you must not trust him, I implore you." Again she lowered her voice. "He's trouble, Frau Schmidt. If ever there was anyone who could get you and your family in trouble, that young man could." She sat back in her chair and surveyed the room.

Diane shivered. I reached up and put my arm around her shoulder.

"However," Frau Berg continued, "I didn't really come here to talk about this young man. I'm more concerned about another shady character that has been hanging around Leer." She paused for breath and to keep us in suspense, as she loved to do when telling one of her tales.

Papa remained standing throughout Frau Berg's tirade and interrogation. I thought he was going to rub the skin off his chin but when he realized that she was about to tell one of her stories, he finally stopped the rubbing and interjected, "Frau Berg, it was very kind of you to stop by and express your concerns." Papa reached over to Frau Berg's arm. "I will just help you up and see you to the door." Papa bent over and extended his hand to Frau Berg. When she didn't respond he put his hand around her ample arm and began to lift her up from the chair.

"But . . . but . . ." Frau Berg looked at Mama as Papa took her arm. ". . . I just want to help." She looked over her shoulder at Mama as Papa escorted her firmly by the elbow. Frau Berg twisted and turned in Papa's grasp and pleaded with Mama. "Frau Schmidt, please, you must listen to me. I have to tell you about . . ."

"Come, come, Frau Berg," insisted Papa, "I'll just walk

you out to the sidewalk and make sure you do not fall down the steps. It is really very dark out at this time of night, is it not?"

As Papa guided Frau Berg out of the parlour and towards the front door she continued to twist and turn, begging for Mama's attention. We could hear Frau Berg imploring Mama, "Frau Schmidt, please, I beg of you, just listen to me." She and Papa were out of sight and still we could hear her calling Mama's name, pleading with her to listen to reason.

The minute Frau Berg left the room, Diane and Marlene started gathering up the cigarettes and candy bars. They would carry them to the kitchen larder to be put out of sight as soon as Frau Berg was out of the house. Eddie's face was pale and his eyes were wide. "I'm really sorry to have caused you such distress," he said as he looked at each of us, his brows knitted. "Will you be having a problem cashing in your payment in this community? Will this Frau Berg cause you some difficulties, do you think?"

Eddie's head snapped around to face Mama as she began to chuckle. "Frau Berg is a busybody, if you did not already notice. She tries to make it her business to know everything that goes on in this town. She has been known to tell a number of very tall tales. No one takes her very seriously. She will not cause us any heartaches, Eddie. Really, she is just a woman who delights in the art of storytelling. Everyone in Leer knows that. It is quite all right. Really it is."

Papa returned to the room, shaking his head. He looked at Mama. "Did you hear that woman calling your name halfway down the street?" He turned to Eddie. "She is quite the character, our Frau Berg."

"You're absolutely sure everything will be okay?" asked Eddie. He turned to Papa. "She won't cause any fuss in the community?" Eddie ran his fingers through his hair. "Otherwise the boys and I will have to rethink our form of payment—if it causes suspicion in the community. I suppose I can understand why they would be so suspicious about you suddenly having possession of cigarettes and candy bars." Eddie was twirling one long lock of hair around his forefinger as he tried to think of possible alternatives.

Papa walked over to Eddie and patted him on the shoulder. "Please do not let Frau Berg upset you, Eddie. She talks a lot but that is about the extent of her interfering ways. She is not taken seriously in our community. We will be just fine, son."

I winked at Eddie. He had taught me to wink like he did, when I was kidding somebody. *Eddie is so much fun!* "She thinks you're a charmer, Eddie. She really won't be a problem. Don't worry. She knows how to keep a secret when she has to." *At least I hope she does.*

Chapter 15

"Johann, I know about your friend, Andreas." Karla looked into my eyes.

My jaw dropped. "How, I mean, what . . ." I stopped stammering as Mama came into the parlour to retrieve the dust mop she had leaned beside the sofa. As soon as Mama left the room I glanced over at Karla and whispered, "What do you mean?"

Karla reached over and patted my shaking hands. "I am proud of you, Johann. That little boy is so lonely. None of the kids seem to like him. They seemed to be his friends when Herr Hitler was alive but now . . ." She shrugged her shoulders. "Now it's like he is poison or something."

A furtive look at the parlour door assured me that Mama was nowhere in hearing range. "Andreas has done nothing wrong, Karla, so why did everybody turn against him all of a sudden?"

Karla's eyes were solemn. "I am afraid it is because of his father. He is not like our Papa, Johann."

Confused now, I asked, "But Karla, how do we know what Andreas's papa is really like? We have not met him."

"Well, Johann, you do know that he is serving in Herr Hitler's *Schutzstaffel*, otherwise known as the SS? These are the most feared people in Herr Hitler's army."

Mama popped her head into the parlour entry, "What is this talk about the SS, Karla? Why are you filling Johann's head with such talk?"

I could barely look at my Mama as I muttered, " Mama, I have been hearing talk about some bad men in Herr Hitler's army."

Mama squared her shoulders as she faced the two of us. "And just where have you been hearing about the SS?" Mama's face had reddened. This was not a good sign. Her nostrils flared and my body trembled. I stood up and walked over to Mama.

"I overheard Eddie talking to some of the Canadians yesterday, Mama. He did not know I was sitting on the bench outside his sleeping car."

"Eddie," Mama sputtered, "our Eddie?"

"Yes, Mama. He called them the Shield Squadron. He said this SS, especially the political police, were brutal and just plain mean," I said.

"Go on, Johann," Mama said.

"Eddie was really upset, Mama."

Mama drew me close. "What else did Eddie have to say?"

Karla fidgeted on the sofa. "Mama, we know that Eddie is our friend. He would not say anything to hurt us."

Mama nodded. "Yes, we do know that." She looked down at me. "Did Eddie say anything else, Johann?"

"He said the SS managed to exert as much political influence in the Third Reich as the *Wehrmacht*, our regular armed forces."

Mama sighed. "What Eddie says is true, I am afraid. Did he say anything else, Johann? Anything at all?"

"Yes, Mama. He was telling some of the soldiers that not all Germans are like the people in Herr Hitler's SS. And then he said, especially not the Schmidt family. He told the soldiers to just get that out of their heads right now. What does he mean, Mama?"

Mama sat down heavily on Papa's favourite old chair. "My child . . ." She tried to give me a reassuring smile. It didn't work. "The SS are feared by all people, Johann, not just us Germans. They are ruthless. They make us ashamed to be Germans. Come here, my son." I crawled onto the chair with my Mama.

"Mama, will they hurt us?" I stole a glance at Karla. "Will they hurt my sisters? Or Papa? And . . ." I couldn't stop trembling as I snuggled closer to Mama on the chair. "What about Arthur? Is he in the ordinary army or is he one of the SS?"

Mama sucked in her breath. "Arthur? Johann, what do you mean?"

I whispered, "Is he one of those SS people, Mama? He had to join the cause so is he a bad man now too?"

Mama's tears slipped down her cheeks. Karla dabbed at her eyes too. Mama cleared her throat. "No, Johann." Her voice was strong once again. "Your brother had to fight in this war but he is absolutely not in the SS."

Another thought occurred to me. "But what about Otto and Friedel? Are they in the SS?"

Mama hugged me tightly. "Johann, we do not associate with anyone who is in the hated SS. We will have nothing to do with such people. You need not worry about that." Mama let me go and rose from the chair. "Now I must get back to work. The cleaning will not get done by itself." Mama looked over at Karla. "You two should get back to your English lessons."

I returned to the sofa and sat next to my sister. We tried to study the English language but we were both too upset to concentrate. I had not seen Karla so distracted for a very long time.

"I think," Karla put the books down, "that we should go for a walk. Perhaps we can concentrate better after a nice walk in the sun."

Mama had no objections so Karla and I strolled down the sidewalk. We saw no action at the barracks across the field so we headed east towards the school. Karla had a friend living in a house just five blocks from our house and she decided to pay her friend a visit. "What are you going to do while I visit my friend? Do you want to come inside with me?"

Andreas's house was just one block up the street and I could see that the car was not in front of the house. *Should I take a chance and see if Andreas is home by himself?* He had told me that sometimes his grandfather took his mother to visit her sister and he was allowed to stay home alone. I had never been inside Andreas's house but I really wanted to talk to him. He had no brothers or sisters. And I knew he had no friends either, except for me. "You go ahead, Karla. I will just walk up the street."

Karla hesitated. "Are you sure, Johann? You will be safe by yourself for a while?"

I smiled my bravest smile. "The war is over now, Karla. Like Papa says, we must learn to live without fear now that the Canadians are here."

"Should we just meet here in half an hour then? Mama will not want us to be too long." I nodded my assent and walked quickly towards Andreas's house. I looked over my shoulder to see Karla's friend letting my sister into her house. Then I ran around to the back of Andreas's house. I hid behind a bush. I threw a pebble at a window. I had no idea what window this was as I waited silently for a reaction. Stillness. There was no sign of movement. I whistled like Andreas and I did when we secretly met by the canal. I threw another pebble and whistled again. This time I saw the curtains flutter only slightly. I stood up and whistled again. The door next to the window opened silently and slightly. I whistled yet again. "Andreas, is that you?"

"Johann? Come inside quickly." Both of us checked to make sure no one could see us and I raced into the house.

Andreas's house was nothing like ours. The furniture was new. He even had what I presumed was a radio in the parlour. I'd never seen one before and I was very curious to hear it. It took up the whole corner of the parlour. I was so intrigued about the radio I almost forgot where I was.

"Johann, why did you come here? Is there something else wrong?" Andreas was jumping from one foot to the other. "You cannot stay long. My mother and Grandfather will be back soon. Johann, why did you put yourself in danger to come here?"

I pulled my eyes away from the radio and realized how anxious Andreas was.

"Come. We must hide," Andreas insisted. I followed him and we hid behind the sofa.

I patted him on the back and tried to reassure him. "Everything is fine, Andreas."

"Then why are you here?" His high-pitched voice alarmed me. "Johann, ever since the war has ended my family has been afraid."

"Afraid? My family is trying to live without fear now. The Canadians are here to protect us now, Andreas. You do not need to be afraid." I offered an encouraging smile.

"Your father was not in the SS, Johann. My grandfather is certain that now we will be in grave danger. I overheard Grandfather and Mother talking about the people who are going to try to hurt the families of the SS soldiers. Mother told me to lock the doors and open them to no one, Johann. You should not even be here!"

"I am sorry, Andreas. I was worried about you. I haven't seen you for weeks now and people are talking about the SS. Mama said the SS makes us ashamed to be German."

Andreas stood up from our hiding place behind the sofa. He was short enough that he could barely be seen over the sofa. He looked down at me as I sat flat on the floor. "My father was in the SS and now he is in a hospital and we do not know if he will ever return to us. Grandfather says Papa had no choice but to serve in the SS. He says Father is a good man. Even good men were forced to serve Hitler, he said, and they did not have a choice when they were ordered to do whatever jobs Hitler chose for them."

Andreas spoke so softly I barely heard his words but I think I understood what he meant. "That is like Arthur," I agreed. "He did not have a choice either. My family is grateful he didn't have to work in the SS. Do you know what that means, Andreas? The SS, I mean?"

"I only know that some of the men in the SS were bad people. I know too that my father is not a bad man."

"I have never met your father, Andreas. I hope that someday soon I will. I have one more question. Why should your family be more afraid than mine now?"

Andreas had a puzzled look on his face. "I think it is because my father was in the SS. Mother and Grandfather do not speak of these things when they know I am here. But sometimes, when I cannot sleep, I creep down the stairs and listen to them talking."

"Do not worry any more, Andreas. The Canadians are here now and they will take care of us." *I know Eddie would not let anything bad happen to me.*

"Johann, you must leave now before anybody knows you have been here. Go to the windows in the front of the house and I will look out the back windows. If you do not see anybody then you should hurry to the back door. You must not be seen leaving my house. Mother said no one is allowed to enter the house when she and Grandfather are away."

I peeked out of the heavy draperies to the front of the yard. I saw Frau Berg waddling down the street. *How long had she been there? Did she see me go into Andreas's back yard?* Frau Berg was the last person I wanted to catch me. I waited patiently until she disappeared around the corner. Then I hurried to the back door. "Andreas, do you see Frau Berg back there?"

"Frau who?"

"Frau Berg."

"I do not know Frau Berg."

"Oh," I replied with surprise. "I thought everybody knew Frau Berg."

"Hurry, Johann, I think it is safe to leave now. Just be careful nobody sees you or we will both be in trouble."

"Will you come to our secret meeting place tomorrow?"

"I will try, Johann, but I cannot promise anything right now. Please hurry before somebody comes along and catches us."

I waved to Andreas over my shoulder as I slipped out of his house. I crept through the bushes and down the street, going in the opposite direction from Frau Berg. I walked two blocks north and two blocks east so that I would be approaching Karla's friend's house from the same direction as the two of us had done just minutes earlier.

"So who do I see here?" Her booming voice startled me and I jumped. Frau Berg peered into my eyes. "You are a little way from home all by yourself, Johann! What are you up to?"

Could she read the guilt I felt on my flushed face? "Karla and I just wanted some fresh air. She is inside visiting her friend. I'm waiting for her to come back out."

Frau Berg frowned. "Johann, I have been trying to tell your parents about all the new people in town since the war is ended. They will not listen to me. I cannot believe they are letting you roam the streets alone."

Karla came up behind Frau Berg smiling. "Hello. Thank you for waiting for me to have my short visit, Johann." She turned to Frau Berg. "And how are you today?"

Frau Berg shook her finger at Karla. "Young lady, you should not leave your little brother out here alone on the sidewalk all by himself. You never know what can happen to him these days. I have tried to warn . . ."

"Thank you, Frau Berg, for your concern." Karla put her hand on my shoulder. "But I was only inside for a few minutes. It is clear that Johann was perfectly safe here on the sidewalk." She nudged my shoulder. "Come, Johann, we must get back to our studies."

We left Frau Berg standing on the sidewalk, her finger still poised in the air pointing at Karla.

"Did you find Andreas at home, Johann?"

I flushed. "How did you know where he lives?"

"Well, Frau Berg told Mama about Andreas's father being in the hospital. You know how she goes into such detail. She described where Andreas's family lived and I realized it was very near to my friend's house. She thinks it is so cruel how people are turning on the SS soldiers now that, as she puts it, we do not need them any more. Sometimes I do wonder about that woman."

"Andreas was home alone."

"I did notice that their car was gone. What did he have to say?"

"Andreas does not know if he will ever see his father again. Was he a bad man, Karla, just because he was in the SS?"

Karla stopped and turned me to face her. She looked deep into my eyes. "Johann, we do not know what kind of a man he is. What we do know, however, is that good men are sometimes forced to do bad things."

"I do not understand this."

"Johann, I think you are now old enough to know that Herr Hitler was a very powerful man."

I nodded impatiently. "I know that already."

"Yes, Johann, but what you do not know is that men were forced to do whatever Hitler ordered them to do. Anyone who defied him was killed. Do you hear me?" Her voice was quiet and shrill all at the same time. She studied my face, hesitated, then declared, "I overheard Papa and Mama talking about a defector. Not only was he killed but his wife and children were slaughtered too. Hitler was a madman. I do not think Andreas's father is a bad man. It was necessary for him to say 'Heil Hitler' and salute. Otherwise he would be made to watch his family perish by Hitler's hand."

I shivered. "Did Andreas's Papa kill people too?"

Karla shook her head. "I understand that Andreas's father was in charge of office procedures. I do not think he had occasion to directly hurt anybody."

I wonder if I will grow up to be ashamed of my nationality. I looked to the west and wondered, as I often did, how different my life would be if my family had been born in Holland. But then I realized I would never have met Eddie. I smiled at my sister as we walked the short distance to our home.

Chapter 16

The stash of chocolate bars and cigarettes had not yet been used to trade on the black market for other goods. My family decided to set most of the first payment in reserve in case it would be necessary to buy the services of a physician or if we needed medicine. I'd had rheumatic fever three years ago and we had no way of paying for the necessary medical assistance. My Mama had to barter her wedding ring for the services of a physician. We did not want to be placed in that predicament again. My health had been fine since then but we knew how dangerous an infection could be for me. I would require medicine immediately or risk losing my life. I had developed a slight cold this week so my family was keeping a close watch on me.

In the meantime each of us was to draw up a list of things we needed. We were to use the categories of food, clothing, and miscellaneous other needs. Medicine was an unpredictable requirement so we decided to keep some of our stash at all times for medicine and any other emergencies.

We decided to spend at least half of the chocolate bars on food alone. We wanted things like canned sausage and any other available canned meat. We were also interested in acquiring fresh meats like poultry, beef, and lamb. We had enough food cards for sugar but not enough for flour if Mama wanted to do any baking. Mama was curious about the flour the Canadians used to make the white bread we had heard so much about. My family had never seen white bread before in Germany. We had heard that our dark bread was quite heavy compared to this Canadian bread. Perhaps the soldiers could get her some of the white flour for payment at some time in the future. She added it to our list.

We were also interested in buying eggs. Eggs could be kept fresh for weeks by covering the shells with lard and storing them in a box filled with salt. We knew that we could get meat and vegetables from the local farmers. They'd had a good growing season in 1944 and were anxious to sell the excess goods from last year's crop. Since the supply was greater than usual, the farmers were in a position to be generous when they bartered. People who had goods to barter with were few and far between. This made our goods even more valuable at the bargaining table. Chocolate bars were highly sought after on the black market. We hoped the local farmers could meet our needs so that we could avoid the black market. Chocolate bars were to be found mostly from foreign soldiers. Eddie told us the soldiers ordered them from home through the Red Cross or they were sent to them as gifts. The candy bars that we were paid with had come from the United States. The soldiers had all Oh Henry bars this time, Eddie said. At other times they were able to purchase Crispy Crunch or Burnt Almond, but it didn't really matter to the locals. A chocolate bar was a chocolate bar. They were unavailable for purchase in Germany at any price.

Papa had made some inquiries with some of the local farmers and he was informed that one chocolate bar could buy enough meat to feed our family for three or four days, depending on the type of meat. There were no freezers or even refrigerators in Germany for us common folk to purchase. Hence, any meat we acquired needed to be canned or used immediately. We did have a larder in our house. This was a walk-in closet with a cement floor. Our larder was on the north wall. That, along with the cement floor, caused the closet to stay cooler than the regular kitchen cupboards. This larder was the closest thing available to an icebox. It only kept milk and other perishable goods for a couple of days in the heat of summer. The larder at our home had been virtually empty all of my life. The empty rows of shelves sat idle, awaiting better times.

My family was able to use their food cards for other, more common foods such as butter and milk. Mama did mention, though, that if she were to do any baking she would require more than the allowed 50 to 100 grams of butter per week. That, too, could be purchased from the farmers.

The second category on the list of desirables was that of clothing. We had all been wearing the same clothing for years. Marlene had grown into Diane's clothing, Karla had grown into Marlene's, and I had a steady supply from Arthur. Even though Diane was the first daughter and Arthur the first son, they had received their clothing from aunts and uncles. No one in the family was accustomed to having new clothes. Years ago Mama had often used old clothing to make new garments for us, but there were no old garments left to make over. She was an excellent seamstress, but what good is a talent without the raw materials to produce a garment? It was impossible in wartime Germany to purchase any fabric unless, of course, you were wealthy. The wealthy always found ways to satisfy their desires. They would import garments and other goods from countries that had them available.

Clothing, therefore, was a category with very few entries. The bigger shops did have a few garments for sale so we listed our wants anyway. Even though Arthur was not home, we made a list of what we thought he might like. Diane's list was simple: a wedding dress for Marlene, who had convinced her that she required only one new dress and that should be for her wedding rather than her engagement. Marlene's list included new shoes and a new hat for her wedding, as well as a dress of course. Arthur's list was a complete new set of clothing. Karla wanted a white dress for her confirmation later this year. She would appreciate white stockings to go along with it. A white dress and stockings were the customary confirmation attire for girls. Since Marlene was 11 years older than Karla, her confirmation dress had been passed on to so many cousins that no one had any idea if it was still in one piece or in shreds from overuse. In any case no one had any idea where it could be. All of our relatives lived far from Leer.

I didn't have anything that I really needed. When Papa saw that I had not made an entry on the clothing list he said, "Johann, the coat you have been wearing for winter is much too small for you now. You are growing tall. It will be necessary to try to get you a new coat before the snow falls, I think." Mama agreed and put a coat on the list under my name. Mama and Papa left their names empty. They said they would consider new clothes for themselves only when all the other clothes on the list were purchased.

The third category was the miscellaneous items. Diane left her spot empty. She insisted that she did not have need for anything at this time. "The only thing I need is to have our boys back with us."

Marlene wrote down a camera. She said she would like pictures of her wedding and Karla's confirmation. She also thought we should have some pictures of Eddie. "After all," she reminded us, "some day Eddie will go back to Canada. When that day comes we may never see him again. I would like some pictures of him to show my children."

Like Diane, Karla didn't add anything to the miscellaneous list. "I just want to have a confirmation dress so that if we have a camera, I can have pictures and look like Diane and Marlene did on their confirmation day."

I did have something to add to the miscellaneous list. I wished for some art supplies. All I wanted was some paper and a few pencils. The only place I could draw was in my art class at school. I had a burning desire to draw more and more these days but, like Mama, I required raw materials in order to create.

Mama said her wish was already on the list. "Our family is growing up and we do not have any pictures of the children for many years. It is the pictures of our boys that have helped us on those occasions when we especially miss them." She looked around the room at the rest of us. "How many times have we pulled out the photos of Arthur and the others in these past years?" She shook her head sadly. "I know that a week does not go by without one of us rummaging through the few pictures we do have for some sort of solace. It is too bad our old relic of a camera had to finally give out. It used to take such good pictures too." She sighed.

Papa chuckled when he saw the list. "I do have one thing to add to this list." He looked around the room with a twinkle in his eye. "I think we will be in need of film for our camera — if we are fortunate enough to get one, that is." Papa looked my way and sighed. "I would like to procure a stamp album for Johann's Canadian collection, too, if that were possible." He patted me on the head as he smiled down affectionately at me.

The list was now complete. We agreed that the first items to be sought after were the food supplies. Papa laid the list on the sideboard. "We will wait to barter until we have a better idea just how Johann is feeling . . ." A knock at the door interrupted him.

Frau Berg entered in her customary grand entry style. "Frau Schmidt, how are you this evening? I just wanted to drop by and make sure everyone is fine. I hear that the farmers are planning to go over to the Canadians' barracks this coming Saturday to do some bartering with the soldiers. The farmers are anxious to acquire some of those chocolate bars and cigarettes. My brother Ludwig is most interested in bartering as well. As a matter of fact, he asked me to come along to assist him in the bartering process. Mmmm, whatever is that delicious smell?" Marlene entered the parlour with a fresh pot of coffee. She poured Frau Berg a cup first, then she refilled the other cups. Frau Berg blew on her coffee, then took a sip. "This is excellent coffee, Frau Schmidt. Did you purchase it from the market? It tastes quite different than what I have been able to buy at the local markets." She took another sip. "It is very smooth-tasting, is it not?"

"I am glad you like it," Mama said.

She took another sip of the coffee. "Mmm, this really is excellent coffee. Where did you say you got it?" She held Mama with her gaze as she awaited a reply. I snuggled close to Mama.

Mama looked over at Papa. He shrugged his shoulders. "Eddie gave us the coffee."

"Eddie? Who is this Eddie? Do you mean that Canadian soldier?" Mama nodded her head. "Why would a Canadian soldier be giving you coffee? What does he want? Has he asked you for some sort of favour? You have to be careful with these foreigners, Frau Schmidt. I know the war is now over but these people were our enemies, we must not forget that." Papa fidgeted in his chair. Mama's burning eyes warned him to remain silent on this contentious issue. Papa sighed and took another sip of his coffee. "What does this man want with your family, I would like to know? Even if this is the best coffee I have ever tasted, you must not trust this man. Where did he get the coffee? Did he say?" Frau Berg raised her eyebrows as she looked up at Mama over the rim of her cup. She sipped her coffee ever so slowly as she kept her eyes glued on Mama. I squeezed Mama's hand.

Mama realized Frau Berg was not going to leave without an answer to her query. She set her cup on her saucer and said, "Eddie got the coffee from his cook. I guess it must come from overseas. I do not know that for sure, though, because I have never even asked him."

Frau Berg wrinkled her brow and narrowed her little bird eyes as she stared at Mama in disbelief. "You never even asked him? You do not know where it comes from? Do you know what he wants with you and your family, this Eddie?" Frau Berg shook her head in disbelief. "I think you should not trust this foreigner. He is an enemy after all."

Papa looked at the clock. He stood up. "Look at the time, Mama. We must get ready for our appointment or we will be late. I will just walk you to the door, Frau Berg."

Frau Berg reluctantly eased her body up off the sofa. "Please be very careful where you place your trust, Frau Schmidt. I am concerned for your safety." She began to move towards the parlour door. She stopped and turned around to face Mama. "Did he happen to mention when he expects his next shipment of coffee?"

Mama shook her head. "I did not even think to ask such a question. What difference does it make, Frau Berg?"

Frau Berg's cheeks flushed. "Oh, I was just wondering, that is all. Now, you mark my words, and do be careful of these strangers. I can let myself out, Herr Schmidt; I do know the way." Frau Berg left the parlour alone. Papa remained standing by his chair, deep in thought. The silence of the room was broken by the approaching voice of Frau Berg. "I almost forgot one of the main reasons why I stopped by this evening. I came to tell you that my brother is coming to the

Canadian barracks to trade with the soldiers on Saturday. It would be my suggestion that you barter with Ludwig first. You will find him to be the most generous of the group. He will bring a wide variety of foods to trade." She lowered her head and mumbled, "That was the real reason I came by tonight. Good night. And thank you for the delicious coffee, Frau Schmidt. I do hope you can find its origin. I believe Ludwig and the others would trade handsomely for the likes of that coffee. Especially after I tell them how delicious it is." Frau Berg gave Mama a conspiratorial smile. She looked somewhat prettier to me at that point. Perhaps Frau Berg wasn't such a bad person after all.

Chapter 17

Eddie popped over to our house every night that week. We were having a wet summer and he said he needed to be assured that I was getting over my sore throat. "Wet cool weather is not good when you have a sore throat, Johann. You must avoid getting a chill." Later I overheard him telling Mama that he was still worried about the rheumatic fever.

I wasn't allowed to go out of doors all week. I desperately wanted to check the stones in the brush in case Andreas wanted to meet but I was under Mama's constant supervision. Eddie's visits helped the week pass fairly quickly, but even so Saturday seemed to take forever to arrive. My health had improved each day and by Saturday it was apparent that I would not likely require medicine or the services of a physician. Nevertheless, Papa set aside a portion of the stash for a medical emergency.

We rose earlier than usual so that we could go to the barracks as soon as the farmers arrived. I sneaked out to the brush. No stones were set out. What could have happened to Andreas? *Maybe I'll have to go by his house to see if there is any activity there.*

Back at the house the stash was removed from the safety of the larder. The 12 packages of cigarettes and the 24 candy bars were carefully placed in the sack Eddie had brought them in. We had decided that we would spend most, if not all, of this stash on food. We could use the next stipend for the other items on our list. Marlene insisted that a dress for her wedding could wait until closer to her wedding date. I overheard her talking to Diane about it one evening. Diane thought the dress should be bought now but Marlene confessed to her that she was afraid that might bring bad luck to Otto. She wanted him safely home before she took any steps towards making the wedding a reality.

I was posted as the lookout person while the others busied themselves with the morning chores. I sat on the front step working on the school English assignments Karla had given me. The morning was sunny and warm. There appeared to be no action over at the barracks. I was about to give up hope when I heard the sound of vehicles in the distance. Three trucks were coming our way. They turned south towards the barracks at the east end of our block. I was about to jump up and rush into the house to tell my family when a familiar voice stopped me. "Well, who do we have here?" Frau Berg waddled up our sidewalk. "I suppose your family is waiting for the farmers. Well, they had better get over there before everything is gone. I hear those soldiers are anxious to get some fresh vegetables and canned meat. It will be all gone by the time you get there."

Frau Berg stopped in front of me. Her face softening, she informed me, "Johann, I've been asking around about your little friend Andreas. No one seems to know what has happened to his family." We heard Mama's voice approaching through the open screen door. "I'll let you know," she whispered, "as soon as I hear anything." Frau Berg patted me on the head, then pushed past me and entered the house, calling, "Frau Schmidt, are you almost ready? The farmers are there now. Ludwig is expecting you. I just thought I would come along with you and introduce you to Ludwig. I will make sure he treats you fairly. He has expressed an interest in the coffee you served the other day as well. Perhaps you can help me, I mean him, acquire some of that delicious coffee." Frau Berg closed her eyes and rubbed her tummy. "Did I tell you that was by far the best coffee I have ever tasted?" Mama nodded her head. "Yes, of course I did. Well, is everybody ready? We must get over there right away."

Papa lifted the sack and carefully slung it over his shoulder. Frau Berg led the way. It amazed me how fast a heavy lady like Frau Berg could walk when she was on a mission.

Most of the soldiers were not at the barracks. They were working at the machinery compound, as they did every day, with the occasional Sunday off. Cook was there and prepared to barter. Frau Berg introduced us to Ludwig. He didn't look anything like his sister. He was short like her but he was almost as skinny as me. His head was balding and he had large round eyes. He was trying to communicate with Cook. They were not able to understand each other at all. Cook was relieved to see me. "Johann, I'm so glad to see you. I was just about to send someone to fetch you. Do you think you could assist this gentleman and me? We seem to be having a communication problem here."

"I would be very happy to help Mr. Cook," I answered with a chuckle.

Cook burst out laughing, much to the dismay of Ludwig and Frau Berg. Karla read the look on their faces and tried to explain to them about the joke of me calling the man dressed in white Mr. Cook when I first started to learn English. My family began to laugh at the joke and that set Frau Berg and her brother off as well. The other farmers stood silently by their trucks. They appeared to be reluctant to join this jocular group. However, when they saw that they had two interpreters, they soon approached and beckoned for Cook and his helper of the day to peruse the contents of their trucks. Cook insisted that my family barter first and get the things we required.

This was the first opportunity our local German farmers had ever had to barter with foreigners. The farmers were extremely interested in the cigarettes and candy bars. Ludwig was insistent that he needed some coffee as well. For their part, the farmers had potatoes, parsnips, turnips, and carrots from last year's crop. They had roasting chickens, eggs, butter, milk, cream, and even some cheese. They also had canned fish, canned chicken, and some fresh mutton.

Frau Berg proved to be invaluable in the bartering process. Mama and Papa were not natural barterers. Frau Berg was. The farmers had expected to be bartering with a whole regiment of soldiers but all they had was Cook and us. This gave us an unexpected advantage. Frau Berg bartered with the other farmers first. She would save her brother for the last, she told us. She managed to get a 100-pound sack of potatoes for us for a single package of cigarettes. After all, she told the farmer, these were hardly fresh vegetables, now were they? Two chocolate bars bought us a 100-pound sack of carrots and two large parsnips. One more chocolate bar bought a 50-pound sack of turnips. The vegetables were bought from the other farmers.

Now Frau Berg was ready to begin bartering with her own brother. He had the dairy and meat products. "You cannot always trust others when it comes to these products. My brother here is completely trustworthy, are you not, Ludwig?" Of course Ludwig did not get a chance to respond before she continued, "Ludwig, how much are you willing to trade for two cigarette packages? Maybe two fresh chickens and ten jars of canned meat, for example? Would that be fair to you, Ludwig? Yes, of course it would. Just set those aside for the Schmidt family then. Now, what about the chocolate bars? Say, six dozen eggs and two blocks of cheese for two chocolate bars? You think that is too much? How about four dozen eggs and two blocks of cheese? Yes. Well then, would another two chocolate bars buy six pounds of butter and one small bottle of cream and, say, two bottles of milk?" Frau Berg, it turned out, was a good woman to have around when it came time to barter. We now had hundreds of pounds of food and we had only spent three of our 12 packages of cigarettes and seven of our 24 candy bars. We could not believe our good fortune. Frau Berg also convinced the farmers to drive the food to our doorstep. "It is not out of your way, now is it, when it is just over the hill there. Herr Schmidt will be glad to help you unload the food once you get there."

It was Cook's turn to barter. "I cannot believe how valuable a few candy bars and cigarettes are around here, Johann. The boys will be thrilled. They've all pitched in to buy food for our meals. We could use some of these goods for variety. I think they're getting tired of the same old grub day after day."

Frau Berg was elbowing me in the side. "Johann, do not forget about the coffee. Ludwig wants to barter for coffee." She stopped talking and let me speak for her. I had never seen Frau Berg silent like this before. I smiled at her and relayed the message to Cook.

"How badly does she want coffee, Johann? I don't have a lot to spare."

"She tasted it at our house and she wants it really badly. I think one can would buy you lots of food, Cook."

"Let's find out just how much a can of coffee is worth to these people. Make sure you tell them it may not be possible to trade coffee because it's in such short supply."

I relayed the message to Frau Berg. She frowned and turned to Ludwig. She muttered something to him. He nodded his head. Together they went over to his truck. Ludwig jumped into the truck box while his sister stood beside the box and discussed possibilities with him. They returned to us with a most generous offer. They would like two cans of coffee and for that they were prepared to offer 20 fresh chickens and 40 jars of canned meat. Cook walked over to the truck and looked inside at the food. He pondered for a while, saying nothing. Frau Berg and her brother had another quick consult. They would add to the offer 10 dozen eggs at no extra charge. Cook looked at me, lifted the corner of his hat, and scratched his head as he pondered the offer. Finally he said, "I think that perhaps I can manage without two cans of coffee, though the boys may be right upset with me. But what can I do?" He shrugged his shoulders. "Tell these people that I agree to their terms." Mama and Papa were astonished to think that Eddie had given us a can of the same coffee for a gift. Now they knew just how valuable that gift really was.

Cook bartered with Ludwig and the others using cigarettes and candy bars. When the other farmers saw what Cook received for the coffee they wanted to know if he had any more to spare. He assured them that he did not have any at this time but that he would order extra next time and perhaps they would be in luck in the future.

Mama invited Frau Berg to stay for coffee after the bartering session. She settled herself on a dining room chair. "I hope Cook does not get into too much trouble with the soldiers because of that coffee he traded with us." She lowered her voice. "My brother has generously offered a can to me. I am so pleased that he thought to do that. Tell me, Frau Schmidt, do you prepare this coffee any differently than our German coffee? Are the proportions of coffee to water the same?" She took another sip and licked her lips. "It truly is the most delicious coffee I have ever tasted. I want to be sure to use the same proportions as you have used. I would not want to spoil it by putting too much or too little coffee into the pot, you understand?"

Mama gave her explicit directions on how to replicate the coffee we were drinking. Frau Berg nodded her head and drained the last of her coffee from her cup. "Oh, well, I really should get going. I have a great deal to do this afternoon." Without another word, Frau Berg hoisted herself off her chair and waddled out the door.

We spent the rest of the morning, after Frau Berg left, putting our food away. Some of the vegetables were taken out of the sacks and stored in the larder. I helped Papa carry the remainder into the tunnel where it was much cooler than the larder. We used the connecting passageway from inside the larder to enter the tunnel. We put some of the butter and cheese down there as well as some of the canned meat. This was the first time I had been inside the tunnel since we moved back into our own house a few years ago. It was hard to believe that we had to actually live in this tiny, dank shelter for over a year. But that's what happened when the Polish officers took over our house. The shelter was barely high enough for Papa to stand up. If I spread out my arms I could touch both of the walls crosswise. The length of the shelter was about three times the width. It smelled musty just like I remembered. It was cool all right, and dark. "The vegetables would keep very well here." *Better than people did, I hope.* A shiver passed through my body.

Papa and I closed up the tunnel door and returned to the kitchen. Mama and my sisters were preparing lunch. The remainder of the stash sat in the middle of the dining room table. We still had 9 packages of cigarettes and 17 chocolate bars to use for some of the other things on our wish list. Yet the shelves in our larder already overflowed with food. We would have a veritable feast today and for many days to come.

We spent the afternoon folding and pressing the soldiers' clothes so that Eddie could return them tomorrow. Mama and

Diane took turns pressing the clothes. We had two flat irons. One kept hot on the stove while the other was used to iron the clothes. When the one being used cooled down it was replaced by the hot flat iron. This way the ironing process was never interrupted. Great pains were taken by the rest of us to carefully fold each item of clothing so that it would not wrinkle. Mama and Diane sang as they ironed. The sound of their sweet voices and the smell of freshly pressed clothes filled our house with a sense of optimism. This was a new concept for me. The only thing that would make life better yet was if Arthur and the others were home with us. We paused for a cup of tea in the middle of the afternoon. I crawled onto Mama's lap. "Mama, when is Arthur coming home?" I snuggled close to Mama, putting both my arms around her waist as I rested my head on her chest.

Mama hugged me back. "We must be patient, Johann. It is only a couple of months since the war ended. I have not heard of any of our men coming home." She paused and looked up at Papa and my sisters. "Have any of you heard about anyone arriving back home yet, with the exception of Anton Degner?"

"No, Mama," said Marlene. "My employer said he heard that our soldiers would be sent to a processing centre somewhere in Germany. Then, once they are processed, they would be allowed to return to their homes." Marlene's voice dropped to a whisper as she continued, "He thinks this process is going to take several more months yet. He does not understand how Anton Degner avoided the processing centre. He speculates that perhaps Anton's health was too poor for him to walk any further."

Papa cleared his throat. "We cannot do anything to bring the boys home any faster. Once again we are helpless." He hung his head and his shoulders sagged. I hugged Mama tighter.

"Maybe we could plan what clothes we could buy for Arthur," suggested Karla, "so that when he does arrive home he can have a brand new set of clothes to begin his new life in."

Marlene put her arm around our sister and hugged her. "What a nice idea, Karla. It just so happens that I was shopping yesterday on my lunch break and I found some trousers I think he would like. Perhaps we could all go for a walk later this afternoon and take a look at them."

"Did you happen to see a dress you would like for your wedding when you went shopping?" asked Diane. "It appears we will have the means to buy all the things on our list," she added, as she directed our attention to the stash on the dining room table.

Marlene sighed. "I did see a few pretty dresses. I especially liked the cream-coloured one with the satin collar. However, I would still like to wait until Otto returns before I buy one for my wedding."

"It would not hurt just to stop in at the dress shop when we go for our walk though, would it?" asked Mama as she helped me and Papa carry the stash to the larder.

Marlene shrugged her shoulders. "I suppose it would not hurt." She need not have worried about shopping. The laundry chores took longer than expected, leaving us no time for shopping.

Eddie popped over for a brief visit Saturday evening. Mama made a fresh pot of coffee. Eddie had the next payment for the laundry. "The boys asked me to bring this over before they spent it on other less important things. I protested, saying that they had not yet received the laundry services for this additional payment but they all insisted that having clean clothes to wear was such a treat they didn't want to risk losing the service."

Diane and Marlene carried the remainder of the original stash out of the larder. They added it to the new payment. Karla counted the stash. Seventeen of the original chocolate bars remained after our bartering session. That was added to the latest payment of 48 chocolate bars, for a grand total of 65 chocolate bars! It was difficult to believe that it was just a few weeks ago that our family saw and tasted our first chocolate bar. The cigarette packages were plentiful as well. We had 9 remaining after today's bargaining. Those added to this payment of 24 packages brought the total to 33 packages of cigarettes.

Everyone sat around the table as we sipped our coffee. Diane was the first to find her tongue. "Marlene, we must go shopping this week for your wedding clothes. It appears we can afford a dress, hat, and shoes easily, right, Mama?"

Mama nodded her head. "It absolutely does. We expect the wedding clothes to cost about six to eight cigarette packages so we will have no problem affording them now. You girls start looking. When you've settled on a few outfits, we will all come and help you with your final decision."

Marlene's head was lowered. She had tears running down her cheeks. "I'm sorry, but I cannot even begin to look for a wedding outfit until my Otto is back in my arms. Only then can I begin to look for wedding clothes."

Karla and Diane went to Marlene to hug her. "Of course not," said Karla, "but when Otto returns we will be ready to help you choose your outfit. Only one month ago we thought it would be impossible to buy you a wedding outfit. Now we have plenty of funds. It will be so much fun, Marlene." Karla gave her sister a squeeze, then returned to her chair.

"When I get my art supplies," I added, "I will be able to draw a picture of your wedding. That way, if we don't have a camera, you will still have a picture."

Marlene smiled and put her arm around me. "You have a solution for everything, don't you, little brother? Even if we do have a camera, I would like you to draw a picture. That would mean more to me than any photo from a camera."

Mama looked at Eddie. "This is all possible because of you, Eddie. You have made our dreams come true. We have a treasure chest resting here on our dining room table this evening. We will spend it frugally so that it will last us a very long time."

Eddie smiled. "There's more where that came from," he assured us, "but we never know when it will arrive. The boys have been together for a year now and we've learned how to be frugal too. We make one cigarette last ten times longer than we did before we joined the army."

Papa rubbed his chin. "Have the Canadian soldiers had plenty of food to eat since they came to Europe?"

Eddie shook his head. "No, we've gone to bed hungry most nights. Food has been awfully scarce for us." Eddie looked at the stash on the table. "But perhaps we can enjoy fuller stomachs now that we're here. We never lived near farmers before so we had no way of trading with them. Cook thinks we will have a better chance of eating fairly well here in Leer. We're all looking forward to that."

Mama smiled and said, "We know just how you feel, Eddie."

"I have no doubt about that, Mama," grinned Eddie. "No doubt at all."

Chapter 18

"Papa," said Diane, as we sat at the breakfast table, "now that the war is over, do you suppose"—she wrung her hands in her lap—"do you suppose that we could destroy the underground shelter?" Diane's eyes were lowered as she posed her question.

Papa rubbed his chin as he studied my sister. "I know that the shelter causes you a great deal of grief, my dear, but I wonder if destroying it would actually help to make you less nervous."

Karla cleared her throat as she looked from Diane to Papa. "It seems to me, Papa, that it is not the shelter itself that is the problem, but rather the memories it elicits from each of us. I do not think any of us has even one good memory of the days spent in that awful place." Karla shuddered.

I gave her a weak smile. "Papa," I said, "the shelter still scares me too."

Papa looked around the table at us. "I would gladly destroy that thing immediately if I were sure that it would not be required in the future. I do not like that shelter any more than the rest of you."

Mama reached over and touched both Karla's and my hand. "Papa is right. We are not at all certain what to expect these days. The war only ended a few months ago. Nobody seems to know what is going to happen next. What if the Polish return?" Now it was my turn to shudder.

Diane began to weep. Marlene got up from her chair and went to Diane. She put her cheek to Diane's and her arms around her. Then she raised her eyes to Papa. "My employer says it is unlikely that the Polish will return to Leer. He says now that the Canadians are here, it is unlikely that any other Allied country will be involved with us."

"And we know," I added, "that the Canadians wouldn't hurt us. They are our protectors, aren't they?"

Diane looked up at me and gave me a weak smile. "Eddie and his friends have been wonderful to us. I have been thinking, and I believe they could be a symbol of better days to come."

Mama's eyes were watery. She blinked and the tears streamed down her cheeks. "It is about time this family had a better life. Papa and I feel so bad that Karla and Johann have never known what we always refer to as the 'good old days.' It is our hope that those days will return to us in the near future, but in the meantime, I agree with Papa that the shelter should remain intact."

Diane nodded her head. "I know you are right. I just hate looking out the kitchen window and being reminded of those dark days."

Later that afternoon, Papa and I were sitting in the parlour. Papa was poring over the antique stamp collection. I was organizing the stamps I had received from the Canadian soldiers. I thought of my older brother as I sorted the stamps. "Papa, when do you think Arthur will get home from the army? He's been away from home for three years now, Papa."

Papa looked up from the stamp collection. He rubbed his chin. "I know he has, son. It is hard to say when he will arrive. Some of the boys are beginning to return, but there is no way to know where Arthur is at the moment. He may be days away, or weeks. We will just have to remain patient."

I looked up at Papa. "Do you think Otto will get home first? Or do you think Diane's husband will be the first to arrive?"

Papa set the stamp collection down beside him on the sofa and turned to face me: "Do you remember when Frau Berg was visiting here a few weeks ago? She said that Otto was not far behind Anton Degner. Do you remember this?"

I nodded. "According to Frau Berg, Anton arrived home about ten days ago, didn't he?"

"I think that is accurate, yes," affirmed Papa.

I frowned. "Then Otto should be home any day now, right, Papa?"

Papa reached over and tousled my hair. "That is quite correct, my son."

"Then will Marlene and Otto get married right away? Will we have a wedding in the family soon?"

Papa rubbed his chin. "That is up to Marlene and Otto, but I do believe we will have a wedding shortly after Otto arrives home."

I set my stamps down on the chair and danced around the room. "I had better practise my dancing, Papa. I want to dance with joy when my sister gets married."

Papa chuckled at my antics. I smiled. It felt so good to see Papa smile and laugh. This had been an unfamiliar scene for me before the war ended and the Canadians arrived. My chest puffed out with pride. I realized that it was I who had found a way to bring joy to my family through my Canadian friend. I realized now that this was a milestone in my life.

Mama entered the parlour to see her husband chuckling and me dancing. A smile lit up her face. I noticed a strange scent when Mama opened the parlour doors. "Would you two gentlemen care to join the ladies in the dining room for some tea? Unless, Johann," she tickled me in the ribs, "you are too busy dancing to come and taste the fresh bread the girls and I just baked."

My dancing abruptly ended. "White bread like the Canadians eat, Mama? Is that what I smell? Did you bake white bread?" I jumped into Mama's arms, my legs dangling close to the floor.

Mama wrapped her arms around me. "White bread it is, my son. Now let's go and eat it while it is still warm." Papa rose from the sofa and shuffled to the dining room, followed by Mama and me.

Marlene placed a slice of bread on each person's plate. Mama sat down at her place as Diane served the tea. "I am very sorry," said Mama, "that we do not have any butter to put on the bread. I am hopeful that we will be able to barter for some cream the next time the farmers come to the Canadian soldiers' barracks. The farmers are certainly anxious to barter for chocolate bars and cigarettes. If they have enough cream available, we will be able to make some butter."

Diane sat down at the table. "It was awfully nice of the Canadian Cook to give us some of his white flour. When was the last time we had cream to make butter, Mama? I simply cannot remember the last time."

Mama stirred a tiny portion of sugar into her tea. "Well, I am sure it was before the war. In fact it was years before the war, was it not, Papa?"

Papa rubbed his chin. "The last time I can remember having homemade butter was in 1934, so that would be almost eleven years ago."

Karla's eyes widened as she looked at Papa. "That was the year Johann was born. I was six years old then. How can you remember that, Papa?"

Papa smiled. "In a way you just answered your own question, Karla. I remember the year so well because Frau Berg brought us a gift of cream when Johann was born." Papa turned to me. "So, my son, it was in honour of your birth that we had our last butter-making session in this house."

I sat tall in my chair. "That means that I have never even tasted homemade butter, not even when I was a baby." I looked at Mama. "Do you think we can make some butter this weekend so that we can serve some to Eddie when he comes over for supper on Sunday?"

Mama smiled. "We certainly will make the butter if we can just get the cream."

I settled back in my chair. "Eddie will like homemade butter, don't you think?"

Marlene reached over and patted me on the wrist. "I think Eddie will love Mama's butter. I was sixteen years old when you were born, so I remember the last time we had Mama's butter very well. Diane, do you also remember? You were just finishing school that year."

Diane shifted her weight in her chair. "I was completing my education, Johann, just as you were being born. I remember the butter well." Diane looked sideways at me and winked as we had all seen Eddie do so many times. "Of course, I also remember your birth, not just the butter." Everyone laughed. It was unlike Diane to wink and tease me. She had been an extremely nervous person in the past decade. I had come to realize that wars did that to some people. I didn't understand why Diane wrung her hands and wept so often while Marlene, who was just two years younger, smiled most of the time.

One night when Mama was tucking me into bed, I asked her about the differences between my sisters. Mama sighed and explained, "Son, Diane has been through some terrible experiences because of the war. Thankfully, Marlene escaped many of these experiences. Diane needs our understanding and our support if she is to overcome these horrors. I am glad that you chose to ask me this question. It would be better if you did not ask Diane about the war. Is that all right with you?"

I yawned and nodded my head. "Yes, I don't like it when Diane cries so much. I like it when Eddie makes her and all of my family laugh though."

Mama kissed me on the cheek and pulled the covers up to my nose. "I am so glad that life is getting better for us. I want you to grow up with good memories."

"My best memory," I said, "will be when my brother comes home from the war."

Chapter 19

All the boys, even Shorty, were beginning to settle into our new lives in Leer. We had only been here six weeks but we had already realized that the German people were no different than we were. Everyone, that is, except for Shorty. He conceded that the Schmidt family was just like any Canadian family but he wasn't ready to believe that the German people in general were of any worth. He was grumbling about the shopkeeper he had tried to make a deal with: "Ed, I just don't know why these people can't speak English. They certainly want to trade with us and get our cigarettes and chocolate bars. You can see the desire for these things in their eyes but how can you deal with somebody you can't even understand? It's ridiculous. They need to learn English. Look at little Johann Schmidt. He learned the language in just a few days because he hung around with us. It can't be all that hard."

I was sitting on my bunk with a pen and writing paper in my hand. "If it isn't all that hard to learn another language, then why aren't you learning German?" I jabbed Shorty in the side with my pen. "Then you wouldn't have any trouble bartering with the people, now would you?" I felt my eyes twinkling as I teased my friend. "Besides, who would want to hang around with a grump like you?"

"Trust you to think of a way to blame me for the problem. It's always my fault, isn't it?" Shorty pouted.

I put my pen down and studied Shorty. "Would you like to tell me just what the problem really is, Shorty? I think I know you well enough to know that all you really need is my help when you get into these moods. So just spit it out, will you?"

Shorty blushed as he turned away from my scrutinizing look. For once, Shorty was speechless. I pressed on. "Shorty? What is the problem?"

Shorty hopped off his lower bunk and faced me, his eyes sparking and his nostrils flaring. "I have to find a way to barter with these ridiculous people. They've got something we need, Ed."

"Something we need, Shorty?"

"Yes. You know how you've been talking about making a bicycle for Johann for his birthday. You said you had all the material you needed down at the compound to make the bicycle except for the tires. Right?"

I nodded my head. "That's right. I haven't figured out where or if I'll be able to find tires for it."

Shorty gave me a sly grin. "Well, I did find tires. There's a shop downtown that sells second-hand items. They have a couple of sets of bicycle tires. I figured I could barter for the tires. That would be my contribution to Johann's birthday gift."

I jabbed Shorty in the ribs again. "Shorty, I do believe you're going soft on me." Another jab and another. "I'm rather proud of you, old boy."

Shorty snorted. "Well, just don't spread this around. I don't want the others to know about it." Shorty put his hands on his hips as he faced me. "I mean it, Ed. Don't you tell nobody. Not even Earl and George. Promise me."

I stepped back from Shorty with a conciliatory gesture. "Okay, Shorty, okay. I promise. Would you like me to ask Karla to go with you and barter for the tires? She already knows about my plans to weld a bicycle for her brother anyway."

Shorty blushed. He ran his fingers through his hair as he pondered the suggestion. "I suppose that would work. She sure knows her English, is what I say. Sure, Ed, go ahead and ask her."

"When do you want to go back to the shop and barter?" Shorty frowned. "I'd like to go tomorrow but you know how it is in this army. You can never do what you want to do. It's always 'Shorty do this and Shorty do that.' You never get to do things you want to whenever you want to do them. I can't wait to get out of this dumb army and get my freedom back." Shorty thumped his foot on the floor.

I just smiled as Shorty ranted on about the army. This was a common occurrence. I knew Shorty's foul mood would eventually blow over. It always did. Most of the boys couldn't tolerate Shorty's negativity. I just shrugged and said, "How about Saturday afternoon? We're supposed to be on parade in the morning, but the afternoon should be free."

Shorty huffed, "They'll find a way to take that free time away from us, as usual. Just you wait and see."

I patted Shorty on the shoulder. "You know that isn't true, Shorty. It does happen sometimes but not as a rule. I'll talk to Karla and see if she's free on Saturday afternoon. Okay?"

Shorty crawled into his bunk. "Yeah, okay. Thanks, Ed."

I looked at my watch. It was only nine o'clock. "It's pretty early to be going to sleep, don't you think, Shorty? You aren't getting old on us now, are you?" Shorty grunted. I sighed and sat back down on my bunk. I picked up my pen and paper and began to write.

Shorty ignored the remark. "What are you up to, Ed?" he asked in a sleepy voice. "Writing another letter to your wife?"

"I'll write tonight for sure. It's our wedding anniversary in less than two months. I want this letter to get to her before our anniversary date because I'm not with her to celebrate. Again."

"I don't see what the big deal is. It's only an anniversary. Anniversary. Birthday. Nobody makes a fuss when it's our birthday, do they?"

"Maybe not, but I really miss being with her on these special days just the same."

"I'm sure glad I don't have a woman to pine over. You go ahead and write your letter. As for me, I'm going to turn in for the night. See you in the morning."

"Goodnight, Shorty." He was snoring in minutes, leaving me with the privacy I needed to write my letter. I dipped the pen nib into the ink and began to write to my loved ones.

09-08-45

Dear Sweetheart and Family,

Happy anniversary, my love. This is the third one I've missed. I surely hope I'll be there for our next anniversary. The mail is so slow I thought I would write to you now in hopes that this letter will reach you before our anniversary date on October 7. I'm so glad I finally have some paper and a pen and even ink to write to you with. Supplies are slowly arriving at our new base here in Germany. Remember how I always wanted us to take a trip on a train? Well, my wish has partly come true. I eat and sleep in a train car. That's what we have for barracks over here. Strange, eh? My sleeping car has four bunks. My roommates are Shorty, George, and Earl, just like when we were in England. It's not so bad really. Our bar-

racks are set off from the community, with a
canal behind us and a field in front. There is
only one house within our view. It's a two-storey
brick house with a tunnel leading to an underground shelter. The house is over a hill and can
be plainly seen from our barracks. You won't
believe this but I've had supper at that house
every Sunday since we arrived. I was so apprehensive about coming here, yet I find myself
involved with a German family already. Their
son, Johann, will soon be eleven years old. He's a
skinny little guy. The family doesn't have much
food to live on so the entire family is thin almost
to the point of being undernourished. The little
boy came over to the barracks on the first Monday we were here and I gave him a chocolate bar.
The next day he helped me unload and arrange
the food supplies so each of the soldiers, even
Shorty, gave up their supper potato and gave it to
him for his family. They are so grateful even for
the smallest of favours. I've gotten to know them
quite well in these few short weeks.

I wasn't sure what the German people would
be like but it seems they are no different than we
are. This family is awaiting the return of a son,
son-in-law, and the fiancé of one of their daugh-
ters. The men were forced to join the war effort at
an early age, some as young as fifteen. There is a
haunting sadness in this family that is difficult to
describe. They did not support Hitler, yet they
were helpless to stop the madness of this war. I am
so grateful to be a Canadian and to know that my
family is safe in our great country. I hope some day

that you will meet little Johann and the rest of his
family. They are helping to fill the gap left in my
heart by our separation. They have made me a
part of their family. Life is interesting, isn't it?
The little girl in the family is having her Confirmation this year. It was delayed because of the
war. She is sixteen years old and is about your size.
She has no special clothes to wear. Can you see if
anyone back home has anything she can wear? If
you sent it here I could return it to the person it
belongs to. Her name is Karla and she has her
heart set on having a white dress and stockings.
I would really appreciate it if you could help us
out with this. Someday we may have a little girl
too. We would want her to have her white dress
for this very special day. Thanks, sweetheart. Well,
I have an early morning tomorrow as usual so I
will say goodnight. Be sure to give my sons a big
hug and kiss for me. As for you, my sunshine, you
are always in my heart.

Your Hubby

I sealed the letter, knowing that it would probably be
opened and read at least once before my wife, Frances,
received it. Censoring of our mail continued even though the
war was over. It was difficult to express what one felt when
your privacy would most definitely be invaded by the censors.
Maybe I shouldn't have said anything about the Schmidt
family. What if the authorities disapprove and make me stay
away from them? How could I help them then? I decided it
was not worth the risk. I would have to rewrite the letter.
Thankfully, Shorty told me to make use of his writing paper

and envelopes. After all, he said, he had no one to write to except for his parents. Then I lit a match and burnt the original before I crawled into my bunk. I would have to find some private time tomorrow to write another letter to my wife. I missed her and our little boys so badly. If only I could have a picture of them. I would ask my wife to try to get a picture to me soon. Surely somebody had a camera back home. I didn't even know what my sons looked like now. It didn't seem fair that the war was over and we still couldn't go home. So many of the boys were back with their families already. Sometimes I almost agreed with Shorty's view of the army. I shook my head. *Enough of that, Ed. Think positive thoughts. You won't be here forever.*

I lay there listening to Shorty's snoring. I focused my thoughts on the project I had given myself a week to complete. I thought about the size and shape of each piece of metal I would require to make a bicycle for Johann's birthday. I wanted this birthday to be one Johann would remember for the rest of his life. I heard George and Earl creep into our sleeping car. They usually went to bed later than Shorty and I did, but they were always considerate and quiet so they wouldn't wake us. Finally, sleep overtook me.

I spent every spare minute at work the next day gathering the parts I needed to weld together a bicycle for Johann. When I wasn't sitting with the others at lunchtime, Earl came looking for me. He found me in the scrap pile as I sorted through the pieces of metal.

"So there you are, old buddy. Why aren't you taking a lunch break with the rest of us? Oh, I forgot. You're making a bicycle for Johann's birthday."

I looked up at my friend. "I'll join you in just a few minutes. I've got all the pieces except for the cross bar." I continued to pull at the scraps on the pile.

Earl went around to the other side of the pile. He pulled a long piece of metal tubing out of the scrap pile. "Will this work, do you think?"

I examined the piece. "That looks like it will do just fine, Earl. Thanks."

Earl put his arm around my shoulder and said, "Don't mention it, old fella. Now can we go and have some lunch before our break is over?"

We sat down to eat our sandwiches. Shorty sauntered over to us. "How's the search for scrap metal going, Ed?"

I swallowed the bite of sandwich in my mouth and answered, "I believe I have all the pieces I need now. I'll work on the project on my lunch hours this week. It shouldn't take much longer than that to weld the pieces together and paint them. Then I'll need extra time to fashion the wheels and attach them. That will be the hardest part of the job, I'm sure."

Shorty kicked the ground with the toe of his boot. "That's good because I don't know now whether Karla will be able to go with me to the market to get those tires."

I swallowed another bite. "Why wouldn't she be able to go with you, Shorty?"

Shorty shuffled his feet. "Well, I don't know. Maybe she's busy helping her Mama on Saturdays. They have all of our laundry to do and I understand that the whole family helps with the job. Maybe she's too busy to help me."

I studied my friend. I stopped eating and said, "Shorty, look at me. I think I've come to know this family pretty well in these past weeks. Believe me, Karla and her family would do anything they could to help us create a dream gift for Johann. Do you realize that Johann has never had a bought birthday gift in his life? The family had no means to buy him gifts. They are extremely anxious to do their part. This will be a gift from all of us, not just me. We're each playing a role in the making of this bicycle. Karla's part is to help you with the bartering. She will not disappoint us. These people are true to their word. Do you understand?"

Shorty snorted. "My life has been full of disappointments. My father used to promise to take me here or there and then not bother to even come home. I used to sit on the front step of our house for a whole day and night waiting on the man. Each time my mother would have to convince me that he was not coming. Again. I would go to bed and cry myself to sleep. That man broke my heart hundreds of times." A tear slipped down Shorty's cheek.

I stood up and put my arm around my friend. "Shorty, I know that you think I pick on you sometimes when I'm teasing you, but the reality is that I'm just trying to help you shake your dark moods. I'll be the best friend I know how to be for you. I'm here any time you need to talk. But you can't always get your own way." I winked at Earl. "Like the next time we go in the canoe, I'll take the back seat so that we don't have to spend the day going in circles." Earl and I burst into laughter at the memory of Shorty trying to steer the canoe and doing circles all the way up and down the canal.

Shorty sullenly looked at the two of us. "There you go again. Making fun of good old Shorty."

Earl stood up and put his hand on Shorty's shoulders. "Shorty, look at me." Shorty and Earl looked like Mutt and Jeff. "We are not laughing at you. We're laughing with you. Do you remember the time I was on guard duty all night? I wasn't used to being up all night. I slept the next morning and part of the afternoon. When I woke up I was in such a daze that I wandered out of the barracks in my underwear. The whole battalion was on parade when I stepped out into the yard. There I was in my underwear wondering why everybody was laughing so hard. When I finally woke up I realized that it was me they were laughing at."

Shorty slapped his thigh as he burst into laughter. "I remember that. You should've seen the look on your face when you finally realized why we were laughing. I wish I'd had a camera to capture that moment. You were hilarious, Earl." Shorty mimicked Earl walking like a zombie in the yard, then waking and realizing that he was not dressed, and covering himself with his hands and walking stiffly but quickly with short steps back to his barracks as he stole several frantic looks over his shoulder at his comrades.

Earl shook his head. "I don't think I'll ever live that one down."

I agreed. "I'll never forget that day, that's for sure." Then I turned to Shorty. "So, Shorty, do you see? Earl doesn't accuse us of making fun of him. He realizes that we are laughing with him, not at him. That is something you really must learn to do as well."

Shorty tilted his head as he looked at me. "I think I see what you mean. I'll try to learn. I really will."

"Good." I looked around to see that we were the only ones left in the lunch area. "Oh-oh, it looks like our lunch break is over, boys. We'd better get to work before we get fired." All three of us chuckled as we made their way back to work.

Later that evening, I got up the nerve to approach Cook. "I have a request for you, Sarge."

Sarge was enjoying an evening cup of coffee in the dining car. "What can I do for you, Ed?"

"Well, it's little Johann's birthday next week. Do you know that he's never had a real birthday party in his life? He's never had a real gift either." I related my thoughts about having a birthday party for my little friend.

Cook shook his head. "The German people have had hard times for decades, I guess. In comparison, we Canadians aren't so bad off, are we?"

I nodded. "I'd say we're pretty lucky to be Canadians. "

Cook set his coffee cup down on the table. "Is that really true about Johann? And now the family wants to help you give him a real present?" With a twinkle in his eye he said, "They really are an amazing family, I can certainly see that." Cook drummed his fingers. "I do have one question, though."

"What's that, Sarge?"

"How do you plan to make the tires for this bicycle?"

"Shorty has that covered."

Cook's eyes widened with surprise. "Shorty? Our Shorty?"

I smiled. "Yessiree. Our Shorty." *I promised Shorty I wouldn't tell anybody but Sarge is not just anybody. He will keep this between us, I have no doubt about that.*

"Really? What about a bicycle seat? That might be a difficult thing to acquire in these times."

"You won't believe it Sarge, but when I was picking through that scrap pile I actually found a seat. It was buried under a canopy of metal and well protected from the elements so it's in pretty good condition, too."

"I see," said Cook. "So what do you need from me?"

"Two things. First of all, I need permission to use the scrap metal."

Cook nodded. "I don't see a problem with that. That compound is piled so high with scraps, we'll never be able to use it all if we're here for a decade."

"A decade, sir?"

Cook chuckled. "I was being facetious, Ed. We won't be here for much more than a year from what I hear."

I wiped my forehead with the back of my hand. "Whew, you scared me there for a minute, Sarge."

Cook patted me on the shoulder. "Sorry about that, son. Now you did say there were two things?"

"Yes, yes I did. You know how we're fixing the motorcycles down at the compound?"

Cook looked straight into my eyes. "Yes, of course I do. What are you getting at, Ed? Just spit it out."

I slowly let my breath out. "Well, you know how we have to test-drive the motorcycles as we fix them?" I stole a glance at Cook. "I know, I know, spit it out. Okay, here goes. I'll need to work extra hours at the compound in order to build the bicycle. I thought I could test-drive a motorcycle by driving it here at the end of the day, then I could return that one in the evening, work on the bicycle until dark, then test-drive a different motorcycle back here in the evening." I stole another glance at Cook. "I would only have to do that a few times, Sarge. I plan to finish the bicycle before the end of the week."

Cook drummed his fingers faster. Finally his drumming stopped. "The motorcycles do have to be test-driven. I suppose it doesn't matter when that happens. You're not proposing to make the bicycle during your regular working hours. Hmm." Cook looked straight into my eyes. "You're a good man, Ed. I don't see any reason why I should stand in your way. Your request is a little out of the ordinary, but not unreasonable. Besides," Cook chuckled, "if I know you as well as I think I do, you'd walk to the compound every evening to complete this project. We don't have so much daylight after supper that you can spare the time to walk. Permission is granted."

I breathed a sigh of relief. Softly I said, "Thanks, Sarge."

"You're quite welcome, son."

Chapter 20

Friday evening my family took their coffee in the parlour after the evening meal. Mama and I sat on the sofa with Marlene. I cuddled into Mama's side. "Mama," I asked, "do you know when Arthur is coming home?"

Mama hugged me close. "No one has heard any news yet, son." She looked over my head at Marlene. "Has your employer heard any news down at the railroad station about our boys coming home?"

Marlene shook her head. "He mentioned a few names of men who have returned, but I did not recognize any of them. It seems they are returning much slower than anyone expected. My employer told me he does not understand what is taking them so long. He also said some of them are returning in deplorable condition." Her voice grew shrill.

I didn't like to hear this news. "Arthur will never get home, Mama." A tear slipped down my cheek.

Mama took me in her arms and rocked me. "Of course he will, Johann; we just do not know when."

Papa reminded me, "We must have patience, son. This is not easy for any of us, but if it is hard on us, imagine what it must be like for Arthur."

I sat up and looked at my Papa. "Will Arthur be just like he was when he left?"

Papa rubbed his chin. "He will look much the same but he may not feel the same. War is very hard on people, especially the combat soldiers. We will just have to see what he is like when he arrives home."

A knock was heard at the door. "Is anyone expecting company this evening?" asked Papa.

Everyone shook his or her head. Papa rose from his chair and plodded to the front door. I watched him from the parlour door. Papa was in the habit of peering through the side window before opening the door. When he saw who was at the door he started to walk back to the parlour without answering it. I guess he thought better of his decision because he returned to open the door.

"Good evening, Herr Schmidt. I was standing on your front step for so long I almost turned and left. I was beginning to wonder if you were not at home, yet I saw the lights in the dining room. Is everyone in the parlour as usual at this time of the evening?" Frau Berg did not wait for a reply. She preceded Papa into the parlour. Her ample hips waddled as she quickly made her way to join us.

"Ah, Frau Schmidt, how good to see you again." She came over to Mama and kissed her cheek. She tousled my hair. "And I hear we have a young man with a sore throat, right Johann? Are you feeling better now?" Without waiting for a response she turned back to Mama. "I also hear that young Canadian friend of yours, the one with the beautiful blue eyes, has been visiting your home a great deal. Is that wise of you, Frau Schmidt?" Frau Berg's heavy chest heaved as she sighed, "We have a few strangers hanging around Leer these past few weeks. Now that the war is over, we may be subjected to many new and uncomfortable situations with these strangers. I just want you to be careful with this Canadian; you do understand, do you not? Now, Frau Schmidt, just how are you doing with the dispensation of your stash of chocolate bars and cigarettes? Oh, Frau Schmidt, that coffee we bartered for with the Canadian cook is just heavenly. I believe you had a hand in persuading the cook to barter his coffee with my brother. Oh, by the way, Johann, thank you for doing the interpreting with the cook. Ludwig is such a generous fellow. He never married and he treats me like a queen. I really am fortunate to have him and my other brothers to take care of me. I get to live in the city and still have all the benefits of the rural life. By the way, is there anything in particular you will be looking for tomorrow when the boys come to the Canadian barracks to barter?" Diane had served her a cup of coffee. She finally stopped her chatter long enough to take a sip of coffee while she awaited Mama's response.

Mama did not hesitate to reply, "As a matter of fact, Frau Berg, there is a special request my family has. We would like some fresh cream so that we can make some butter. We just realized today that Johann has never eaten homemade butter and we think it is time he did."

Frau Berg's small, bird-like eyes widened. "Never eaten homemade butter? That is very difficult to believe. My brothers supply me with cream on a regular basis. I suppose I have come to take it for granted." She looked at me curiously. "Never had homemade butter, not even once?" I shook my head. "Hmm. Well, I am sure that one of my brothers can spare some fresh cream. I suppose I could go without it for one week if it came to that." She looked at me again as she raised her eyebrows. "I think you will like the butter, Johann. And what about you, Karla? Have you ever tasted butter?"

Karla balanced her cup delicately on her knee. "Mama says that I did but I was only six years old at the time, so I do not remember the taste."

Frau Berg stared at Karla and me. "Well, we will just see if we can remedy the situation for you two." She turned to Mama. "I guess that means that you have not tasted homemade butter for at least ten years, is that so?" Mama nodded. "Yes, of course it does. You will have to try putting a little cream in this delicious Canadian coffee. It tastes wonderfully divine with cream." Frau Berg closed her eyes and drew in a long slow breath as she thought about the aroma of the cream in her favourite coffee. "Why did you not tell me you needed cream sooner? I could have arranged for one of my brothers to supply you with some long before this if I had known."

Papa cleared his throat. "That is very kind of you, Frau Berg, but we had no means to pay for it before now."

"Oh. Oh, I see. But now you have plenty of means, do you not? The one time I dropped by for a visit—that was a few weeks ago now—you had a whole stack of cigarettes and chocolate bars, did you not? I remember that they were piled on the side table over there. Do you still have some left? I should tell you that the word around town is that you have fallen into a wealth of these products. I would lock my doors at night if I were you. You never know what kind of scoundrels are lurking around Leer these days. I've heard reports that there are renegades running around Germany trying to get even with Hitler's cohorts and their families. Apparently, they've been allowed to get away with brutal beatings, lootings, and whatever they choose to do."

Frau Berg glanced at me. I had to stop shaking before anyone got suspicious. I don't think anyone else noticed me. Diane had the spotlight, as she was wringing her hands and weeping. Frau Berg continued, "It seems we have no order in this country. There seems to be a number of new faces in the city lately. I guess we can expect that with the boys slowly returning. Say, have you heard from any of your boys yet?"

Mama shook her head. "No, not yet. We are hopeful that they will be home soon. Have you heard any more about our boys from the men who have returned?"

Frau Berg shook her curly head. "No, not a word. I would not worry too much, though, because apparently they have to walk for hundreds of miles to get home. Some of the boys are having trouble walking because of illness or injury, you understand. So it is taking them much longer than we expected to get home."

I nestled closer to Mama's warmth. "Mama," I whispered, "is Arthur sick? Or injured? Is he, Mama?"

Mama sighed. "We have no idea what is happening with Arthur. Remember what Papa said about patience, Johann." She hugged me closer.

Frau Berg put her coffee cup down and wiggled her chunky body closer to the edge of the chair. "I must be getting on. I have many chores to do today. I must not forget to stop by the post office on my way home to catch up on all the latest news around town. I was wondering what time you were planning to be at the barracks in the morning. Ludwig told me that he would be there by eight o'clock. Would you like me to stop by just before eight? I will catch a ride over here with him and go with you. I think I can procure you a good price on the goods. Not just from my brother either, but also from the others. It worked very well for you the last time I assisted you with the bartering, I thought." She hoisted her bulky body off the chair and stood still a moment as her legs adjusted to the shock of the weight they were being asked to support. "Frau Schmidt, there is one little favour I would like to ask of you. Do you suppose you could persuade the Canadian cook to barter some of that incredible white flour they use for making bread? I have never tasted it but I hear from other folks that it is absolutely divine. Have you ever had the pleasure of tasting it? I have only spoken to one person who has actually had the experience of eating the white bread. I am terribly anxious to taste it for myself. I would be in your debt if you could do that for me." Frau Berg walked towards the door.

Mama put me down and followed her. "We will expect you tomorrow morning then, Frau Berg. It was good of you to stop by."

Mama returned to the sofa. "We should review our list of items we wish to acquire tomorrow when the farmers arrive."

Papa rubbed his chin. "How many chocolate bars and cigarettes do we have left over from the last bartering session? Does anyone know?"

I was not surprised when it was Karla who responded. "We have exactly thirty-three packages of cigarettes and sixty-five chocolate bars left, Papa."

"We must remember though," reminded Mama, "that this stash will not last forever. We do not have any idea what sort of jobs will be available for Papa and Diane once the men return from the army." She looked over at Papa and Diane. "Many of the jobs you two have been doing will be taken over by the young men as they return, I am sure. It is wonderful to know that you, Marlene, will be able to keep your job. That will be a blessing, at least."

Papa shifted his weight in his chair. "Shall we discuss the things we need in the immediate future?"

Diane agreed. "We have already decided that we need some fresh farm cream. Do you think Frau Berg's brother will bring some for us tomorrow?"

Papa chuckled. "He will if he knows what is good for him. I think Frau Berg will make certain of it. That will be her bargaining tool for the cook's white flour, I would suspect."

Mama tapped her cheek as she pondered the family's needs. "We shall try for the cream. We could also use some other vegetables. We got potatoes, carrots, and parsnips the last time. Hopefully the farmers will have some different vegetables tomorrow. It is still too early for this year's crop of most vegetables, except perhaps for lettuce, tomatoes, and green onions. They may have some canned corn on hand from last year's crop this time." My mouth was watering at the thought of all these delicacies.

Diane clasped her hands together. "Perhaps we can get some more of the canned meats and fish. They will keep well in our larder."

Marlene added, "Yes, that is a good idea. We have enough eggs to do us for quite a while. They do not keep all that long, even in the larder."

"And of course," chimed in Karla, "it would be nice to have some fresh meat for the week. I really enjoyed the chicken. I think Eddie did too."

"Me, too," I said. "I think chicken is my favourite meat."

"They may have canned chicken as well," Papa said. "I ate that once several years ago and, as I recall, it was delicious."

Mama looked around the room. "Does anybody have any other requests? We do not know for certain what the farmers will bring but we can always put our desires on the list just in case."

Papa folded and refolded his napkin. "I do have one concern about our present circumstance." Papa glanced up to see our puzzled looks. "I am worried that we will become accustomed to having plenty of food to eat. Then when this all ends we will have to go back to the hard times again. It is always harder to go from good times to bad times than the other way around." Papa lowered his eyes and continued with the napkin folding. "I think this is something we need to consider."

Mama nodded. "I can certainly understand your point, Papa. However, it seems to me that we must give our family a taste of what could be. Life has been so difficult for us for the past fifteen years. One can only hope that our circumstances will improve with the end of the war. We now have a wealth of chocolate bars and cigarettes. These items will purchase many of the things we need and some of the things we want. If we can just relax, Papa, and enjoy our good fortune no matter how short-lived, then Karla and Johann will have some idea of the possibilities life can offer them." Mama touched my cheek.

Karla nodded her head. "Papa, we will be frugal with our stash. The cigarettes and chocolate bars are extremely valuable, as we learned last week. Who would have ever guessed that one chocolate bar could purchase enough meat to supply our family for four days! If we used the chocolate bars we currently have on hand only for meat, we would have enough chocolate bars to buy meat for, let me see . . ." She looked up at the ceiling as she calculated in her head, then she looked at our parents and said, "two hundred and sixty-eight days."

Marlene's eyes widened. "Wow, that is truly amazing, is it not? We have had so little meat in the past that we are not accustomed to eating it every day. Imagine if we ate meat only every other day. Using those calculations and multiplying by two, that would mean we would have meat for . . ."

Karla spoke up immediately. "Five hundred and thirty-six days. Or . . . one year and one hundred seventy-one days."

I gasped. "Really?" I faced Mama. "Really, Mama?"

Mama nodded her head, a smile spreading across her face. "Now that is truly amazing."

"And," Diane reminded us, "the Canadians will be here for several months to come. They will continue to pay for their laundry. We could possibly purchase meat for our table for several years to come with these chocolate bars. It is like we have a gold mine in our larder. I think Frau Berg is right about the fact that we need to ensure that our doors are always bolted." Diane's eyes darted from Mama to Papa and back again.

Papa reached over and patted Diane on the shoulder. "Of course, you are quite right. Perhaps I should inform you that Johann and I inspect the shelter every morning and every evening as well." He reached over and patted me on the head. "That way if anyone tries to break in, I will be aware of any changes in the shelter's appearance. I want to be prepared for any future intruders. I am going to ask each of you to report anything you notice to Mama or me immediately. Does everyone understand?" Heads nodded. "Good. Then let's continue with our list."

"I think," said Mama, "that we have fully discussed our food needs, so let's discuss the other items on our list. We have clothes for Arthur, wedding clothes for Marlene, confirmation clothes for Karla, and a winter coat for Johann."

I giggled. "I think I can wait for my winter coat now that summer is here." I screwed up my face and pretended to be floundering in the water as I was swimming. "Besides, a winter coat would only slow me down when I am racing with Arthur in the canal." Then I pretended to be swimming smoothly. "I plan to beat him in our first race. Just you watch me."

My family giggled with me, then Diane spoke up. "Perhaps we should wait for Arthur to return before we purchase his clothes. We can set the funds aside and let him choose his own clothes. He has been gone from us for three years. He may have changed quite a lot in that time."

Mama sighed. "Perhaps you are right. That leaves two items on the list."

"Mama," said Marlene, "I still do not wish to buy wedding clothes until Otto returns. That means there is only one item left on the list requiring our immediate attention: Karla's confirmation clothes."

Mama nodded. "When shall we begin our search?"

Papa suggested, "Why not tomorrow afternoon? We will barter with the farmers in the morning, spend time doing the Canadians' laundry, and go to the markets after that. Does that sound like a reasonable plan?"

My chest puffed out as I realized none of this discussion would have taken place if it weren't for my friendship with Eddie. We would simply be having another sombre evening in our parlour as we'd had almost all of my life.

Chapter 21

The plans for building the bicycle for Johann occupied my thoughts most of the time these days. I rushed over to the scrap metal pile on my lunch break again today. I assembled the pieces of metal on the ground in the shape of a bicycle frame. I would have to cut some of the long pieces to fit the frame, so I measured and marked each piece. I stood up and pondered the best tool for the job.

"Looks pretty good to me." I jumped at the sound of Earl's voice. "Haven't you eaten any lunch yet, Ed?"

"Not yet. I wanted to get the project ready for the cutting stage; I'll return tonight to do at least that part of it. Then all I'll have to do is weld the pieces together and paint the frame."

Earl ran his fingers through his straight blond hair. "And just when do you plan to do all this? You can't skip lunch, Ed. You know how shaky you get when you don't eat on time." Earl handed me a sandwich. "I figured I would find you here when I didn't see you at lunch. Now eat while you still have time."

I accepted the sandwich. "Thanks, Earl, you're a good fella."

Together we sat on the ground. The only sound was that of me chewing my food. When I swallowed my last bite Earl asked, "So when are you planning to work on this bicycle?"

"I plan to come back here to the compound every evening until I'm done."

"By the time you walk all the way here you will have very little daylight time left to work."

I nodded. "Yes, I know. So I asked Sarge about test-driving the motorcycles we're working on."

Earl stared at me. "And?"

"And Sarge said I could test-drive at night. I'll drive it home at suppertime and back here after supper. That way I'll have plenty of daylight time to work on it."

Earl smiled. "Oh, I see. The motorcycles have to be test-driven anyway, so this way you're actually working on the motorcycles in the evening. Clever, my friend, very clever."

I chuckled. "Well, I guess we'd better join the others before they send a search party out looking for us, eh?" We picked up the pieces of metal and placed them in a neat pile against the fence.

* * *

Early the next morning Shorty and Karla set out for the open market. Shorty scanned the booths. "I don't think we'll have any luck finding tires here. These people seem to be selling mostly food, with the occasional piece of footwear and clothing. I don't see any white dresses or stockings either."

Karla picked up a pair of white shoes. She turned them over carefully and ran her fingers along the top of the shoe. Then she abruptly turned to Shorty. "I think we should go and try to find the shop you told me about." Karla turned on her heel and walked away.

Shorty rushed after her. "Are you sure you don't want to try them on? We have time if you want to."

Karla shook her head. "No, thanks. I would rather find the bicycle tires before I consider looking at anything else."

"Okay, I think the shop is this way. But I must admit, I'm not really sure. I have a bit of a problem with my directions. When I found the shop the other day, I was coming from another direction. I definitely did not see that open market. I'm sorry, Karla, I'm not sure which way to go."

They reached the end of the street where the open markets were. Karla looked to the left, then to the right. "Do you remember what the shop looked like?"

Shorty shook his head. "Not really. I'm afraid I wasn't paying that much attention. I thought you would be able to find bicycle tires anywhere. I should've known better. It was one of the first shops I looked in. I searched through several more and didn't find even one more shop with tires." Shorty ran his fingers through his hair. "It seems to me the shop had a green sign. I'm afraid that's all I can remember."

Karla shook her head. She was not all that familiar with the marketplace since her family had not traded here for years. She could not think of a single shop with a green sign. "Well, let's just go to the left and see what we can find."

They visited shop after shop. Finally they found the shop they were looking for. They could see the bicycle tires through the window. The sign was not green. It was blue. When Karla pointed that out to Shorty, he laughed and said, "Oh, yeah, I forgot to tell you. I'm colour blind."

It seemed there were very few bicycle tires to be found in Leer. This shop had two pairs of tires. One set was in perfect condition. They appeared to be brand new. The other pair was quite badly worn. The shopkeeper approached Shorty as he examined the new tires. "How can I help you, sir?"

Shorty examined the tires closely. He set them down and asked, "How much are you asking for these tires?"

"Would you be paying with British money or American cash?"

Shorty faced the man with his hands on his hips. "Neither."

The man's eyebrows lifted up over the rims of his glasses. "Neither, sir?"

Shorty reaffirmed, "Neither."

The man's eyebrows were furrowed as he looked at Karla. "Can you explain to me what your friend is talking about. What other kind of money is there?"

Shorty pulled a chocolate bar out of his pocket. "There's this kind of money, that's what."

The shopkeeper's eyebrows rose in surprise. He looked from Karla to Shorty, then back again. He rested his eyes on the chocolate bar. "Is that a chocolate bar? Is that what it is?"

Shorty nodded his head. "That is a real bona fide American chocolate bar. Here." He held the chocolate bar to the shopkeeper's nose. "Take a good whiff of this."

The shopkeeper took a long whiff. He kept his eyes closed long after he had finished inhaling the sweet scent of the chocolate. Finally he gave his head a shake and opened his eyes. He looked from Shorty to Karla and back again. Then he asked Karla, "Have you ever tasted one of these?"

She smiled and answered, "Yes, as a matter of fact, I have."

"What did it taste like?"

"I think you could find out for yourself. All you have to do is barter with this man."

The shopkeeper tugged on his moustache. "I wonder what you would expect to purchase for a chocolate bar."

Shorty put his hands on his hips and said firmly, "I will do you a real favour today since I'm in such a good mood. These two bicycle tires would do nicely. I get the tires, you get the chocolate bar."

The shopkeeper hesitated. "I have never traded for

chocolate bars before. I do not know how much they are worth."

"Well," Karla said, "I can tell you what they are worth to the local farmers. Last week we traded one chocolate bar for enough meat to feed our family for four days."

The shopkeeper studied Karla. "How many people are in your family?"

"We are a family of six and we had a guest on one of those days."

Shorty was nodding his head. "Now, do you suppose this chocolate bar is of equal value to those two bicycle tires or not?" Shorty held the chocolate bar up to the man's nose one more time. "Either make a deal or we'll leave and find someone else who is interested."

The man hesitated. Shorty started to walk away. "Come on, Karla, we're wasting our time here." When Shorty and Karla reached the door the man called out, "Wait! I will trade you the chocolate bar for the bicycle tires." He picked up the two tires and handed them to Shorty. Shorty smiled and gave the shopkeeper the chocolate bar.

As they left the building Shorty said to Karla, "I would have given him two chocolate bars for those tires if it would have been necessary, you know." Shorty chortled.

Karla looked puzzled. "Then why did you not give him two?"

"Because," Shorty smirked, "he didn't ask for two." Shorty walked Karla home. "Thanks for helping me today. I couldn't have done it without your help."

"You are quite welcome. I cannot wait to see the look on Johann's face when you and Eddie give him the bicycle. He was upset today when he offered to go with you, and the whole family told him that only I could help you today. I am afraid I left him quite puzzled. I expect a lot of questions when I return."

"Good luck. I'll see you later." Shorty turned south and sprinted to his barracks.

* * *

I was just pulling up on the motorcycle as Shorty crossed the field. I got off the motorbike and waited there for Shorty. "Well, Shorty, I got most of the metal pieces welded together for Johann's bike this afternoon. How was your day? It appears you had some good luck."

Shorty handed the tires to me. "I had great luck, is what I say. I got two brand new tires. It took us most of the morning to get the shopping done, though."

"Why did it take so long? Did you have trouble bartering?"

Shorty looked a little sheepish. He lowered his eyes and confessed, "I forgot where the shop was. There was only one with bike tires, so I guess I lucked out."

I examined the tires carefully. "I'll say you had good luck. These will be just perfect."

Back at our sleeping car Shorty put the tires on his bunk and asked me, "So you've got the frame together? What's the next step?"

I sat on my bunk. "Well, the next step is probably going to be the hardest part. I'm sure glad you were able to get the tires today because the next thing I have to do is make the wheels. Now that I have the tires the job will be a little simpler."

Shorty studied me closely. "Have you ever made a bike before?"

I shook my head. "Uh-uh. But the frame was easy. I'll figure it out, though it may take me a while. I have a brother back home who is always inventing things. I've worked with him on a few projects. He built an airplane, a bombardier, and a windmill. A bicycle should be relatively simple after that, wouldn't you think? "

Earl came along and heard the end of the conversation. He chuckled. "It may be easy for a guy like you, old buddy, but some of us couldn't build a tower with wooden blocks. So, Shorty, I see you had some luck with the tires. Good for you. Did they cost you an arm and a leg?"

Shorty swayed his hips as he faced Earl. "Not at all, my good man. I paid one chocolate bar. I think I got the best of that deal."

"I would say you did. Now me, on the other hand, I had to pay a fortune for my contribution to the bicycle."

My eyes widened in surprise. "Your contribution, Earl?"

Earl held out a package to me. "You mentioned to me quite a while ago that you were wanting to make a bicycle for Johann so I wired my cousin James in Britain. Do you remember meeting him on our trek to Germany, Ed?"

I nodded. "Yes, of course I remember. We visited his parents in London."

"Well," said Earl, "I thought Johann would enjoy having a horn on his bicycle. James has so many connections that I hoped he could round one up for me. I received this parcel just a few hours ago." He handed the opened package over to me. "Take a look and see what you think."

Shorty and I examined the horn. It had a ball-shaped device on the end. When you squeezed the device the horn blew. It had a deep sound, something like the foghorns we heard at the port in Halifax. I studied the construction of the horn and pondered the possibilities of attaching it to the handlebars. I looked up at Earl as Shorty played with the horn. "Johann will be delighted with this fine accessory to his vehicle. We're going to make this an unforgettable birthday for our boy."

Chapter 22

Saturday afternoon I sneaked away to our secret rendezvous spot. I was sitting in the brush wondering what had happened to Andreas. My imagination ran wild as I pondered some of the horrible explanations for Andreas's absence. I hadn't seen him for weeks now. And Frau Berg hadn't reported any news either. Something awful must have happened to him. I began crawling to the exit from the brush when I heard footsteps approaching. I sat down on my haunches and held my breath. The person began to push the branches aside. Fear overwhelmed me. Was it the renegades Frau Berg spoke about? I heard no voices so I assumed the person must be alone. I took in a shallow breath. The person pushed more branches aside. I could see the outline of the man's shape against the sun. A croaky voice demanded, "Come out of there, you scoundrel. You are trespassing. Now come out!"

That was Papa! I heard anger in the shaky voice. I couldn't ever remember Papa using a really angry voice before. "Come out at once!" Fear too. *Should I just stay still and hope he gives up?* Footsteps continued to invade my safe spot. "I will not stand for this. Come out at once!"

I crawled towards another exit. Papa was now deep into the brush. I crawled around the outside of the brush and hid just to the left of his entry point. I heard him pushing the branches aside as he tramped through the thick brush. It sounded like he was coming towards me now. I slunk down closer to the ground and buried myself under the overhang of the brush. Footsteps approached closer. Now I could see him. Finally he emerged just one metre from my head. *Should I stay hidden? Should I show myself and pretend I was just playing in here?*

Papa came closer. He tapped at my foot. "Johann? Is that you?"

"Papa? Papa, is that you?" I jumped up and hugged my Papa. "I was so afraid. I thought you were one of those scoundrels, Papa."

Papa released me and looked into my eyes. "Johann, what were you doing in there? You scared me half to death."

Truth? Lie? Half-truth? I settled on the half-truth. "I was just looking for birds' nests, Papa. I thought there might be some hidden here." I actually did think this would be a good place for a bird to hide her nest.

"Well, I'm relieved to see that it isn't one of those renegades. It's so easy to be paranoid with all the rumours floating around." Papa put his arm around me. "Come now. We must go on home. Your Mama will be wondering what has become of us."

* * *

Sarge put out the word that we were going to have a meeting in half an hour in the dining car. Shorty snorted, "Now, what do you suppose they want with us? Always something with this army, is what I say."

George looked up from the book he was reading. "It's probably not anything much. The army is still trying to figure out what our roles are supposed to be here in Germany."

Earl looked from me to George and Shorty. "My cousin James wrote me and said there seem to be some problems in other parts of Germany with looting and such now that Hitler is supposedly dead."

I looked at my watch. "Well, I guess we'll find out soon enough. We'd better hit the trail if we don't want to be late. You know what a stickler Sarge is for punctuality." I started for the door, with the others close behind.

We poured ourselves a cup of coffee. Cook had told me that it was all right for me to have coffee at the barracks even though I had taken a can to the Schmidt family. He said we owed them at least that much because of their assistance with the bartering process with the farmers.

Sarge called the meeting to order. He was our cook but he commanded authority when he acted his part as Sarge. "Listen up, boys." He took a sip of his coffee. "I have received a directive from the Major. The authorities have clarified the whole issue of occupation. We have been ordered to do the following to keep order in post-war Germany: One, report all acts of violence or unlawful conduct to the authorities. In our case you are to report to me and I will contact the Major. Two, be vigilant in your observances of strange faces. Of course, this will be difficult for us because we are so new to the community. The Major instructed us to inform the local people we have come to trust to notify us of strangers entering the city. Three, take an inventory of all equipment owned by the army, especially that which is not under our direct surveillance. In our case we will have to keep an eye on the vehicles at the compound as well as the canoes. The Major said there has been a problem with stolen vehicles all over the country. Four, and the final point is the most crucial, we have been declared the official law enforcement authority in Germany. Each Allied Occupation battalion has been given specific directives. In our case we can defer any law-breakers to the Major since his barracks are just a few miles from ours. However, the Major made it quite clear that we are to assume the role of law enforcers to the locals. It must be presumed by the public that our authority is unquestionable. We must be firm in our dealings with all law-breakers when we apprehend them."

Sarge took another sip of his coffee. "Any questions?"

George spoke up. "Sarge, what are the laws of the land?"

Sarge nodded. "Good question. The Major has indicated that whatever laws we are accustomed to in Canada should be enforced here." He surveyed the group. "Is there anyone here with any law enforcement background?"

Again George spoke up. "Yes, Sarge, I have had some experience. I served on the city police force back home for a few years."

Sarge frowned. "Really, George? Then why did you join the RCEME? We're all mechanically inclined here."

George glanced at me. I nodded. His cheeks flushed. "I got out of the police business because of all the violence I witnessed. The car accidents were one thing, but the deliberate acts of violence against humankind were the clincher."

Sarge nodded. "Does anyone else have any experience in the field of law enforcement?" He looked around the room. He scratched his head and returned his attention to George. "Okay, George, it appears you will be our resident expert. Your role will be to advise me when we face a matter that falls into the grey area of the law, as we know it." He looked around the room again. "Any other questions? No? Okay, you're dismissed."

The four of us returned to our sleeping car. Shorty elbowed George as we entered the car. "So, you're a policeman, are you? Hmmph. No wonder they picked you to head up the guard duty roster." Shorty glared at George. "I hate cops almost as much as I hate Nazis."

This was news to me. I studied Shorty. "Why do you hate

cops, Shorty? Have you had a run-in with them somewhere along the way?"

Shorty kicked the floor with the toe of his boot. "No, not me. They hauled my old man to jail more than once though."

Earl shook his head. "Really, Shorty? What for?"

Shorty looked up and stared at each of us in turn, his face crimson. He whispered, "If I tell you, you won't be my friends any more."

George, Earl, and I exchanged looks of confusion. I put my hand on Shorty's shoulder. "Shorty, the sins of the father do not get passed on to the son. Our feelings for you won't be affected by your father's wrongdoings. It's all right, you can tell us—if you want to, that is. It's entirely up to you."

Shorty shoved his hands deep into his pockets. He stood before us like a convict facing a jury, his face red, contorted, his left eye twitching. His voice was barely audible. "My father used to beat me and my mother up. He broke her ribs several times. One time he even made her ear bleed. She still can't hear much out of that ear."

Earl asked, "Where is your father now?"

Shorty kicked the floor with a fury now. "He drank himself to death, that's what. And good riddance to him is what I say."

George shook his head, his brows knitted. "But, Shorty, you're always talking about your folks back home. I didn't know your dad was gone."

Shorty put his hands on his hips. "Yeah, right. I sure wasn't talking about him. My mother remarried after the old man died. I was about twelve years old then. I only talk about my dad, not the old drunk. He isn't worth . . ."

Then we all heard it. It sounded like somebody calling

for help. We rushed out the door to hear "Eddie! Eddie! Help!"

It sounded like Johann. "Over there," said George, as he pointed to some distant figures near the north bend of the canal.

Johann screamed, "Eddie, help! Hurry, Eddie!" We raced over there to see three young men beating on a little boy. Johann was hanging from the back of one of the men, trying to wrestle him to the ground. The other two were ruthlessly kicking the kid.

George grabbed the taller man and pinned his arms behind his back. He threw him down and sat on top of him. Earl wrestled the other attacker to the ground. I pushed on Johann's back, knowing that would cause the third man to fall forward, thereby decreasing the risk of hurting Johann as he clung stubbornly to his back. Johann fell off the man and I was able to pin the man's hands behind his back. Several of the other soldiers from our barracks heard the commotion and joined us. They hauled the three bullies to our barracks to meet Sarge.

Johann rushed over to where Shorty was kneeling down at the child's side. He looked up at me, his eyes pleading. "Will he be okay, Eddie?"

Shorty patted Johann on the shoulder. "I think he has a broken leg. I wouldn't be surprised if he has other broken bones too." He turned to Earl. "Would you go to the barracks and bring something to splint this leg? We could use a gurney too."

Earl turned to leave. George said, "I'll go with you and ask Sarge to send out a search party in case there are more of these culprits in the vicinity."

"Good idea." Then I knelt down beside Johann. "Johann, are you all right?" He was as white as chalk. He was kneeling beside the child. He looked up at me. "I'm okay, Eddie, but what is wrong with Andreas? Why isn't he awake?"

"You know this boy, Johann?"

"He's my secret friend, Eddie. Mama and Papa don't know about him."

"They don't?"

"No, Eddie. I couldn't tell them."

"Why not?"

"Because his father was a member of Hitler's Gestapo."

Shorty instantly removed his hands from the boy and stood up, shouting, "What? What did you say, Johann?"

I stood up to face Shorty. I put my hand on his shoulder and said softly. "You heard him. The sins of the father. Remember, Shorty? This little boy has done nothing wrong, Shorty. We both know that, right?"

Shorty shook my hand off his shoulder. He looked for-lornly down at the broken child. He knelt back down and stroked the child's hair. "It's not your fault. We'll take care of you."

As if on cue, George, Earl, and Cook appeared. Cook did a quick examination of the child. "His left leg is broken here just above the ankle. It looks like we may have two bro-ken ribs too. We'll have to be careful when we transport him. The ribs could easily rupture the lungs." Sarge stood up. "I'll let you boys handle getting this child to the hospital. I have some culprits to deal with." Sarge looked down at the child's still body. "He needs medical attention immediately. God only knows what damage has occurred inside this little boy's body."

Johann swooned against me. I caught him. "He will be just fine, Johann. We'll make sure of that."

George and Earl carried the child away on the gurney. They drove him to the hospital while I accompanied Johann to his home. On the way there he said, "I must tell Mama and Papa about Andreas but I'm afraid they will not understand."

I tilted his chin to meet my eyes. "We have to go and tell Andreas's mother about his injuries and take her to the hospital. So, Johann, you really have no choice. You're the only one who knows where Andreas lives. You do know, don't you?" Johann nodded.

"Good then. We'll tell your folks and then you and I'll drive one of the army trucks over to their place to tell Andreas's mother."

Johann smiled at me. "Thanks for coming with me, Eddie. But we will not have to drive. His house is only six blocks from here and his grandpa has a car so he can drive her to the hospital. I always thought Andreas was so lucky because his family had a car."

We entered Johann's home with great trepidation. I thought I knew the family pretty well but I had not lived through the horrors of the war as they had. It was easy for me to forgive Andreas for being a child of a member of the Gestapo; I'd never had any personal dealings with any of Hitler's men.

We found the family sitting at the dining room table having a cup of coffee. Papa greeted us with a smile. Clapping his hands he declared, "Well, who do we have here? What a surprise, Eddie."

Mama read the gravity of the situation on Johann's face. "Johann? Eddie? What is wrong?"

We took our places at the table. Diane's shaking hand attempted to pick up a fresh cup to offer me some coffee. "*Nein*," I said.

Johann explained what had just transpired. Papa's mouth fell open in shock.

Mama's lip trembled. Diane wrung her hands in her lap.

Marlene sat straight in her chair but her eyes softened as she leaned over to hug her little brother. Karla's voice shook as she interpreted German to English for me.

I asked permission to take Johann to Andreas's house to break the news to his family. Mama came over to Johann and examined him. "You are quite certain you are not hurt, Johann?"

Johann nodded. "I'm fine, Mama, but I think Andreas is not. May I go now with Eddie to see his mother?"

Mama looked over her shoulder at Papa. He sighed. "Yes, Johann, of course you may. We are not angry about your friendship. We are just disappointed that you thought you had to keep it a secret from us."

Johann's shoulders shook as he gave in to the sobs he'd been holding back. He looked up at me and I gave him a reassuring smile. He turned to Mama. "Andreas said no one should know because everybody hates Hitler and his hit men now. He said it would not be safe for me to tell anyone, not even my family, because that might put us in danger."

Mama hugged him tighter. "It is fine, Johann. We do not hate children. They are not responsible for any of this madness. Now, you go ahead with Eddie, and break the news to Andreas's mother. Go on now."

Johann was right. Andreas's grandfather put Andreas's mother and her sister in the car immediately. Before he drove away he said, "I knew of your friendship with my grandson, Johann, and I would like to thank you. You are the only friend that little boy has ever had."

As they drove away I said, "Well, Johann, I was right about one thing."

Johann's eyes reflected his confusion. "What do you mean, Eddie?"

"I mean," I replied as I slung my arm over his shoulder,

"people are people no matter where they live. This family of a Gestapo member seems no different from your family or mine. They're normal just like us, not the monsters some folks make them out to be."

Chapter 23

Eddie was not able to come for supper on Sunday. He said it was his turn to do kitchen duty again. Eddie said he hated this KP duty but everyone had to take his turn. He just wished his turn hadn't been on a Sunday, but when you're in the army, you do as you're told. My family had gotten quite used to having him at our table Sunday evenings. When we sat down to eat our meal we realized just how much we missed him. There was no laughter. We ate our meal in silence. Every time we tried to make light conversation we found ourselves looking at the empty place at the table. Sadness was all around the room.

The whole next week was a strange one for me. I was allowed to visit Andreas at his home every day. He had a cast on his leg and he was therefore on crutches. I tried walking with them and soon discovered that they were not that easy to use.

Eddie was never at the barracks in the evenings. Whenever I went over to see him, the soldiers wouldn't tell me where he was. All they would say was that he wasn't there. Once I ran into Shorty, and I gathered the nerve to ask about where Eddie was. He just tousled my hair and said, "Oh, he's off inventing something."

"Inventing something?" I asked.

Shorty smiled. "Yeah. He'll be done soon, I think." Shorty walked over to the dining car and disappeared inside, leaving me staring after him in confusion.

I noticed several times when I walked into a room at home that people would abruptly stop talking or I would catch them whispering if I was close enough to hear their conversations. My family was acting very strangely. One afternoon, I walked into the kitchen. Mama and Diane were making butter from the cream we had been able to buy. Frau Berg had been true to her word. Her brother, Ludwig, did bring cream to trade with us at our last bartering session. Diane was shaking a jar of cream as Mama was scraping a batch of butter they'd just made into a bowl. Diane's voice was jerky as she continued to shake the jar. "Mama, have you decided who we should invite?"

Mama smiled. "The decision is not just up to me, my dear. Did you have someone in mind?"

"Eddie must be here, of course, and I was thinking . . ."

Diane looked up to see me standing there. She stopped shaking the jar and said loudly, "Oh, Johann, I did not see you standing there. Have you been in the room long?"

"What are we inviting Eddie to? Is he coming for supper this Sunday?" I asked hopefully.

Mama smiled. "Yes, Johann, I think Eddie can come this Sunday. We are planning a special meal with all the food we have been able to acquire with the stash. Is there anything in particular you would like for supper on Sunday?"

This was a curious question. I had never been asked what I would like for a meal. We always just had to eat whatever was available. I scratched my head. "I really like the roasted chicken we had once. I know Eddie loved it too. Could we have that again? If we can get some fresh chickens, that is."

Mama nodded. "I will ask Frau Berg to see if any of her brothers could provide us with some on Saturday. Is there anything else?"

"That is enough, Mama. Thank you."

Sunday finally arrived. Eddie walked home with us after church and asked if I would like to go out in the canoe after lunch. He had some chores to do but he would be free by four o'clock. Mama and Papa agreed.

I rushed over to Eddie's barracks at precisely four o'clock. Several of the men were out in the yard. They all waved at me and greeted me with smiles. It seemed like I had known them for years. I remembered being so afraid of some of them, especially Shorty. *Eddie was right about him*, I reflected, *he is not such a bad fella after all.*

Eddie was waiting for me in his sleeping car. He was writing another letter to his wife. He looked up when I entered and smiled. "I'll just be a moment, Johann. I'm just finishing this letter."

I nodded and waited silently. Shorty came into the car. "Well, look who we have here. So you're brave enough to go out in the canoe with us, are you, Johann?"

Eddie winked at me and I teased, "Only if Eddie is the driver. I don't want to go in circles all day like you do."

Shorty jabbed me in the ribs. "You've been hanging around Ed too much. You're getting to be as big a tease as he is." His eyes were smiling.

Shorty, Eddie, and I walked to the compound down by the dock to get a canoe. I stepped carefully into the middle of the canoe as Eddie and Shorty put it in the water. It felt so peculiar to be sitting in a moving boat. I had never been in any kind of vehicle before in my life. The canoe bobbed up and down with the waves. My tummy felt a little queasy at first as the canoe bounced in the water. Soon I became used to the craft and enjoyed the adventure. I did not have a paddle so towards the end, Eddie asked me to move to the back with him so that he could teach me how to paddle. I stood up and tried walking to the back but a wave hit the canoe and it rocked. I lost my balance and fell flat on the bottom of the canoe. I quickly got back up on my knees and crawled to Eddie. He taught me how to steer with the paddle. Eddie looked at his watch and said, "Where did the time go? It's twenty minutes to six already. Shorty, we'll have to row fast or we'll be late."

Shorty began rowing quickly. "You're not kidding. We have to dock this thing first. I need a few minutes to change my clothes first, too. Let's hurry, Ed."

I looked over my shoulder at Eddie. "Are you going somewhere with Shorty tonight, Eddie? Aren't you coming to our house for supper?" The tears were welling in my eyes.

Eddie smiled as he pushed the water with his paddle. "Of course I'm going to your house this evening. Your parents asked me to invite Shorty to come along this evening as well."

My family didn't really know Shorty but I was delighted that they would invite him for a meal. We finally had enough food to invite guests and I guess Shorty would be a good candidate for a guest. They had certainly heard a great deal about him. Maybe they just wanted to meet this man we'd had so many chuckles about. My family had been acting kind of strange all week. Maybe it was the stash that was causing them to act so funny. *Who can figure adults out anyway?*

We rushed back to the barracks knowing that we were a few minutes late. Eddie and Shorty changed their clothes while I waited on the bench. It was pretty quiet at the barracks. I guessed that the men were all inside the dining car having their supper. A couple of minutes later Shorty and Eddie emerged dressed in their dress pants and white shirts. Shorty had his hair slicked back. "Okay, Johann, are you ready to go?" he asked as he put his arm over my shoulder.

We entered my house but there was no one there. Fear instantly surfaced and I panicked. "Eddie, where is my family? Something has happened, Eddie. Something is wrong." I was trembling so hard that my knobby knees knocked together.

Eddie put his arm around my shoulder. "I don't think anything is wrong, Johann. Watch this: Hello," he shouted, "we're here." The kitchen door burst open and the dining room was instantly filled with people. The men from the barracks were all here along with my family. They shouted in unison, "Happy birthday, Johann."

I looked up at Eddie. "How do they know it's my birthday?"

Marlene came over to hug me. "Because we invited them here to help you celebrate your eleventh birthday, that's why." That same boisterous bunch of Canadians that I had secretly observed only a few weeks ago immediately surrounded me.

The door opened behind me. I turned to see Andreas standing on his crutches between George and Earl. "I couldn't miss your first birthday party, Johann."

Mama greeted Andreas with a gentle hug. "Papa and I paid a visit to Andreas's family this week. They agreed that he should be here today. Happy birthday, my son." She kissed me on the cheek.

We did not have the space to seat so many people at our house so we returned to the barracks and ate in the dining car. Mama and my sisters had spent the afternoon preparing food at our house while Cook and his helpers worked at the barracks. I had never seen so much food set out on tables in my life. We had roast chicken, potatoes and gravy, turnips, carrots, cabbage salad, and . . . fresh bread and butter. I spread the butter sparingly on the warm white bread. I closed my eyes and allowed myself to focus on the taste as I appreciated the new experience. Frau Berg was quite right. The combination of fresh butter and the equally fresh Canadian bread was absolutely wonderful. I wanted to imprint this moment into my brain, just in case I never had the opportunity to experience it again. I finally realized that Karla was waiting patiently for me to take the bowl of carrots from her. I opened my eyes to see my family thoroughly amused by my expression of joy. Diane's eyes twinkled. "I see that the taste of the home-made bread and butter agrees with you, little brother. I am so glad that you have finally had the opportunity to understand what all the fuss was about."

Andreas took a bite of the white bread. "Mmm, Johann, this is delicious. I've never tasted such good bread before."

Papa passed me the potatoes, then the chicken. My plate was almost full. It did not resemble the plates of other meals. They were always at least half empty when each of us had taken our small portions. Tonight, however, each of us filled our tummies. This was a new experience for me. I imagined that the older members of my family had only faint memories of the days of plentiful food. I also knew that the Canadians often went to bed hungry. Tonight was special for all of us. At the end of the meal I noticed that my tummy was bulging out from my trousers. It seemed so strange to look down and see roundness where there had always been emptiness in the past. Maybe Papa is right, though. It might not be a good idea to get used to good times because then one has so much disappointment to deal with when they are over. I decided to shake the bad feeling and simply enjoy the bounty set before us on this evening. The soldiers' banter around the room helped lift my spirits. Andreas was all smiles as he, too, enjoyed the company of his rescuers.

Soon everyone had finished the meal. Mama and my sisters rose to help clear the dishes. Eddie stood up and announced, "Ladies, you will not be doing any dishes in this dining car. Each soldier will take care of his own dishes and those of our guests." The men cheered and began to clear the tables. Cook disappeared with the others close behind him. Eddie and Shorty remained at the table with my family, Andreas, and me. Eddie looked at my tummy. "Is there any room in there for dessert?"

Mama's face flushed. "Eddie, I did not have the ingredients to make a dessert for tonight's meal."

Just then, Cook led the men back into the dining car. He was carrying something on a huge tray over his head. He set an enormous cake on the table in front of me. One of the men I knew to be a guard named Danny stood beside him. "I'm a chef, but since I joined the army I've had no opportunities to practise my craft. Today, Cook and I had all the necessary ingredients to make you a birthday cake." I looked down to read the words "Happy Birthday, Johann," written in red letters in English on the cake. "Earl found some berries growing on the brush behind the barracks. I used them to dye the icing red for the letters. Sorry, we didn't know how to write this in German."

Mama and my sisters were in tears. Papa sat stone-faced as he always did when he felt very emotional. I couldn't sit still in my chair. I almost wiggled right off it as I looked from the cake to the men to my family. I whispered to Eddie, "Is this what a birthday cake looks like?"

Eddie chuckled. "This is a birthday cake all right. I think Cook wants you to cut the first piece."

I took the knife from Cook and held it in my shaky hands. I trembled so hard I couldn't get a good grip on the handle. Eddie reached over and put his hand over mine. "Here, Johann, let me help you with that." Together we cut one piece of cake. Then Cook lifted it off the tray and placed it on a plate. He handed it to me but I shook my head. "Thank you, Mr. Cook, but I think everyone else should have a piece first. I will have mine last, if you don't mind." Cook looked at me, then at Eddie.

Eddie squeezed my shoulder and shrugged. "I guess we have to obey the wishes of the birthday boy, Mr. Cook." The men's laughter filled the dining car. Andreas and my family were served before the soldiers. No one touched their cake until all had been served. When the last piece was placed before me the men burst into song as they treated me to the English Happy Birthday song. Karla must have been teaching my family because they joined in, except for Diane. She could not stop weeping long enough to sing.

We gathered out in the yard after the meal. Earl and George helped Andreas down the steps. Eddie told me to close my eyes and not to peek. He said they had a surprise for me. I heard a door open and close. No one spoke. It was so quiet that I wondered if I was all alone like the time Arthur told me to hide my eyes because he had a surprise for me. I was hiding my eyes and waiting and waiting. In the meantime, someone came to the door and Arthur forgot all about me. Apparently I held my hands over my eyes for over half an hour waiting for Arthur to return. Arthur was devastated when he realized what he had done.

Finally, I heard the sound of crunching gravel. Eddie spoke up. "Johann, you can open your eyes now." I slowly removed my hands from my eyes. Eddie was holding the handlebars of a shiny red bicycle. "Johann, this gift is from all of us."

My mouth dropped open and my hands trembled as Eddie handed the shiny new red bike over to me. It had my name written on the back fender in small block letters. "A bicycle, Eddie? For me, Eddie? Thank you everybody." Then I whispered to Eddie, "I have never ridden a bicycle before."

Shorty sauntered over to me. "Don't worry, Johann, Old Shorty here will show you how to ride this fine vehicle." He looked up at Eddie. "May I?" Shorty took the bike and tried to get on it. He swung his leg up but he couldn't quite get it over the cross bar. George held the bike while Shorty stood on his tiptoes. He finally managed to get onto the bicycle. George gave him a shove and off Shorty went around the yard. He shouted out instructions to me as he rode around and around. He honked the horn each time he passed by me. Finally he hopped off the bike and brought it back to me.

George helped me get on the bike. Andreas clapped his hands. "Go, Johann, go."

Eddie held the bike as I settled myself on the seat. "At the rate you're growing I figured I should make it just a little too big for your current height. You'll grow into it before the summer is over I would think." I rested my tiptoes on the pedals as I had seen others do. I didn't know many people who owned a bike. I couldn't believe my good fortune. The tears slipped down my cheeks as I thanked everyone for an unforgettable birthday party. I would learn to ride the bike another day.

Earl and George took Andreas home after the party. Eddie returned to my place. We enjoyed a cup of coffee in the parlour. Karla and I had our coffee white with cream and sweet with sugar just the way we had come to love it. Marlene was speaking with her British mannerisms: "Sir Eddie, it was jolly good of you to construct a bicycle for my brother's birthday. Whatever made you think of such a gift?"

Eddie aimed his little finger in the air as he held his coffee cup. "I say, I do believe the idea struck me when I realized this household has no mode of transportation."

"Do tell. Are you planning to go into the business of constructing vehicles, or is it more of a hobby?"

"Construction of vehicles, you say? No, I do not believe I will. It was a challenge, though, I must say."

The rest of us giggled as we listened to their banter. Diane spoke up. "Johann, you have had quite a day, have you not?"

I reached out and patted Diane's hand. "I sure have. You see, things are getting better for our family all the time." I looked up at Eddie. "Our lives were filled with darkness before you arrived. Now even Diane smiles and sings. You've changed our lives forever, Eddie. You've shown us that on the other side of war is a new world filled with light and joy." I snuggled beside Eddie, content that my family had a bright new life to look forward to, one with full tummies and the friendships and protection of a whole battalion of Canadians. At that moment I finally understood that this day would be the beginning of my story, as I would someday tell my children about my very own good old days.

Epilogue

1998

The gracious silver-haired lady sat erect in the armchair in her daughter's home in Germany. A small gathering of people were present to meet my Mom, including Diane's daughter, son-in-law, and grandson, as well as Johann's widow and Karla's widower. Through Diane's grandson she spoke to my Mom and brother about her memories of my Dad in 1945-46. Dad was in the Occupation Force with his regiment, the RCEME, the arm of the military responsible for the restoration of all of the dilapidated machinery in post-war Germany. She looked directly at my Mom as she said, "It is by way of Eddie that we were to be fed."

A tear slipped from my Mom's eyes. She had waited 52 years to meet someone, anyone, who could tell her about those lost years. She knew Dad was torn when the army sent his troop back to Canada. He had spoken of "the family" many times and had expressed his desire to take Mom and the three little sons he left behind to go back to Germany to meet them. He missed "the family" enormously and worried about them incessantly. However, he had his own family to take care of and get reacquainted with now. And there was the matter of finding a job. Mom smiled at the lady whose family Dad had known so many years ago. "We had to leave our home in Alida, Saskatchewan, and move 30 minutes away just across the Manitoba border to Tilston.

We bought the local hotel, and life got in the way. Sadly, that trip never happened."

Diane spoke of the fond memories her family had of my Dad. Mom, my brother, and his wife soaked in all the stories being shared with them. The family had suffered many atrocities because of their nationality. They were German in citizenship only, but that mattered not to the rest of the world.

Diane's shoulders sagged a little as she declared, "We were powerless to stop the madness created by Hitler. And we dared not express our views for fear of death. That is how it was in Germany during those trying years."

Mom turned her eyes away from Diane and asked her grandson to tell her, "Ed was so grateful for your family. He was the kind of man who needed a family and you and your parents provided that for him. We suffered too during the war but not like you did. He knew that and a piece of his heart was left here with you. To his dying day, you never left him. I knew the day he returned from Germany that you saved him just as much as he saved you. I"—she looked at her youngest child—"or I should say we, came to thank you for filling a void in his lonely life. He was quite despondent before he met you." She asked Diane's grandson if he could read the letter she received from Dad just before he left Holland. It was dated approximately two days before he arrived in Germany and met the family.

Mom continued, "I'm sorry that some of the letter has words missing from the torn airmail paper and the censoring process. We made a photocopy of the original letter. The dotted lines represent words that were either on the missing pieces or from the ink spill, but if you can just do your best I would appreciate it."

Diane's grandson nodded his head and said in excellent English, "I will do my very best."

He turned to face his grandmother as he read the letter:

Dear Wife and Family,
Well here I am again, still in Holland but I don't think we will be here long. Well how is everybody at home? I suppose that the kids are really growing, eh? Gee, I sure made a mess of this letter [Author's note: The ink had dripped all over the page] but I have to use this form anyway, because I could only bum the one form from Shorty. Say, is there anybody else but you that sent me parcels? When did you send the one with the oxfords in it? There was one boat of parcels that got all burnt, I suppose that would just be my luck that my parcels were in that one. Say, when you order cigarettes order 900 every month, will you? I think that I will write to Louis and ask him to send me cigarettes too. It would be too funny to have all your relations there [page is torn for the next few lines] and none of them ever sends you a few chocolate bars and gum or soap. . . . that I have told you before, but you . . . that in Holland we can't buy anything to . . . all. All we can get to [blot over next word] what they gave us at meal time. And some time when we go to bed we are pretty hungry, specially when some of the boys have received parcels and are eating right next to you before they go to bed. I sure hope that we don't have to stay here a year or two. Anyway, when they asked me to enlist, I said no I want to go back home. Tell Frankie that if it keeps up this way he will be a big boy before Daddy gets home.
Gee, I sure hope that I get some mail soon,

sure makes you lonesome when the mail don't . . .
know why the mails don't come maybe is because
. . . . Have been moving to much. I am writing
this at noon hour, if I get a chance I will also write
to-night. Give my love to all those that are dear to
us, give the kids each a big kiss for me, say hello
Dad and Mother. Well Sweetheart, with all my
love,

Your Hubby

Diane rose from her chair, as did my Mom. They
hugged, then wiped tears from their eyes. Mom said to those
in the room: "The circle is now complete for me, thanks to
all of you. I want you to accept my gratitude for helping Ed
out of his depressive circumstances. I'm not so sure he could
have managed without you."

Mom returned home from Germany feeling at peace at
last. She had made the long-desired journey many years after
Dad's death. Dad had died suddenly in a car accident. Once
she finally accepted his death she made a promise to herself.
Now, she had finally met the family. Mom could relax now.

My work, to tell this remarkable story, however, had just
begun.

Welcome to The Other Side Series
by Marie Donais Calder

Marie Donais Calder has authored a series of books based on real people, centring around her father, Edmond Joseph Donais. The first several books are set in the city of Leer in northwest Germany between July 1945 and July 1946. Marie's Dad, Ed, was stationed there as a member of the peacekeeping force. The remaining books in the series are set back in Canada when Ed returns from Germany. There is magic in these pages . . . the magic of human decency, tolerance, caring, and understanding. They illustrate how small gestures become life-transforming events in a time when the things we take for granted meant life or death for some. In our world these days, people have much to gain from such an inspirational message. Several more books are to be published in the near future.

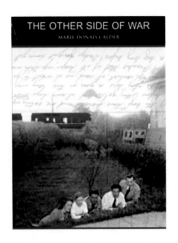

The first novel in this series is *The Other Side of War*. In a 1998 visit to Germany my mother was told, "It's by way of Eddie that we were to be fed." Eddie, my Dad, served in the Canadian Occupation Force in Germany for one year following the Second World War. My Mom was back home in Saskatchewan caring for their three little sons. Soon after arriving in enemy territory, Eddie met ten-year-old Johann. Unlike so many others, Dad didn't view Johann as a Nazi. He was just a starving little boy. This story illustrates how one man and one family rose above the vile hatred caused by war. It highlights the best of humanity—even between enemies. (225 pages)

The second novel in the series, *The Other Side of Fear*, continues the Canadian soldier's (Eddie's) relationship with the German family who, like other people of Europe, faced fear of epic proportions. Sometimes this fear was produced by Hitler and his hit men, and frequently by the treatment of the German people by members of the Allied countries. For example, the family in these novels was forced by the Polish military to evacuate their home, dig a hole in the ground in their back yard, and live in it for almost a year. (220 pages)

The third novel, *The Other Side of Pain*, serves to illustrate the depth of the bond between Eddie and Johann's family. Even Shorty, Eddie's army buddy, is instrumental in helping the family. Earlier Shorty couldn't understand why Ed would even bother with the Nazis. To him all Germans were Nazis. Otto, Marlene's fiancé, comes home from the war and must have his leg amputated. Eddie helps him to deal with this. Then the Russians come back to try to finish the job they started in the second book. There is still incriminating evidence hidden in the Schmidt home. The Russians kidnap Karla. Eddie, his regiment, his superior officers, and a trained rescue team are deployed to find Karla. We realize what Eddie has been saying all along: people are people no matter what they look like or where they're from. (221 pages)

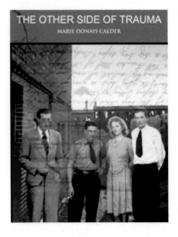

The fourth novel, *The Other Side of Trauma*, continues to illustrate the commitment Eddie has made to the family. Trauma comes from various life experiences. It is complex and unique to the affected individual. This book illustrates the syndrome that is known today as Post-Traumatic Stress Disorder. Eddie, his sergeant, superior officers, and others band together to assist the family with the challenge of dealing with yet another blow: shell shock. Johann's older brother, Arthur, and Diane's husband, Friedel, arrive home together. Arthur has a serious case of this debilitating condition. He's catatonic at times and suicidal at other times. Once again Eddie is instrumental, along with others, in helping Arthur heal from his emotional war wounds. (202 pages)

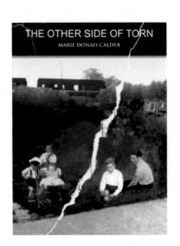

The fifth novel in the series, *The Other Side of Torn*, continues the story of Eddie's life in Germany. He has to make a major decision that will affect both his wife and children as well as the German family. He is desperate to confer with his wife on the matter. However, communication between a Canadian soldier and his family in the 1940s was painfully slow. Letters typically travelled by boat and took several weeks and sometimes even months to reach their destination. Telegrams were expensive and therefore rarely used. A soldier's family was often notified of their death by telegram. Hence, the soldiers rarely used this method of communication. Eddie will have to make his decision without the luxury of hearing his wife's thoughts on the matter. In the end he will make the right decision. (221 pages)

The sixth novel in the series, *The Other Side of Rebellion*, illustrates the point that not all German people were accepting of the Allied Occupation of their country. Fuelling the rebellion were the many sightings of Hitler being reported around Europe. The rebellious faction was threatening to reclaim their country on behalf of the madman. Once again, Eddie and his Canadian army must intercede. *The Other Side of Rebellion* will have you on the edge of your seat. It has proven to be another novel in the *Other Side* series that you just won't be able to put down. (217 pages)

In *The Other Side of Capture*, the seventh novel in the series, the rebel leader is still at large. The Canadian army is determined to capture him and rescue his captives. A woman's hand drops an envelope, addressed to Frau Berg, in front of Eddie and Shorty. Frustration builds as Frau Berg refuses to reveal critical information that would facilitate the capture of the rebel leader. In the meantime, Ed's wife, Frances, is dealing with an accident involving one of their little sons. She needs her husband, but currently he is available to no one. (213 pages)

The Other Side of Rescue is the eighth novel in the series. The tension continues to build beginning on Valentine's Day, 1946. Johann's devotion to Eddie is palpable. He fears that he might lose his mentor and best friend forever. And he may be right. Johann and Earl had pulled Eddie out of the water in that canal in Germany but now Eddie's fate is terribly uncertain. Johann is helpless once again. This eighth novel poses many questions. Will the rebel leader finally be captured? What has happened to Herr Keller? Who is driving Sarge's jeep? Will Frau Berg ever settle down? She laments incessantly: "Oh, Frau Schmidt, whatever am I to do?" On the Canadian front, Eddie's wife has learned some unsettling news from Doctor Jones. (220 pages)

This ninth novel in the series, *The Other Side of Devotion*, highlights the devotion of those in Germany who remain by Eddie's side during grim times. Thankfully, he is unaware that his future is in jeopardy. An army friend of Eddie's visits Frances and the children. He has unsettling news of an atrocious act carried out by the Allies at the end of the war. Frau Berg finally learns of the fate of her friend, Herr Keller. She must make a heart-wrenching decision. Oh, what should she do? (252 pages)

The Other Side of Starvation is the tenth book in the *Other Side* series. It serves to reveal the reality of life in Germany in the aftermath of the Second World War. Millions of people died of starvation in Germany, as well as in other countries. However, there was a difference between the reasons for the deaths in Germany and those in other countries. Have you ever wondered what that difference might be? Meanwhile, Johann's family's stash is dwindling—there is a thief in the area. Who could it be? Will this culprit ever be apprehended? (230 pages)

The eleventh novel in the *Other Side* series is *The Other Side of Liberation*. This novel evokes powerful emotions as it celebrates the liberation of the Netherlands by the Canadians while, at the same time, exploring the plight of children when their family members perished before their eyes. Who was left to care for these destitute children? Can you imagine hiding within the walls of a house, in some cases for years at a time? *The Other Side of Liberation* shares a view of the liberation of the Netherlands as recounted by a young Dutch boy in his later years. He and his family immigrated to Canada and spent decades trying to find the Canadian soldier whom they billeted for a short time in 1945. They found Clifford in Saskatchewan and remained lifelong friends.